PC Feroc Hans
LB 599

Someone had spray-painted WE R CANCER on the wall of the
youth centre. Whether it was an acknowledgement and
acceptance of the contempt society seemed to hold young people
in, or a statement as to the zodiac sign of the person with the
spray can, wasn't clear.

"Bloody vandals," Tony muttered, stroking the Area Car through
the slight camber of the road, hands barely seeming to touch the
steering wheel. Watching Tony Raglan drive was mesmerising, at
least at normal speed. At high speed, when his eyes flashed with
the thrill of the chase, his knuckles went white against the
steering wheel, and he became like someone possessed,
something beautiful and feral, deadly, yet delightful. A werewolf.
A *loup-garou*, transformed by blue neon moons.

For now, though, Tony was calm. Everything was calm, even the
gulls, turning lazy circles overhead, and ignoring the people
coming out of Greggs with their sausage rolls and sandwiches.
Tony's stomach growled.

"They're not vandals." It's a fundamental instinct in all animals to
mark their territory; humans just do it with ink, rather than urine.
"I wouldn't put it past the yobs who did this to have pissed up the
wall afterwards. And anyway, it's not their territory."

I shrugged. "Scotland isn't ours. Jerusalem isn't Israel's. In fact,
the whole of England wasn't Rome's. We have a long and
illustrious history of taking territory, Tony – often by force. At
least whoever did this hasn't done any harm."

"Except for the poor sod who's going to have to clean it off. And
the tax payers, who probably have to fork out for his wages. It's
selfishness, Feroc. That's all it ever is." Without seeming to move
his arm, he flicked the indicator.

"What are you doing?" I could guess the answer.

"I'm starving. Nip in and grab us a sandwich or something, would
you?"

Turns out they were right, the people who claimed that marriage was just acceptable servitude.

I got out of the car, smiling back at Tony, shaking my head in mock disapproval. Tony pulled a face. I laughed. This was what marriage was – not servitude, but a recapturing of childhood.

PC Tony Raglan
LB 265

The future potential, or lack of it, of common vandals was one of those things Feroc and I would never agree on. He saw stuff like graffiti as art at best, a simple expression of understandable frustration at worst. I saw it for what it was; criminal scum being criminal scum. I'd nick Banksy, given half a chance.

Feroc loped out of the newsagent's. I loved watching him walk; he didn't stride, trot, or jog; he wasn't one of life's dawdlers He moved at an unhurried pace that, nonetheless, kept him at least 100 yards ahead of anyone who happened to be walking behind him, a pace that he was able to up effortlessly in the event of a chase. And when he *was* in a chase, running after someone who'd done wrong... well, let's just say you didn't want to be in his way. Feroc Hanson running flat out was beautiful, but terrifying.

He pulled open the passenger door, folding himself in, and handing me a sandwich, a can of coke, and a chocolate bar in one fluid movement.

"Anything over the main set?"

I shook my head, tearing open the plastic wrap on the sandwich. "No. All quiet at the moment."

"It does seem a little..."

"Dead?" I took a large bite of bacon and egg, enduring the taste of bread. "Make the most of it. I plan to."

Feroc laughed. "Maybe the Rapture that Facebook Christians keep going on about has happened, and we're the godless remnant."

"Not a chance. When Ragnarok happens, we'll know about it – we'll be run off our feet dealing with people who see no reason to carry on the pretence of being decent human beings." I chewed my sandwich, feeling the hairs on the back of my neck prick up at the mention of Ragnarok. That had been the name used by a woman, a serial killer, who'd almost ended my life down on Lothing's shore, a couple of years ago.

Lothing. It was an odd, almost foreign-sounding, name. The town was named for the large lake that split it more or less in half, flowing into the sea, and forming a harbour that could do with being a lot busier than it was. The whole town could do with being busier than it was, really. Like just about everywhere else in the country, Lothing was struggling; as a decent human being, that bothered me. As a copper, it delighted me; failure and poverty keeps people like me and Feroc in work, even if we do end up doing more with fewer resources, less money, and a hell of a lot less support.

Lothing suited me, though; faded, run-down, not quite as successful as it could be, not quite as good as it could be. It didn't help that the town was pretty much used as a dumping ground for everyone else's undesirables – although there were plenty of the "born and bred here, mate" brigade who spent time as our guests, too. Not that you'd hear them admit it – every problem Lothing had was down to immigrants, entitled kids, the unemployed, or "posh sorts from London."

"You alright?" Feroc was looking at me strangely. I wondered if I'd missed something on the main set; I cocked half an ear, but the chatter was the same as usual; the bored small talk of restless coppers with not enough to do.

"Just thinking."

"What about?"

"Everything and nothing." I gunned the engine, pulling away with a smooth kick of speed. There was no traffic. There wasn't much of anything at all.

The truth was, I was thinking about Feroc, about how Lothing didn't really seem to suit him. About how it seemed too small for his potential. Feroc was the kind of copper I could see making Superintendent, one day, if objectionable elements home and abroad didn't set the country back fifty years.

I sighed. I'd lived through the threats, the jokes, the aggression, and the dismissals. I'd coped with the knock-backs, vaulted the barriers that had been slammed down in front of me. I'd done it before, I'd do it again. Feroc's generation, though... they were still bewildered and hurt when they encountered ignorance and prejudice, having only ever really known tolerance.

"Tony?"

"What?"

"Just checking you were still with us – did you even see the lights back there?"

"They were about to change. And there was nothing coming. There's nothing about at all. What the hell's going on?"

"Make the most of it – wasn't that what you said?"

"Yeah..."

"Tony? Is this about the physical?"

"No – why should it be? I've got no worries on that score."

Feroc raised an eyebrow. I looked away, pretending to scan the road.

I'd be fifty this year, and, for the first time, I was starting to feel my age. Fifty wasn't the new forty, not for front line coppers; for us, fifty was the beginning of the end.

I thought of the people you heard every day on radio phone-ins, who's letters you read every other day in the papers, screaming in outrage about having to work another three, four, five years before they could get their State pension. I'd give anything to have another fifteen years doing this job, patrolling these streets – my streets. I'd give anything not to be thrown on the scrap heap in ten years' time. I'd give anything not to have to start thinking about what the future might hold.

I'd outlived my life expectancy as an Area driver – most of them had stripes, or a cushy job in the private sector, by the time they were my age. Others were dead; mostly heart attacks, a couple in the line of duty. One had killed himself. Too many others had tried to. I shouldn't be here, shouldn't be as sane as I was. But I'd survived too much – the only thing I could do, now, was to keep on surviving. It was one of the very few things I was good at.

I was thinking about all of that – and I was thinking about Colt Devereux, too. He had been a mistake, but, in a way, everything that had happened had been his fault. I wasn't saying he'd led me on, nothing like that, but I *was* a Response driver; I couldn't help but give chase.

Colt should have known that.

Inspector Bill Wyckham
LB 81

"Aimee... we need to talk."

I'd meant it to come out sounding ironic, casual. Like I knew exactly how much of an idiot I sounded. Instead, it come out sounding like I was telling my wife I wanted a divorce – something I could never imagine doing, no matter what the provocation.

My sergeant simply nodded, her expression as grave as my statement had sounded. In her case, however, it was intentional. "About Tony Raglan?"

I blinked in surprise, "No – I was intending to talk to you about Feroc Hanson. But go on – what's up with Tony?"

"It can wait, sir."

"You sure?"

"Yes, sir." She didn't look sure, but experience had taught me – repeating the lesson several times – that there was no point pushing Aimee Gardner any further than she was willing to go. Her stubborn resolve made me glad she'd decided to stay on the side of the angels; she would have made a very good, and very competent, criminal.

"So – Feroc?" Aimee pulled back a chair, and folded herself neatly into it.

I nodded. "He's got, what, four, five years in? About the time most coppers of his calibre would be thinking of putting in for their first try for Sergeant."

"Absolutely. I haven't pushed him so far because, frankly, he's been through hell, on a fairly regular basis, since he started." Aimee smiled wryly. "Or, at least, since he started going out on patrol with Tony Raglan."

I chuckled. "I don't think we can blame Tony for what's happened to Feroc; it's not as though he's come through the past few years unscathed, is it?"

"No, I suppose not, sir." We were both quiet for a moment,

remembering things we presumably weren't alone in wishing we could forget. I found myself thinking about Tony Raglan, about why so much seemed to happen to him. He'd always been a strange blend of trusted stalwart and loose cannon, better in a crisis than he was at the everyday tedium. I wondered how Tony Raglan saw himself. I wondered how Feroc Hanson saw him, in his more honest moments.

"Do you think he'd go for promotion?" I watched my Sergeant's face as she considered the question. Aimee Gardner had a good poker face; it was constantly in motion, a very fluid, expressive canvas, that told you absolutely nothing.

She looked up. "I think he would, if Tony Raglan were on board. That's what's going to keep Feroc here, what's going to clip his wings – his loyalty to Tony Raglan. I think he sees promotion as a betrayal of Tony's principals as a beat copper. If Tony were openly supportive, if he encouraged him – then yes, I think Feroc would be more than happy to start moving through the ranks. But he'd need Tony's backing – he'd need him to openly approve. Tony knows he won't be here forever, and I think he knows that Feroc could go all the way – if he's give free flight."

It was a jolt of awareness, the thought of Lothing existing without Tony Raglan's compass. Imagining the streets of Lothing, bereft of Tony's particular brand of professional driving.

I shook my head. "I can't imagine Tony going quietly, but it's going to happen." I realised something. "You know, he's the only long-service officer who hasn't come storming in here, demanding to know what the hell was going on when they announced the reforms a couple of years ago. I should probably try and suss out what his thoughts on retirement are."

Aimee smiled. "I'm torn – part of me wants to be there for that conversation, the other part doesn't want to even think about how things might go during that kind of talk."

"I know the feeling. At least I'll be walking out with him, like as not."

"You're staying on, then?"

I nodded. "I thought about going sooner, but I like this job. I like this team."

"I can't see you or Tony Raglan going for a security gig, to be honest, sir."

"Not a cat's chance. For either of us." I paused, twirling a pen around in my fingers. "Nor Feroc, neither. The lad's bright, and we need to make the most of that."

"I agree. And if you want me to do the groundwork, find out where the land lies with him?"

"Yes – that would be a good idea. I don't want to spook him." I sat back. "And you, Aimee?"

"Sir?"

"What are your plans for the future?"

PC Feroc Hanson
LB 599

"Did you never think of trying for stripes?" Even as the words took form, I was surprised that I'd asked. I'd never questioned Tony about his ambitions directly before, and I wasn't sure why I was doing so now.

 Tony laughed. "It's not really me, is it?" His hands played over the steering wheel. I relaxed into the motion. Tony's weary brown eyes never left the road, warmed by a light I never saw when he wasn't behind the wheel.

"I don't know – you've got the kind of quiet confidence that would make you a good leader."

"Yeah, but I don't have the desire to *be* a good leader." Tony paused. I don't think he intended me to hear him sigh, but I caught the ragged edge of it nonetheless. I glanced at him, an expression that told him he should carry on, should finish the story. He drove in silence. Something had changed in his energy; he seemed distant, distracted. He hadn't seemed that way a moment before.

"Why not?"

"Doesn't matter."

It did to me, but I'd learned not to push Tony when he was like this. He tended to push back – a hell of a lot harder.

"What's brought this on?" Tony didn't even glance away from the road. His grip on the wheel seemed awkward, suddenly, as though driving were a skill he was unfamiliar with. "Fer? What's up? You're not thinking of going for promotion are you?"

My heart began to thump, slowly, a powerful echo. A struggle with honesty, which, in that moment, seemed like a demon. I wasn't used to thinking about being honest; it normally came as naturally as breathing.

"How would you feel if I were?"

Tony's eyes flickered over to me. "It's natural. You're young, intelligent. The world belongs to people like you."

"It's your world, too."

"No." Tony wouldn't look at me. His grip on the wheel still seemed awkward, as though he were somehow suddenly afraid of the car. "It hasn't been my world for a long time. And it never will be again."

He sounded sad. His voice was soft and quiet, and utterly unlike the Tony Raglan I knew. It didn't escape my notice that he was deliberately keeping his gaze away from the rearview mirror, that he was putting a lot of effort into not looking at me at all.

"Come on, Tony – you don't believe that."

"Don't you *dare* tell me what I believe!" He looked at me, a short, sharp snap of his head away from the road. His eyes were shot through with a rage that couldn't quite disguise the tears that danced at their edges. I wondered what about the discussion had upset him – I'd never seen Tony Raglan cry, not through any of the kinds of hell we'd been through in the past five years. And I wondered how he really felt about the idea of me going for promotion.

PC Tony Raglan
LB 265

Feroc was going places. His type were set to inherit the world, and Feroc had it in him to lead the rush to claim. And people like me? We'd be left behind, shut out of the city to die. Out of sight, out of mind, disenfranchised from the world we'd always believed we were building, and serving.

How did I feel about Feroc going for promotion? It rubbed my nose in the fact that I didn't have any prospects left. It grabbed me by the scruff, and made me face the fact that I'd given my life to a job that wasn't going to give me anything, once I couldn't be useful to them. Feroc's thoughts of the future made it clear I didn't have one; or, at least, I had the same future a greyhound who couldn't run any more faced; a bullet.

In all the articles I'd read about relationships with an age difference, in all the documentaries I'd watched, no one had ever mentioned the moment when the older partner realised that the world wasn't interested in them any more When that partner had to face the fact that they were yesterday's news, detritus that society was anxious to sweep away, lest any casual observer realise that the glittering image was built on a rotten core.

I closed my eyes on saltwater shards, feeling my heart twist in my chest, a feeling that echoed all the times I'd been knifed, with the added burn of a wound no one could be hunted down for causing. Suddenly, Lima Bravo One felt too cramped, a moving coffin that would suffocate me if I stayed behind the wheel a minute longer. I couldn't breathe. The road in front of me started to swim, grey spinning off into a thousand fragmented shades, each one a little more blurred than the other.

Get a grip, Raglan. You can't afford another POL-AC.
I pulled over, braking too sharply. Feroc glanced at me. I indicated the curve of the public toilets up ahead. "Call of nature." Feroc watched me walk away. I didn't turn back. I wouldn't let him see the tears I couldn't fight.

Sergeant Aimee Gardner
LB 761

"My plans, sir?"

I looked at Wyckham, trying to work out what he was asking.

He nodded. "Yes. Where do you see yourself in five years' time, say?"

"Why is it always five years?"

"What?"

"Sorry – I suppose that was a bit facetious. But I've always wondered, why five years? Why not three, or ten?"

Bill Wyckham's eyes flickered with light humour. "I don't know; I suppose some bright spark in an office somewhere decided that five years was long enough to fulfil an ambition, and short enough to keep it in sight. I expect they worked it out with graphs. Flow charts. Ignore five years, then – pick a number, any number. Where do you see yourself, in however many years that number represents?"

I thought about it, my mind playing out several possible scenarios, considering each of them in turn. I was aware of Wyckham watching me, aware that he was waiting for an answer. It wasn't that I wanted to keep him waiting; it was simply that I wanted to give him the *right* answer.

The problem was, I couldn't work out which of several possibles that answer might be.

"I'm not sure, sir. I mean, I'm enjoying being a sergeant. I like the team here." Something occurred to me, a chilling thought.

"You're not thinking of moving on yourself, are you, sir?"

"Not a chance – I've reached my level, I think. This is the point of competence for me. If I took it further, I'd only come a cropper."

"Should you be telling me this, sir?"

"Probably not. But here we both are, sergeant. So – I'm not going anywhere. What about you? Where are you going?" He grinned.

"Will I one day be watching the appointment of the first black, female Commissioner, and telling everyone how I made her the woman she is?"

I shook my head. "No, sir. That's not what I want."

"You seem very certain about that?"

"I am, sir. I know I don't want to be taken that far away from the front line."

Wyckham's grin spread. "Ah. So, I've got a minority-status Tony Raglan, with a dash of ambition, on my hands, have I?"

I laughed, feeling waves of dopamine wash through me, taking the edge off the anxiety I'd been feeling since Wyckham had asked me about my ambitions. "You're forgetting, sir – Tony Raglan's a minority-status individual himself."

"Don't let him here you say that. The term 'straight-acting' could have been invented for Tony Raglan."

"You're not wrong about that." For some reason, the thought of Tony Raglan having deliberately set himself apart from the wider gay community saddened me. I mean, I was hardly a bra-burning, flag-waving bulldagger myself, but I spent time on the Norwich scene when I could. I kept up with people online. As far as I was aware, Tony Raglan's involvement began and ended with his personal relationships. At the moment, there was nothing wrong with that. One day, though, people like me, like Tony, like Feroc, might well find ourselves in need of all the friends we could get. If we didn't bother to make those friends, though? What happened then?

"So," Wyckham continued "you don't want to be one of our bright lights, but you've already taken some quite definite steps away from the rank and file. You want to stay a sergeant?"

Did I? I was surprised to find the answer didn't come to me immediately; I'd expected it to be an immediate, resounding 'yes'. It troubled me that it didn't.

"I'm not sure, sir. Am I allowed to say that?"

"Of course – there's no 'allowed' here. No rank, no pack drill. If you're not sure, that's what I want to hear. You don't have to wonder what the right answer is for me, Aimee – the right answer is the truthful one. Truth, Aimee. We're nothing without that, are we?"

"I suppose not, sir. The thing is..." I took a deep breath, felt myself shaking. "I'm not sure I know what the truthful answer is. I know I want to be a copper, but, from the moment I made it out of Hendon, I... well, I suppose I've been taking it one day at a time, seeing where I am at the end of it all. I know it doesn't sound like much, but it's worked so far,"

Bill Wyckham nodded. "And have you ever had days where it hasn't worked? Where you've questioned what you're doing?"

I nodded. "Yes. That evening in the Heart of Darkness. I went home, sir, and I seriously thought about chucking it all in. I stayed up the whole of that night. I drove around town, down to the beach. I just sat there, until the moon set and the sun started to rise." I sighed. "And then I went home, had a shower, changed my clothes, and came back. I still hadn't made a decision, so I just kept on doing the same thing I'd always been doing. And I did it long enough, and well enough, to make sergeant. I want to keep being good at what I do, sir. I want to keep doing my best for the team out there. But I don't think my best involves promotion, or transferring to CID."

Wyckham got up, slowly walking over to the window that looked out onto the corridor. He pulled the blind down, drumming his fingers on the windowsill.

"That night...did it change the way you felt about the Job? About your progress?"

I should have been expecting that question, and it surprised me to realise I hadn't.

"I... probably, sir. Yes, it probably did, sir. I think... I think, that night, when I didn't know anything else, when everything was up in the air, I knew that I couldn't walk away from Tony Raglan." I paused. "Something like that... it changes you, doesn't it?"

Wyckham nodded. "In my day, they called it First Blood – the impact it had on you, the first time you saw a colleague bleed. It was always held that you didn't really know anything about a copper until they'd been through their First Blood. Tony Raglan

getting shot... it was Feroc Hanson's First Blood, too, wasn't it?"
"Yes, sir. It was."
"And he seems to have a very striking lack of ambition, given
how bright and forward he was before that night." Wyckham
regarded me, a tiredness in his eyes.
"Much like me, eh, sir?"
Wyckham nodded. "In a nutshell, yes." He shook his head, a wry
grin flicking at his lips. "And we come back to the five years
thing, don't we? Five years, give or take, since that night in the
Heart of Darkness – and we're starting to see that Tony Raglan
wasn't the only one wounded that night, aren't we?"
"Yes, sir. Perhaps there's something to the five years thing after
all."
"Perhaps there is, Sergeant. Perhaps there is."

PC Feroc Hanson
LB 599

"It's like that bloke in the Bible, where Yahweh threatened to blast the daylights out of some city, and this bloke bargains with him over it; starts off with if he can find a hundred righteous people, then he gets it down to fifty, then ten, then one, and, when he can't find a single person who meets the criteria, he says to Yahweh; "Look, *I'm* a good man; I'll stand between you and them." That's us – standing between the government, and everyone else. It was alright when it was scum, but it's not, not any more. They're going after everyone they don't like, everyone who threatens them, and they see us as their private fucking army." Tony hurled his polystyrene cup through the window, beige-brown liquid arcing, a stain against the sky's blue and white promise.

Tony rarely swore. And he'd usually find a bin for coffee cups. He gunned the engine, yanked the Area Car into the flow of traffic with a squeal of tyres, and a barely suppressed rage. I watched him without looking at him, seeing the warning signs; his knuckles white as he gripped the wheel, eyes narrowed to dark slits of swirling chaos, a rasp to his breath that came close to being a growl. I took in the set of his broad shoulders, the sight and set conjuring a ghost of memory.

When it matters, Tony – I won't stand in your way.

Blood and sweat. Torn clothing. Engine grease. Dust and dirt. The looks of others.

Tony Raglan was on the verge of something – either a transformation, or a breakdown. I sensed that it mattered, but I wasn't prepared to simply get out of his way. Not if he needed me – and I had a feeling he would, soon, even if he didn't know it, and wouldn't admit it.

PC Tony Raglan
LB 265

I knew I was out of control, knew I had to stop this, get a grip. But I couldn't. I wasn't myself, and I couldn't just go home until I became myself again. The Job didn't work like that.

I could almost smell Feroc's fear, and I hated myself for frightening him. Whatever he was planning for the future he'd have without me, he didn't deserve this.

I found myself remembering words spoken a long time ago, when things were so different, we may as well have been living in another country.

When it matters, Tony – I won't stand in your way.

I could still feel the subtle weight of Feroc's touch. Could still remember the exact way the rhythm of my heart changed. That had been the beginning of what we'd become, the two of us, but I was coming to realise it was a beginning that didn't reflect the ending.

In the end, I had nowhere to go; it wasn't going to be Feroc who'd stand in my way – it was me who needed to get out of his way, to give him the space to spread his wings, and the freedom to fly. It was an awful realisation, and I understood, all too well, how falconers must feel, probably each and every time they sent their birds up. You had to do it, you had to let them fly, because it was what they were born to do, but your heart was in your mouth, every time, afraid that they wouldn't come back, that they'd fly farther and faster than you could follow.

I was angry, almost wild with it, and I couldn't be around Feroc when I was like that. I needed to be with someone who'd let me give in to the wildness, to the animal rage that felt like raw power flooding my veins, blurring my vision, giving me a headache even as it sharpened my senses.

One name yelled above the clamour in my head. Colt Devereux. I hadn't seen him since Killjoy, but I needed to see him now. He understood. He'd let me be the beast, so that Feroc only knew the beauty of a partnership in full flow, and perfect harmony.

Inspector Bill Wyckham
LB 81

I watched Aimee Gardner stride off along the corridor, took in the
confidence in her bearing as she paused to speak with one of the
CID team, a harried young DC who'd come in a couple of weeks
ago, fresh out of graduate entry. She'd make a great Commander,
but, at the same time, she was the perfect front line officer.
 I sighed, wondering if the cult of ambition that seemed to have
infected every sector in the country in the past few years was
making us lesser, not greater. If we weren't losing the very best of
our talent to roles that paid more, offered more opportunities,
gave greater respect, but didn't allow those talent s to shine to
their fullest and brightest. We wanted people to be impressive –
we didn't want them to be good. I'd meant it when I'd talked about
having found my level as an Inspector; perhaps Aimee didn't need
to be pushed to achieve hers.
 Tony Raglan, though... I tapped flicked the plastic slats of the
blind with one finger. I had a feeling that Tony Raglan did need a
push. Or a slap. He had his physical coming up, and I got the
feeling that, for the first time since I'd come to Lothing, he wasn't
confident he'd make it through. That didn't worry me. What did
was that Tony seemed to have forgotten that it wasn't a way for us
to kick coppers out of a job. It was just a way to pick up any
major red flags, really. I'd always go to bat for Tony Raglan – I
wondered when he'd stopped believing that. When - and why.
 I let the slats fall back into place, and walked over to my desk,
glancing up at the clock. A couple of hours of paperwork, and
then Tony and Feroc would be in for refs – and I could have a
word with Tony Raglan. The kind of word that was steel-honed,
and guaranteed to get to the bottom of whatever was bugging
him.

Colt Devereux

If you're not afraid, it's because you're not looking. I saw the
world for what it was, knew exactly what that world thought
about people like me – trans people, coppers – and I was terrified
of it. Mostly, though, I was able to keep that fear at bay, channel
it into something useful, something that made the world I feared a
little safer for others.

I hadn't been afraid during Killjoy. In the run up, yes. Right up,
in fact, until I stepped into that flat, and saw Tony Raglan. Even
though I'd never seen him before, he looked like safety. He'd
survived being shot – that was impressive enough for me. Tony
Raglan's legend went before him, and created a sense of safety I'd
lost long ago.

Killjoy had helped kickstart the process of my life getting back
on track. I could go back to being the copper I'd been before, the
copper I'd always wanted to be. I could work with the security of
a measure of respect – from the outside, Killjoy had looked a lot
more intense than it had felt from inside; I'd felt as though I was
treading water throughout most of Killjoy, while the impression
among the troops was that I was swimming through some pretty
deep water. Everyone knew about Tony Raglan being shot, at the
showdown, and some of that blooded glory washed back on me.
That was a kind of safety; it was a beginning, but it didn't build
the kind of safety other people took for granted. It didn't give me
the kind of safety I wanted.

I had a feeling I could get that safety from being around Tony
Raglan on a more permanent basis – and that was something I'd
decided to concentrate on. Everyone needs ambitions, and my
ambition was to get transferred out of Bethel Street. A life by the
sea could be good, in more ways than one – and I'd be working
with a copper who knew me, approved of me, and trusted me.

Whether Tony Raglan loved me, I didn't know – but I definitely
wanted to find out. It hadn't seemed like a one-night stand thing,
those nights I'd spent with Tony, but who can ever be sure? He'd

certainly seemed genuine when he married Feroc, after all.

PC Feroc Hanson
LB 599

I was worried about Tony. It had been a quiet shift, and he didn't cope well with having too little to do. He hadn't become a copper to offer a visible symbol of peace and harmony to the good citizens of England's green and pleasant land; Tony had told me once, only half joking, that he'd become a copper because he couldn't be a cowboy. It was clear to anyone who spent more than a day with him that he saw the streets of Lothing as his own personal Wild West, despite the town's reputation as the most Easterly point. I wondered what role I played in all this, whether Tony had thought beyond his own need to escape a reality he was temperamentally unsuited to.

As Tony drove, I thought back over the years we'd been together. We'd seen a lot, been through a fair bit more, and I'd thought we'd come out okay. Maybe I'd been wrong; maybe what was up with Tony was that he was approaching a point of needing his fantasy to become reality. A point where he wasn't able to cope with the demands that an ever-changing world put on all of us, but especially coppers like Tony, who'd been around the block enough time to spot an old dog in a new collar when they saw one. A lot of barking, muddy paws and fur everywhere, when you thought you were done with training, when you thought the days of frustratedly explaining what was expected were over.

We were coming up to Imbolc – not a big deal for Heathens, but I'd always been more eclectic, and liked to take some time to reflect, set intentions, and focus on plans for the year ahead. The beginning of spring, green shoots and fresh starts. Hopefully, it would work its magic on Tony Raglan, bringing him round from whatever slump he was going through.

Of course, taking a more practical, earth-plane approach, that change would probably begin once the annual physical was over and done with. Tony had always got through without a problem before, and he would do again – unless he was keeping something from me. And I was almost certain he wasn't. Not Tony. I'd know.

Sergeant Aimee Gardner
LB 761

I needed to get out, get some fresh air. Put the fear of whatever gods they may or may not believe in into a few PCs who weren't doing anyone any harm – because the coppers on my relief didn't exist to be harmless.

I hated being cooped up indoors. It always made me irritable, and it was part of the reason I didn't want to progress further up the ranks; the higher you climbed, in this job as in any other, the less time you got to spend on the ground. And, if I was honest, I was deeply worried about Tony Raglan. I knew people, had always had a kind of sixth sense about them, something that helped me survive the curse of adolescence, and that got me through the minefield of being a young, untried copper – who also happened to be black, and female. It meant that, when I took the decision to enter into an in-depth romantic relationship, I was able to identify a woman who didn't have skeletons in her closet, and wouldn't cause any problems for my professional life. Now, that sense was telling me that Feroc Hanson was starting to think about testing himself, spreading his wings, finding his own level in the game of life we played in the Force. He'd had a rough start, seeing more in his first five years than some coppers saw in a lifetime, but things had been calm for a while, and I got the feeling that, now he was no longer preoccupied with Tony Raglan's various crises, Feroc was starting to feel the seven-year itch, starting to wonder what the future held.

Selflessness is always heralded as a supreme virtue, but, in my experience, selflessness often came about because an individual had been so thoroughly stripped of their sense of self, either by chance and circumstance, or by deliberate abuse, that they were simply incapable of putting themselves first.

Feroc Hanson had been no more or less selfless than anyone else when he'd first started as a probationer at Lothing; he could be selfless at times, and he had moments of harmless, necessary selfishness. He'd talked about his ambitions, then; and then the

Heart of Darkness had happened, a single, shocking incident that had destroyed any sense of self Feroc Hanson had come into the Job with.

I couldn't imagine how it must feel to realise that you love someone, and then, on the same day, see that person's blood pooling beside them as they sprawled on the floor. Tony's shooting had been bad enough for me, and I wasn't in love with him, I couldn't begin to process how much it must have messed with Feroc's head.

I'd spoken with Con, since. He was doing well up north, enjoying himself. He'd found himself a girlfriend, the last I'd heard. I got the feeling that Lothing had expected him back, at some point; as of six months ago, I got the feeling that Con had no intention of returning to Lothing. I didn't blame him; he'd spent fifteen years pretending to be someone he wasn't; I could understand his need to spend plenty of time becoming himself, finding a comfort in his own skin.

I'd never really known Con until the night of Tony Raglan's shooting. Two black coppers in a town that hated anything different, a town that had howled for Brexit, a town whose residents spoke out, at every opportunity, about how "downhill" things had gone "since they started letting anyone and everyone in." It was inevitable we'd exchange words. I think Con fancied me, at least at first, until I put him wise on which team I played for. That had surprised him; it surprised most people. Like Tony Raglan, like Feroc Hanson, I had never been obvious. Being black helped; we were always assumed to be sex-crazed wild women, rather than dykes. Sometimes, both were true.

I smiled to myself as I stepped out into the yard. The sun was shining, a soft breeze took the edge off the heat, and, so far, there were no reports of anyone starting a riot, committing arson, or terrorising their neighbours.

Give it time. My smile broadened as I imagined Tony Raglan's voice, his likely comment on observations about good days and calm citizens.

Tony Raglan. What was I going to do about him? And more importantly, what was Feroc going to do?

Geraldine

"You want him to be successful, though, don't you? You want him to achieve whatever he's capable of? You wouldn't want him to feel that he'd been held back by you, would you?"

Tony flinched – it was the first time he'd reacted in nearly an hour. To be fair, he'd been the one doing most of the talking, disjointed, unconnected, half-formed sentences, mostly relating to fears and Feroc. Because, with Tony Raglan, it always came back to Feroc Hanson. He'd never been as caught up with his previous partner, Max, and I had my own ideas about why he felt as strongly for Feroc as he did. At the moment, though, the depth and strength of those feelings wasn't the issue.

"I...of course I do."

"Do you? Or do you just want me to think you're a nice guy, who wouldn't dream of stopping his spouse achieving his ambitions?"

It was the wrong question. I could see that as soon as I'd asked it, the split-second flash of something unreadable in Tony Raglan's eyes, the way his face fell, closing in on itself. "Okay, let's come back to that. For what it's worth, I get the impression you've never just rolled over and given someone the answer you think they want to hear, and I can't see you doing so now. So... you've spoken a lot about how you're afraid of losing Feroc. Let's try and go deeper with that, shall we? I mean, you're married now – surely that should give you additional security, rather than making you feel more worried about a breakup?"

Tony shifted on the sofa, swirling the dregs of his coffee as though he could read his future in the grounds. He sighed, shook his head.

"I'm not worried about him finding someone else...I'm worried about him *becoming* someone else. He's starting to think about his future... I'd always just assumed... I mean, he told me..."

"You assumed he wanted the same as you – a life on the streets?"

"You make it sound like I was proposing homelessness."

I chuckled. "Sorry – I didn't mean it like that. But you did assume that's what he wanted? To be a beat bobby, like you?"

"Yeah. Only... " a shake of the head. "...I'm not sure it was ever really what I wanted, to tell you the truth. I sort of ended up as a copper, and happened to be good at being a street cop, the same way I'd always been good at driving. The only thing I ever had been good at." I heard Tony swallow, hard, as though choking down a truth he wasn't ready to admit. "Other than the driving – I'd been doing that since I was in my teens, been good at it from my first time out – I wasn't really used to being good at anything."

I remembered things Tony Raglan had told me before. "And you liked the feeling of people praising you? Being proud of you?"

Tony nodded, stretching long legs out in front of him, staring down at his hands. "I didn't want to lose that by pressing for something I turned out to be rubbish at."

"And you assumed you *would* fail, if you tried something new?"

"Yes."

"Why?"

Tony's deep, brown eyes were bright with wounded honesty. "Because I'm stupid and lazy. I don't know a good thing when I see it."

"Tony – I asked *you* why you assumed you'd fail. I didn't ask your mother."

I thought I'd gone too far, pushed too hard on the wrong buttons. Tony was halfway to his feet, face twisted into a mask of rage, when he suddenly slumped back, tears in his eyes.

"I don't know anyone else's answers."

I leaned forward. "That's okay. I don't want someone else's answers – I want yours. Why does Tony Raglan think you'll fail?"

He shook his head. "I don't know."

"Does he believe you would?"

"I don't know." It was a whisper, shot through with agony. I got up, and came across to the sofa, sitting beside him, a slight distance between us. Giving him space, whilst being fully present. I didn't speak – the silence allowed us both to say enough.

After about five minutes, Tony took a deep breath. "Sorry. I went a bit flakey there. I don't know what came over me."

I smiled. "It's okay. You're allowed to be flakey sometimes."

"No, I'm not." He sighed. "I suppose that's part of the problem – everyone's always looked up to me, relied on me. I've got a reputation to live up to; good old Tony, a diamond bloke, completely bombproof. I'm like Lestat to the Lothing pack, and I can't step down from that. I can't let them down."

"Why not? If you did take a break from your life, from the responsibilities you've taken on – and I feel it's worth mentioning that these are responsible adults – what's the worst that would happen?"

Tony stared at me for a long moment, as though he'd never considered the question before. I pressed on. "Nothing would happen, would it?"

"It would, though..."

"Go on."

"If I let them down...if I didn't keep everything going... people wouldn't trust me. They'd feel that they couldn't rely on me. Every time they stepped onto the street, they'd be wondering if I was going to be there, if things got tense. Then they'd start to wonder if it was worth risking their necks to back *me* up, since I couldn't be relied on to back *them* up. I'd go from having mates to having colleagues, and that's no good for any copper. Coppers don't need colleagues. They need mates. A copper without mates is like a lame deer in hunting season, and I'm not ready to go down just yet."

"Is that what you're worried about if Feroc pursues other ambitions? Do you feel that a lot of your mates are actually his mates – and that he'd take them with him if he moved onwards and upwards?"

I couldn't imagine what the silence must have felt like to someone who had never cultivated a relationship with it. I was always relaxed in silence, even when I could practically reach out and touch the tension that ran through it. Tony Raglan, however, was visibly uncomfortable, fighting to try and find the words to break the threat. He swallowed hard, turned, and met my gaze.

"Any chance of another coffee?"

I got up, smiling softly. "Of course. Same again?"

"Please."

"You owe me, you know – all this coffee from me, and no real talk from you? Can't go on, officer."

"Yeah, well... it's not easy, putting everything into words. I've never been much of a one for naval gazing and yappery."

"That's not what this is, Tony. You know that – if you thought for a moment it was, you wouldn't have stayed more than five minutes, that first time, would you?"

"I suppose not."

"And I *know* not. Now – I'll get your coffee, we'll take a break – and then I'd like to try a slightly different approach. Give you a change from talking."

PC Tony Raglan
LB 265

I held it together until I was out of sight of Geraldine's office, then allowed myself to collapse against a wall, sliding down into a feral, wounded crouch, fingers clawing at my temples, tears streaming down my face.

I'd never had a session that rough before. I'd got the trick of not talking down very early on in my relationship with Geraldine, and had prided myself on controlling the sessions.

Today, though... I'd always mocked regression therapy, thinking it was just New Age claptrap, encouraging deluded girls into behaving even more entitled than they already did, because they'd 'been an Egyptian princess in a past life.'

Regression therapy with Geraldine, though, had left me feeling small, cold, and vulnerable. I wasn't sure whether I needed icecream, or a hug.

I'd go home via Tesco, and see if I couldn't get both.

PC Feroc Hanson
LB 599

I sat on the sofa, looking at the TV, not watching it, listening to Idaho, scratching about and talking to himself, waiting for Tony to come home. I remembered that he'd gone to see this woman, Geraldine, once before, after we'd... was it a row? An argument? I still wasn't sure exactly what had gone on between us, that night. I knew I regretted it, knew that it had left a bitter taste in my mouth. We'd been having an intense discussion, that was an indisputable fact. Tony had reacted badly. Perhaps, if I was honest, I had, too.

Maybe that was why people seemed to awkward when we attended their domestics; they genuinely didn't know how things had got to the point where a neighbour was concerned enough to call the police.

Whatever had happened between me and Tony hadn't been a domestic. We were coppers, and coppers tried very hard not to have domestics – because we knew how much the coppers who got called to them hated them. Coppers went to a great deal of trouble to avoid involving other people in our problems. Except that Tony had involved Geraldine, was probably involving her again.

And I didn't know who she was, or why Tony went to see her when he got wound up enough. I sighed. Tony had assured me I didn't have anything to worry about on the Geraldine front, but he'd never proved that I didn't.

The door opened. Idaho began squawking, furiously, hopping around the walls of his cage, eyes rolling in delight. He'd always preferred Tony to me, which made me wonder just how close Tony had been to Idaho's original owner, a wheelman who'd taken a job with a drugs gang. The pursuit that followed had been the first domino to fall, the pack finally collapsing in the Heart of Darkness pub, blood and beer, the adrenaline of not knowing.
"Heya. You okay?"

"Yeah. You?"

"Better now you're home." I got up from the sofa, grabbed the remote, and went to turn the TV off.

"Leave it, if you want."

"I don't."

"Put the news on, then – let's see what madness we've got going on in the world."

"You sure?"

"Yeah. I mean, there's nothing we can do about it, but at least we won't be surprised by it."

 I turned the TV off, and got up. "You look terrible." I went over to Tony, taking in his ashen face, the way his hair fell, as though he'd spent the past three hours trying to tear it out by the roots. Getting close, I noticed the redness in his eyes, the small, glittering trails his tears had left.

 I put my arms around him, laid my head against his chest. His heartbeat sounded too slow. "Tony... what's wrong?"

PC Tony Raglan
LB 265

Everything was wrong. Nothing was wrong. I wasn't suffering, at least not any more than I deserved to.

Keeping secrets was a kind of adultery, and adultery was something I'd always sworn I'd never get involved with. Max had cheated on me; I knew how it felt. But I'd still done it. I'd slept with Colt, and I continued to keep secrets from Feroc. I was guilty, and the pain I felt was my punishment. I pushed Feroc away.

"I'm fine. Just tired." Feroc couldn't know about Geraldine – he'd try and make things alright, and I couldn't let him do that. Couldn't let Geraldine do it, either. Not being alright was my punishment, and I just had to keep my head down, and get through it.

Be a copper long enough, and you realise almost all the problems in the world come down to lies. The lies we tell others, and the lies we tell ourselves. Why do we lie? It's something I've spent a lot of time thinking about, over the years. There are seven types of killer; those who kill for profit, the hired guns, the hitmen, and women, of the world, the mercenaries. There are those who kill from jealousy, those who kill to defend themselves or others, those who kill for financial benefit, those who kill for love, from misguided passion, those who kill to avoid punishment, and those who kill because they love killing. The last kind is the hardest to catch, and impossible to rehabilitate. Thankfully, they're also the rarest kind.

We don't all kill. We do all lie, and perhaps we lie for the same reason some people kill. Total honesty isn't possible – it destroys relationships just as quickly and completely as lying does, just in a different way.

Why was I lying? Partly to protect myself – that was obvious; I didn't want Feroc to find out about Colt, because he'd walk out over something like that; Feroc didn't do betrayal. But I was also

lying to protect Feroc, too. I couldn't let him meet all of my
demons. I couldn't let those demons catch his scent. They'd
destroy him. I'd been round the block, I was strong enough to
survive them. Feroc wasn't. Feroc didn't know nearly enough
about the dark side. It was never going to be safe to let him meet
more than one or two of my demons.

That led on to another thought – the difference between "protect"
and "defend". The two words were similar, but not the same, and
I wondered what the difference was, exactly.

Perhaps it was more about the person behind the action than the
action itself; you defended people who might've done wrong, and
protected people who were incapable of it. Criminals were
defended; children were protected.

So... was I protecting myself, or defending myself?

"Tony?"
I shook my head, clearing the fog of thought. "Yeah?"
"Are you okay?"
*No. Hold me close, Feroc; hold me close while I break your
heart.*
"Yeah. I'm fine."
"What were you thinking about?"
"Did you always want to be a copper?"
Feroc stared at me. I didn't blame him – the question took me as
much by surprise as it did him. Feroc stepped away from the
embrace he'd been holding me in, and shook his head slowly.
"No, actually, I didn't."
"What did you want to be?"
Feroc turned away, wrapping his arms around himself. "I wanted
to be an artist. I wanted to paint, and I wanted to teach others to
paint. I wanted to work on novels. I wanted to live a life that
involved going to galleries, meeting and greeting. I wanted a
relaxed, languid workload, that didn't really seem like work."
"That's hardly the Job, is it?"
"No."

"Then what led you here?"

Feroc turned back. "I saw you in action. I was down in Yarmouth for a friend's stag do, and I was bored with the whole drinking and gambling scene – I took a bus out to Lothing, change of scene, chance to be on my own for a bit. I was walking on the beach, and suddenly -"

I burst out laughing. "Let me guess; you were walking on the beach, the tide was coming in, you were turning to come up the slip ramp, back onto the prom, and you nearly got knocked flying by a bloke on a motorbike – and then, just as you got your balance again, a police car slammed down, handbrake turn, blocking off the ramp. One copper was already running, kicking up sand. The driver jumped out...."

Feroc smiled. "...he was a big guy, but he moved well. Everyone was watching. The tide washed over the wheel of the bike. The copper, the big guy, splashed through the edges of the surf... grabbed at the rider's jacket, pulled him off...his bike went over, surf lapping metal, plastic, rubber...The sun was starting to set; it caught them at just the right angle. The copper looked like a painting of a cowboy, something beautiful and terrible."

We took each other in, like two friendly dogs, meeting for the first time.

"All that time."

"Yeah..."

"I wish I'd noticed you then."

"You were probably pretending to be straight, then."

"Yeah – I probably was."

"Do you remember who your colleague was?"

I shook my head. "No. Do you remember what they looked like?"

Feroc shook his head. "No... I remembered you, though. And I decided that I wanted to be just like that bold, beautiful copper, one day. What had he done, anyway? The guy on the bike?"

"Drugs."

"And he went down?"

"Yeah. He went down."

We were both smiling, the soft smiles of memory. All those years
A whole career. I'd changed the direction of a young man's life.
And I wasn't entirely sure how I felt about that.

Chris

It pisses me off when people are all like "But what do you want
to *do* with your life,Christopher?" For a start, I ain't Christopher
to nobody – I'm Chris. Always have been, even to my Mum.
Christopher is some poncy nob in the Houses of Parliament.
Chris? Chris is a guy who knows where it's at, knows that it
doesn't matter what he wants to do with his life – he's got a set list
of things society'll *let* him do, and he'd damn well better know
enough to pick one of those.

I'll spend my life in a series of council squats, cleaning up after
strangers and savages who can't string a sentence together. If I'm
lucky. Otherwise, it'll be some privately rented shithole I can't
afford, where the landlord kicks me out the first time I explain
that I don't want to die from mold poisoning, and while rats make
great pets, I'm not sure I can tame the ones running round the
skirting board.

That's just how it is, these days. Council don't want to waste a
whole house on one person, so, if you're under 35, you get to
share with the junkies and care in the community cases, whether
you like it or not. Landlords want money without hassle, so good
luck getting your repairs sorted, or finding someone who doesn't
run a revolving door, kicking people out every six months so they
can get another wedge of deposit and "administration fees."

It's alright for girls. If they're pretty, someone'll give them a job,
however thick they are. Or some bloke'll take them in, grinning
all over his face for landing some nice arm candy, a living doll
that just wants a nice house and plenty of cash. And if they're not
pretty? They can always go on the game. Or just open their legs
for some skank chav in a club, get up the duff, whine to the
council, get a nice flat, in a nice area, and nice people coming
round to make sure everything's nice for the baby.

That's probably not fair, really – I mean, the girls in the crew
ain't like that. But a lot of girls seem to be. Women, too – them as
should be old enough to know better. If you're female, you have it

easy – that's how it appears, anyway.

And don't go on at me about how I should "get a job, not sit around moaning all day." I applied for loads of jobs when I left school. I worked for bugger all, I wrote speculative letters, I even put up ads saying I'd work as a drivers' mate, a gardener, a dog walker.

 Nothing. I can't afford to buy stuff to sell on, I haven't got a car to take my art and that round to fairs, and no one's interested in employing me. So; I'm stuck here, because, unlike the rich twats who constantly get at me, my life is dependent on other people. People who don't want to help people like me. It doesn't matter what I want to do with my life – I wouldn't be able to do it anyway.

Adam

Thing is, people shit on graffiti, but they'll hang abstract paintings on their walls at a couple of hundred a go. I've seen enough of those paintings to know I'm not exaggerating about the price; if anything, I'm being conservative. And this isn't even in London.

When I talk about graffiti, I'm not talking about tagging; but using words or phrases thoughtfully, as part of a wider artistic expression – that's what I do, and it's completely different from tagging. Genuine graffiti isn't vandalism – it's art. Genuine graffiti brings life to an area – and, if people don't like the kind of life it brings, maybe they shouldn't have abandoned the life that was already there, the shops and expressions of entrepreneurship that didn't make it, because people are selfish, snatched their money tighter to them. What was there before wasn't good enough, and what's been put in its place is "awful"; you can't have it both ways.

Graffiti should make people think, and that's what we do with our tagline; the word "cancer" always worked into every piece we create. People see it, and, whatever they think of our work, the wonder what the cancer reference is about.

Chris. Adam – that's me – Nicole. Charlie, Evie, and Rick. Charlie's Nicole's girlfriend, and Ricky's my younger brother. We're all into graffiti, and, together, because of our initials, we're the Cancer Crew. No one ever thinks of that, though, so it keeps them wondering, keeps them guessing. Which is exactly what I want. People guessing, wondering. People unsure and confused. We need more confusion in the world. People need to be unsettled, they need to be made apocalyptic with rage, they need to be tested beyond endurance. Because it's only when people reach the end of their rope that you see what kind of creature they really are.

Getting back to the girls. I'd been wary about having girls in the crew, but, once I saw their work... That was it, for me. I'm not an artist, not really; I do cartoons, and will always be thankful that the "stick figure style" is coming back into fashion, thanks to meme creators wanting to get something on Facebook quickly, and the limitations of Paint.

I will always admire people who ARE artists – people like Nicole. She already had a rep for her photography; I knew about that. I didn't know just how good she was at using those skills in a wider setting until she started running with us. She's got a photographer's eye – she can simplify things down to a single shot, get something up quickly and cleanly. She's got real talent, the kind I can only dream of having; she makes proper money at it, too. That must be great – I'm currently trying to save up the money to go to art college, with a view to hopefully learning a way to make a bit of money from artistically presenting words. God knows, there's nothing on offer unless I go self employed. And I'm not really suited to the brickie trade, which is about all there is for the lone wolves round here. So; art has to save me. And, in order for it to do that, I need to find someone who can teach me to create the kind of art people actually want to buy.

Nicole

People think that digital art isn't "real" art. They don't want to pay for it. "Hmm...twenty pounds? For *digital?* That's a bit... pricey, isn't it?"

 Of course, digital art IS worth something, sometimes – when someone's looking at work they believe to be by a household "name" - work that's usually one of the name's underpaid assistants. Then, they'll pay the GDP of a small landlocked nation, just so they can brag about owning a piece of that over-hyped action. Otherwise? They think twenty pounds is "pricey."

 Let's do the maths on that. To create even the simplest of my pieces takes me an hour and a half on the computer, absolute minimum. At minimum wage, that's at least eleven pounds. Then I have to print it – the paper I use is quality, ten pounds for fifty sheets. My printing inks cost fifty pounds every time I replace them. They run to about fifty of my pieces. One fifty to print. Then I mount my pieces, and frame them in a basic wooden frame. The frames cost me four pounds a throw for A4. The mounts are a pound for that size. Five pounds. Six pounds fifty. Seventeen pounds fifty – just for my time and materials. Never mind the electricity. Never mind if I spend longer on a piece, which I usually do. And that's not including the fact that I include original photos that I've had to take, which costs, in terms of travelling to a location, the time it takes to get the shot. But no; I don't deserve to make even two pounds fifty of profit. While other people can make hundreds.

 It's why I stopped doing fairs, other than a couple that are art-specific. It's why I only sell online through my own website – that, and the fact that everywhere else takes a commission, or charges me to list in the first place.

 Oh, yeah – I forgot the fact that fairs charge for space. At the main fair I do, every year, space costs eighty pounds. I have to sell four pieces, just to cover the cost of the space.

 Why do I carry on? Why keep doing it, when the returns are so tough? Because I love it. Because, in the end, it's worth it.

[

Charlie

We're not a gang – I want to make that clear. People see more
than three people under thirty together, and the assumption is,
they're a gang. We're not, we're a crew – we work together, we
don't cause trouble together.

And yes, I know plenty of people think that graffiti *is* trouble,
but, really, what worries you more – some brightly-coloured
paint, or shops boarded up, the fabric of the buildings behind
them disintegrating from the inside out? Rotten shells. Empty
tombs. Or gardens of creative growth? Well? Which is it? What
do you want?

I know what I want. I want the wild brightness of my mind,
sprayed large on some wall, somewhere. I want my girlfriend's
photo-mosaic inspired pieces splashed all over city skylines. I
want Adam's words, I want Chris's wild arcs of technicolour
anger. I want Evie's careful naivete. I want Ricky's splashes of
incoherence. I want all of that, in place of emptiness and slow
decay. I want the place where I live to look as though people care
about it.

That's the other thing people get wrong; people who do graffiti
actually *do* care about the places we work; it's why we do it.

Graffiti gave me everything I have; it gave me Nicole – we met
when I was admiring a piece of hers; I hadn't even gone out to
paint; I'd been shopping, browsing charity shops for vintage-
inspired gear, and cheap furniture I could upcycle; I tuned a
corner, coming round to the Red Cross shop, when a glimpse of
something had me crossing the road, jumping the low fence that
ringed off a patch of land that hadn't been used in years.

I'd been staring at the wall, a Ferris wheel arcing over the sombre
exterior of a bank, two dogs with cats' heads walking out of the
bank.

"I made a stencil from the original photos. Then it was just
scribbles with permanent markers."

I'd spun round, to find myself staring at a tall, lean woman,

chocolate brown hair pulled back from a cat-like face that
stopped just short of being sharp, bright, intelligent green eyes
adding to the impression that, any minute, this woman would
drop to her knees, and become the kind of sleek creature you
wanted to stroke, but knew better than to even look too long at.
 "You did this?"

"Problem, if I did?"

I smiled, took a step forward. Breasts front and centre, testing the
waters. No flicker of disgust, no half step back. "Nope. Not at all.
Whose were the original photos?"

"Mine."

"Woman of many talents, then."

She'd smiled, becoming the cat I'd imagined – and the one that
got the cream. "Not all of them related to photography."

"Oh yeah?"

"Yeah. I'm on Facebook – Nicole Grayson."

"Charlie Reeve."

Nicole had nodded. "I'll keep an eye out for you." Then she was
gone. I could have chased after her – could have caught up with
her easily. But, for once in my life, I played it cool. I snapped a
photo of Nicole's work, saving precious diversity to my phone,
hedging against the likelihood of the powers that be painting over
it, finished my shopping, went home – and did a full clean on the
house, put a load of laundry on, and had a long, leisurely bath
before I even glanced at Facebook.

 There was a message on my wall from Nicole Grayson – her
profile picture was a camera, but I could hear her voice in the
words.

 LIKED WHAT YOU SAW EARLIER? I KNOW I DID.

There was a friend request. I hit "Accept"faster than I'd intended,
but not nearly as quickly as I would have liked.

 We've been together four years since then. We were both fifteen
years old, that day. I was living with parents who hated me,
Nicole was living with a mother who quietly, politely, ignored
her. Now, we had our own flat, Nicole was working part time at

an art gallery, a little more than part time at the local supermarket. I worked for the local council. We were talking about marriage.

Evie

I'd never intended to get caught up in graffiti culture. When I'd first taken my doodles off paper, and onto a wall, it had been out of boredom. Nothing more or less than that. No grand motivation, no wild resentment. I was just a thirteen year old kid who had too little to do, too little respect for the world around her.

I've been graffiting for five years since that first, terrifying, heart-stopping line on someone else's plaster, and the only thing that had changed was that I now had more respect than most people for the property of others – that's why using them as a canvas for great art mattered so much.

I'd met Chris's crew a couple of years ago. They weren't the Cancer Crew, then; just a group of people making art, without a name. The name came a few weeks after I started running with them, once we realised what the initials could stand for.

I'd always been a "good girl" - top marks at school, Girl Guide, plenty of friends, loving parents, adorable little sister... But puberty hit me the way it does most of us, and I'd found myself wondering what the point of everything was, found myself resenting the fact that other people had things – even though they'd worked for them, were still working for them. I suppose I should just be grateful that graffiti caught my energy and attention, rather than anything more harmful.

A lot of people grow out of graffiti; I grew into it. I honed my style, experimented, tested myself, proved myself.

Became part of the pack, part of the Cancer Crew.

Ricky

People always think Adam got me into graffiti – it's what our dad thinks, for sure; the truth is, I got him into it.

I started tagging when I was twelve – the year my mum died. Cancer, although I didn't know that back then. I missed her, and I hated all the people who got to carry on a life she couldn't have. The first place I tagged was our doctor's surgery. Her initials, made out of a chaos of dots. That was my theme, for the next eighteen months.

One night, Adam followed me. I think he'd wanted to be angry, but, instead, he looked at what I'd done – I'd just started moving into other things in dots, other initials, acronyms, stuff like that – nodded once.

"That's good. How long've you been doing stuff like this?"
Adam always liked arty stuff. He wasn't really any good at it, but he knew good stuff when he saw others doing it. He had some pretty hot calligraphy skills, and I told him so – they could add a whole new element to the work. I told him that – and the rest, like they say, was history. Adam met Chris a couple of years later, and we tagged along with him and his two girls. Then Evie came along, and Adam, ever the wordsmith, worked out that the first letters of everyone's name spelled "cancer"; he liked the way it would almost certainly worry people, the way its meaning was ambiguous, and it became a central part of our identity, worked into every piece we painted up.

I never really got every part of my anger, grief, and frustration out, but perhaps we're never supposed to; perhaps that's what fuels us, what keeps us going, what helps us create art, compose music, write poetry.

Perhaps, without that pebble in our shoe, we never really achieve anything.

The one thing I know is that every member of the Cancer Crew has been through some kind of personal hell – even Evie, who comes across like she wouldn't know a bad day if it bit her. We all live with a pain we can't talk about – so we paint it, instead.

PC Tony Raglan
LB 265

It had been an awkward evening; even the parrot was quiet, focused on doing his own thing. Feroc had suggested getting a takeaway; I hadn't felt hungry, but had agreed, and made an effort to eat, acting like everything was normal. I spent a lot of time pretending I was fine, for the simple reason that I felt Feroc's generation had been put through enough by people my age. They were already inheriting a broken world, because we hadn't asked any questions when the government of our day had made promises that, in retrospect, we should never have believed. They were struggling, but, for the most part, they were stoic about their struggles. They kept their collective head down, and kept on keeping on. My generation, the generation of traitors, should feel obliged to do likewise. And I, at least, do; it's one of the legacies of emotional abuse, believing that the blame and guilt for everything should rest firmly on your shoulders, no matter how improbable it is that you could actually be responsible for whatever's happened.

It's easy to feel aggrieved, to believe that, because we didn't *mean* to be selfish – because we didn't even realise that's what we *were* being, we shouldn't have to apologise for anything that's happened, but we're deliberately selfish if we refuse to accept that we've caused harm, whether we meant to, or even realised that's what we were doing. Sometimes, I wonder if the crime rate would be quite as high as it is if my generation hadn't assumed that "everything available" was simply our due, and taken all of it, without a thought for those who would come after us. I'm not saying there'd be no crime at all if we'd played fair – there's always been crime, and there always will be crime; even when we look back at the decades everyone claims were so amazing, there were plenty of villains. People like to claim that the difference was when drugs came on the scene, but, in truth, the drugs chased something else; the beginning of genuine unfairness. Up until the eighties, when drugs started becoming a serious issue, there'd been rich people, and poor people, but the rich people had either inherited their wealth, or grafted – legally or not – for it. Now? People have to watch their inferiors achieve insane wealth, seemingly effortlessly.

"You okay?"

I snapped back to Excelsior Street, to twenty-eighteen, and Feroc, sitting beside me.

"Fine. Why?"

"You've barely touched your chow mein. Are you feeling alright?"

I thought I'd pulled off the trick of eating enough to keep Feroc's curiosity at bay – apparently not. I shrugged.

"I'm fine. Just not as hungry as I thought I was. Stop *worrying*, for pity's sake." I took a couple of large mouthfuls of chow mein, chewing, swallowing, and trying not to wince. Anything to ensure Feroc was happy. Anything to avoid burdening him more than my generation had already burdened his. Then, suddenly, I actually was hungry, wishing I'd ordered more than just chow mein, pork balls, and chips.

Feroc touched the tips of his fingers to my wrist. "Tony? Whatever's going on, just let it go, okay?"

I turned to Feroc, smiling. "It's already gone. I'm just tired. Nothing more than that, fella."

"Early night, then."

I raised an eyebrow.

"I *mean*, you go to bed, within the next hour, and go to sleep."

"Oh. Shame."

"Sensible."

"Maybe I don't want to be sensible. Maybe I need to be a bit daft."

Feroc laughed, all patience, for now. "Or, maybe, you need to go to bed, and get some sleep."

"Come with me?"

"I'll come up once I know you're asleep. I don't trust you, Tony Raglan."

I pulled a face, which saved me from having to admit that Feroc was probably right not to trust me – I didn't go in a whole deal for being trustworthy, but it was a bit disappointing to realise Feroc had been around me long enough to realise that.

PC Feroc Hanson
LB 599

It couldn't be easy for Tony's generation. I expect that they genuinely believed they were building a better life for my generation, and they don't really understand how come it hasn't worked out. Perhaps some of them, those without kids, those who don't have much to do with their kids, those who didn't have much to do with anyone more than five years younger than themselves, had managed to convince themselves they had created that better life, had built a better world. Their anger was the righteous kind, the fury of people certain they're being lied to. I could imagine how it would feel, believing you've given someone your very best, and then hearing them claim that it's not enough, that you've short changed them. And those who do have kids? They only see the trappings – the tech, the car, the new clothes every couple of months. They hear the numbers in the pay cheque, without realising that inflation means a hundred pounds no longer buys *their* idea of a hundred pounds' worth of goods. They don't understand that a twenty year old needs a decent car, because they'll be driving hundreds of miles to jobs that don't pay much more than the minimum wage. That, sometimes, only pay the minimum wage. We all believe our world can only endure, or improve, so Tony's generation wouldn't understand how it could be that renting wasn't the affordable option, that it didn't offer stability.

I worried about Tony. I knew he had his physical coming up, and I got the impression it was affecting him more than he'd ever let on.

I watched as Tony made his way upstairs, listened to the familiar, comforting sounds that meant that, for once, he was doing as he was told, and getting ready for bed. I heard the creaking of bed springs, the strangled curse as Tony turned over, his back causing him pain I was too familiar with. I closed my eyes, as though that would help Tony, and finished my coffee. I should go up to him. I should make sure everything was okay with him.

Sergeant Aimee Gardner
LB 761

I slept badly that night, worries of various kinds chasing around my mind.

I was worried about Tony, about how he'd cope without Feroc, if Feroc did go for promotion. About his upcoming physical. I worried about Feroc, about the attitudes he might encounter if he went for promotion, and about how his career would go – or fail – if he chose not to.

And I worried about my own future, about making the right choice. I wasn't convinced that was something I could guarantee. I didn't do broken sleep. I was a cop, and cops slept when and where we could, in spite of anything that might be happening around us. It was how we survived, how we found the strength to keep putting one foot in front of the other, day after day, night after night. We didn't do stress, and we didn't do insomnia.

All the same, I couldn't sleep, and I was worried – about myself, and about the men who'd become my favourites on the relief. Was I allowed to have favourites? Probably not.

I got up, kicking the duvet to the floor, and headed through to the kitchen. It was at times like this I wished I had a girlfriend, someone who'd get up with me, sit with me in the kitchen, and let me talk about trivial things, until I finally got around to admitting what was wrong. Someone who'd listen without trying to solve my problems for me. Instead, I just had me, myself, and my thoughts. And coffee, friend of many lonely people through long, dark nights of souls in various states of grace.

As I drank the coffee, bitter warmth chased by the sweet, cloying edge of sugar and cream, I wondered if what I really needed was a holiday, a chance to get away from Lothing, from the suffocating embrace of its citizens, struggling to cope in a world they believed was new, but which had, in fact, been around more than long enough for them to get to grips with – if they'd wanted to, only none of them had.

I had a cousin who lived in Bridlington, and she was always talking about how resilient the place was, how it managed to attract tourists, and keep them coming back, without becoming a caricature of a British seaside town. Her only complaint was free bus passes; "You can never have a decent day out without taking the car, because you get on the bus at just after nine – nothing much opens before ten o'clock, up here, except the big shops, and you can see them anywhere – and it's rammed with oldies on their jollies. Half of them would just as soon settle for a potter round their own high street, if they had to pay the fare! Sixteen quid, if I want to get into Whitby, and don't fancy the drive! I don't mind subsidising someone to get an education, or get them back into work, but what are these people going to do to repay me, I'd like to know?"

Yvonne was like that, always ranting about something, yet, beneath the bluster, she was kindness itself, quick to help, and with the kind of practical comfort I probably needed right now.

I made a note to call her in the morning, and switched on the telly; the great thing about Freeview, you have a hundred and one channels broadcasting repeats, which make for comfortable viewing, as you don't have to worry about what happens. I made a nest of blankets on the sofa, and settled in for what was left of the night.

I'd go and stay with Yvonne – but I'd do it on the way back from the Lake District; Conor had settled in up there, and I wanted to know what life without the Job looked like. I had more than enough leave owing; I'd take a couple of weeks, spend a couple of days with Conor, a few more with Yvonne, and the rest thinking about what they told me, and what I'd seen for myself. That, and finally getting round to sorting the flat out. My parents had been disappointed when I'd chosen to buy a flat, pointing out that Lothing had some perfectly nice houses that were cheap to buy, but I'd known what I was doing. I wanted the security of owning property, but I wanted it small, with the comfort of knowing that whoever owned the freehold was responsible for major external work. Besides, the only houses that were cheap were on streets like Excelsior – no offence to Tony, who'd lived there as long as I'd known him, but somewhere that regularly made our hit list for drugs, domestics, and anti-social behaviour wasn't top of my list of places to be chained to long term.

I wondered how Feroc was getting on, living there – he didn't seem the type to relax into calling streets like Excelsior home, but maybe being with someone he loved made that easier. I probably shouldn't be such a snob, but, at the end of the day, we all have our preferences, for everything. I wouldn't want to live on a street like Excelsior. Some people wouldn't want to date a woman who looked like me. As long as you acknowledged your reasons were personal, and didn't try and force other people to agree with you, there wasn't a problem.

Conor

I was only supposed to be in the Lake District for a few weeks, long enough for a new gaff and new identity to be sorted out, but I'd ended up liking the place. Six months had become a year, and a year had become half a decade.

I'd realised, in that first year, that I didn't want to go back to the Job. I wouldn't settle as a regular officer, and I was tired of being deep cover. Fifteen years, moving around Lothing's drug scene and its supply chain. It had been long enough.

I avoided the cliché of buying a pub or a B&B, and, instead, found myself a job as a jack of all trades, helping out Fi, a woman who felled trees, and carved stunning ornaments and furniture from the wood. She also happened to look hot with a chainsaw, too.

It had been a bit of chance, me getting the job; she'd been in the newsagent in town, writing up a card to go in the window. I'd asked her what she was selling, she'd explained she was looking for someone to help her load and unload her van, and "give me a chance to pee once in a while" - there was finally enough work, on the carvings front, that she was doing roadside sales, and getting requests to attend fairs. Which, being on weekends, often clashed with people wanting their gardens cleared.

"It'd be good to do a few of the outdoor fairs, but I just haven't got the time. If you can take care of those, you can keep whatever you make – just pay me back the cost of the stall."

"You sure?"

"Yep – I'm making enough that I don't need the extra, especially now I've got my bits of paper to say I know about tree diseases, and how to handle them, as well as knowing which trees to plant where for best effect – that's taking off very quickly; I might need to look into getting an assistant; I don't suppose you'd be interested in training up for the role, at all?"

So, now, I wasn't just working; I was studying, too. And hoping that, one day, Fi and I might become a little bit more than boss and hired help. I liked her; she was funny, intelligent, laid back, and practical – a breath of fresh air after a decade and a half spent around needy women who were constantly trying to prove themselves to some bloke or other. She seemed to like me, too; it was just a matter of the right time, the right words. A matter of who made the first move.

I'd had an easy transition out of the Job, perhaps because I'd spent so long only ever existing on its edges. That night in the Heart of Darkness had made it clear to me that I didn't want to be so involved in so much potential for violence again. And, in the weeks afterwards, it had become clear that I'd be dragged back into that world, whether I wanted to be or not, if I stayed in the Job.

In fifteen years, the Job had changed anyway. I'd seen the looks, over time, on new faces fresh to command. The distrust of deep cover officers, the sense that I was probably already "native", helping to sow the seeds of a growing dislike and distrust of the police. What I never saw from the brass, but always heard from the grass roots, was an acknowledgement that dwindling resources, ever-changing priorities, and an obsessive focus on technology, were already banging nails into the coffin of respect for the police. We sifted out certain things, not responding to them. We took out our frustration at having to step into the gap created by the loss of social services and mental health support on those least able to cope with our anger. We joined in with the witchhunts the media whipped up against anyone who was different, and we disappeared from sight. And then we blamed the people we'd attacked, dismissed, and walked away from for losing affection for us. It was madness, but we believed we were sane. We should've seen it coming – but we were blind.

Perhaps we always had been. Perhaps it had always been too late.

Whatever the reality, I was happy here, in the life I was living now. That had surprised me, at first, and it still surprised others, but it was the truth. And I needed the truth, needed the reassurance of knowing that my life was simple, that I was who and what I claimed to be, and that no one was judging me. Here, I had all of that, and it felt good.

Inspector Bill Wyckham
LB 81

The mention of Tony Raglan's retirement – postponed, thanks to certain difficulties, not least financial, in recruiting sufficient new coppers to manage the flourishing crime and disruption of civil privileges sector, had got me thinking about my own. I knew I wasn't going to be promoted above Inspector, and I didn't want to be – too much politicking and making nice, not enough boots on the block – but I was starting to wonder if I wasn't ready to get out of the firing line altogether. The Job wasn't what it had been, and I wasn't the man I was once; I wasn't Tony Raglan; I had a family, and I wanted to live long enough, without having to go to work every day, to feel that I'd made the most of them, and that they'd had the best of what I could give. I wouldn't leave yet – I still loved the Job, still looked forward to coming in at the start of every shift, including the nights and riotous weekends, and, right now, I still couldn't imagine a life without my team. Right now, Lothing nick and its crew still felt like a second family. When I lost that, when I wasn't feeling part of things any more, it would be time to walk away. It wasn't, yet, but it was time, probably, to begin to think about what came next, about where I'd been, and where I was going.

The stereotype of the copper who couldn't cope without the Job was often true, but only because coppers suffered from the same tunnel vision that made the public despise us or idolise us; they believed they could only ever be coppers, and, when they suddenly weren't, and suddenly couldn't find a job that was very much like being in the Force, they struggled to cope. Plan ahead, though, get things in place long before you needed them, and it didn't have to be like that.

I knew I didn't want to work as a security guard, and, while running a B&B appealed, I knew the appeal was a surface one. I liked the *idea* of playing the charming host – in reality, I'd probably be longing for a convenient cell to throw ill-mannered guests in, or forgetting that Joe Public liked their sheets washed on a daily basis when they went away for their jollies. Although I could always grab a niche market, set up a B&B that would appeal to coppers. I smiled – it was a nice idea to play with, certainly.

And that was the good thing about planning ahead – I had time to play with ideas, to have fun, to explore, the way a child would, before I had to settle down, and make concrete, realistic plans.

I wondered whether Tony Raglan would use the extra time the government had given all coppers his age to plan ahead, or if he'd become one of our casualties, suddenly jolting to a stop at sixty, and wondering what to do with the rest of his life.

That was the other problem; this job, more than most, got into your mind, and under your skin. It took everything from you, and left little time for hobbies and interests, the kind of outside activities that would see people through their retirement. It set you apart from your community, too – perhaps especially so when you were any kind of minority. I hoped Tony would cope, but, in my heart, I strongly suspected he wouldn't. Feroc was sensible enough to try and guide Tony towards having a plan, making arrangements – but Tony Raglan had never been good at being guided. Someone once asked me what the difference between confidence and arrogance was; until I'd met Tony Raglan, I hadn't known. Having met him, the difference is as clear as night and day. Confidence is an innate certainty, and, as such, is open to suggestion – there's an infinite store of quiet competence that underpins a confident person, so they don't feel a loss if they ask for advice, or heed it. Arrogance, on the other hand, is a cover doe insecurity, which leads to the belief that someone giving you advice means they think you're not capable of making the right decision for yourself. That means that, at best, you'll ignore the advice, and, at worst, you'll react angrily against the person who gave it to you, alienating someone who could have been a useful ally, as well as doing yourself out of the chance to get where you needed to be, physically, emotionally, or intellectually.

Confident people had been treated well by the world; the arrogant hadn't. Tony Raglan had already been damaged by the time I met him, and I wondered who'd done that harm, Wondered, too, if the uniform was helping him heal as much as he believed it was.

I sighed, and stood up. The tide was starting to come in, and, behind me, Lothing was beginning to darken to the kind of low threat that men and women like me, Aimee, Tony, and Feroc were employed to keep away from decent people.

My phone chirruped, and I smiled as I answered it. "Yes, I know, love. I'm just heading back now. D'you want me to pick up a takeaway on my way home, or have you two already had something?"

In the background, a teenaged voice, pitched in the mid-register of a young woman who was far too cool to squeal, demanded kebabs. On the phone, an older woman laughed, informing me that they'd had sandwiches and a salad, since I'd "gone off for a wander" rather than coming straight home, but a takeaway might be nice. Perhaps something other than the kebabs, for adult digestive systems.

I returned the laughter, and suggested I pick up some sort of pizza – Mediterranean vegetable, perhaps? Then, turning my back on the sea, coming to reclaim, if only temporarily, what it would one day own for good, I headed back up to my car, feeling soothed by the couple of hours on the beach, but no more certain of where anyone's life went from here.

Tonight, all I had to do was provide pizza for myself and my wife, and a kebab for my daughter, chips, onion rings, and spiced wedges for all of us to choose from. After that? I had to keep my team safe where I could, teach them what I knew, and stand between them and an increasingly hostile government. The former was easy, the work of a few minutes and some cash. The latter could take a lifetime, and cost more than I would ever imagine.

As I pulled away, the pier came alive, a klaxon howling across the town, summoning men in h-vis wet weather gear – a lone jogger, at first, then a car, then two, three, four people running from the roads leading down to the beach. A second car screeched hard across the front of mine. The lights were up in the harbour – a lifeboat call. I hoped they got there in time. I hoped everyone made it back. I hoped no one's world ended, suddenly, tonight.

Nicole

˯ ghost through the open window, and glanced up
...˯ collage I was working on; if I leaned out and back at just
the right angle, I could see the approach to the pier. It looked like
a lifeboat call. I wondered what had happened, and hoped
everything would work out okay, for everyone out there. I
frowned back at the collage, struggling to see how to move
forward with it. I felt suddenly tired, but I needed to get this
finished; there was a big competition coming up, and winning
that could really put my name on the map in the art world. The
theme was "the water's edge", and I knew I needed an obviously
connected, yet completely novel, interpretation to be in the
running. Judges always told you that you could interpret the
theme any way you chose, but every artist worth their salt knew
that meant "be interesting, but not *too* interesting." It's like those
essay competitions where they ask you to comment on anything
to do with technology, tell you that you can write from any angle
you like, but they actually just want a stream of invective against
technology, they want you to argue that it's destroying society,
causing people to lose the ability to think for themselves, etc. It's
usually obvious what angle the judges of writing competitions are
looking for if you read the question closely, and definitely if you
read the previous winners. With art competitions, it's always "be
interesting, but don't make us think too hard to see how you've
referenced the theme." Depressing, but predictable. You can't
change it, you just have to live with it, and work round it.
Unfair? Yes, but that's life, really; it isn't fair, and you can't whine
about it, you just have to accept it, and work around it. It's a pain
in the backside, but it's a fact. You can't fight facts, you just have
to circumvent them.
"Nic? What's that noise?"
I smiled, turning round to look at Charlie as her head popped up
from under the duvet.
"Lifeboat call. That's what it looks like, anyway."

"Shit. D'you reckon it's something bad?"

"Probably – it could just be a drill, though."

"Mm." I watched Charlie unwrap herself, and get out of bed. She hadn't been sleeping; her preferred place for relaxing was burrowed under a duvet and several blankets. "How's the collage going?"

I pulled a face. "Slowly. I think I have artists' block."

"Is that even a thing?"

"Absolutely. It's like writers' block, only you don't get to fling yourself in bed and give up while you wait for the muse to alight."

"So..?"

"So, I just fiddle about with things, hoping that, sooner or later, they come right, and I'm able to finish something that's halfway worth looking at."

Charlie came over, dragging the duvet, wrapped around her shoulders, behind her, and peered over my shoulder. "It doesn't look too bad. You just need more confidence in yourself, that's all."

"I need more talent."

Charlie stroked my hair, a gentle gesture. "You've got plenty of that going on, sweetheart."

I grinned. "Yeah, but the problem is I'm not sleeping with the judges."

"You're not sleeping with me, right now – you need to do something about that."

I got up, stretching. "I need to get out."

"Spraying?"

I nodded.

"Want me to come with?"

"Always." I was already scrolling through my phone, texting the other members of the Cancer Crew, seeing who was about, who wanted to meet up. Graffiti was always better in numbers, not least because you could rely on at least one lookout.

My phone bleeped four times in quick succession – Adam and

Ricky were already out, Evie couldn't make it, as her aunt was visiting, and Chris was "spewing it out from both ends" - charming image. I grabbed the rucksack I kept packed and ready, and grinned back at Charlie.

"Let's go."

Charlie carried her gear in a battered leather satchel – sorry, a *vintage* satchel, which would, she assured me, have been used by "a professional gentleman", for carrying papers and the like. Charlie was big into vintage, and I had to admit, I loved her style, which was kind of 1950s tomboy – an anachronism, probably, but it looked good on her.

She swung the satchel off the bed post, pulled on a pair of canvas deck shoes that – as usual – she'd spectacularly failed to take off at the door, a habit I was trying to indoctrinate her into. I wasn't having much luck with that. We were off, trotting down the three flights of stairs from our top floor flat. We didn't know any of our neighbours, but we imagined their lives; the guy across the hall, who never managed to shout louder than his dog barked, the woman on the second floor, who we often heard singing, and who regularly played music that sounded Middle Eastern in flavour, the couple across from her, who had their television on loud enough to be heard from the foot of the stairs, and who we'd glimpsed twice, coming back with shopping, the old man on the first floor, who walked his Siamese cats on leads, and had a rainbow flag in his window – whether he was gay, Christian, or both, we didn't know. Across from him was a single mum who, no matter what time of day or night we came or went, always seemed to be screaming at her kids. In the single ground floor flat lived the only neighbours we'd actually spoken to – Jess, barely thirty, and already in a wheelchair, and her husband, Raf. They'd created a beautiful, vibrant garden, rigged up in empty bottles, washed out cans, hanging baskets, and window boxes. Lavender waved to rhubarb, tomatoes shook themselves at strawberries. Jess was a vibrant personality, seamlessly blending hippie and steampunk into an eclectic, striking style. I wanted to get to know them better, but I knew from brief conversations we'd had in passing that they were Christians, and that worried me. When you're gay, or trans, Christians are a frightening species, because you can never predict whether they'll be benignly patronising, or violently outraged. It didn't make for a particularly restful life, when you couldn't afford to live with degrees of separation between you and people who might hate you.

Out on the street, night was rising, wrapping itself around the town. I could hear the shrieks and snarls of people out later than was good for them, the howl of different tones of sirens – police, ambulance; the lifeboat siren wasn't sounding, now; boat and crew would be out at sea, doing whatever it was they'd been called out for. Car doors slammed, music fell from second and third floor windows.

Adam and Ricky were down at the bowling green, a place called Kensington Gardens, because Lothing was desperate to pretend it was just London-on-Sea; it would only take about ten minutes to walk there, a stroll made atmospheric by the darkening sky and the sound of the sea so close you felt that you could reach out and touch it.

One of the things that always seemed strange was that Lothing didn't smell of salt. It didn't have the tang of the sea. The sound was there, but not the scent. It felt unsettling, as though the town were only pretending to coastal. Given the way some of its inhabitants carried on, the town itself would probably prefer that its seaside situation was nothing more than pretence. There were a lot of people living in Lothing who didn't want to live on the coast. They didn't want the unpredictability of water and wind; they wanted the certainty of Primark and River Island, and it wasn't good enough that these shops could both be found just ten miles away.

When we got to Kensington, Adam and Ricky were both sitting, innocent as the dawn, on one of the benches, swigging from cans of energy drink.

I went straight over to the farthest wall, smiling as I drew close.

Ricky's trademark dotwork had rendered the Leaning Tower of Piza, with a pineapple set jauntily on top of it, chunks spewing from a gash in its skin, splatting onto the street below. Adam's brash, bold text danced around the sketch, proclaiming: "I BELONG." I took out my camera – an actual digital camera, with a flash, rather than my phone. I took a photograph, checking that the flash had shown the sketch at its best.

"I like it – you should put this on t-shirts."

Adam nodded. "We're going to. It's one of the pieces that will really work on a shirt."

Adam pulled out a couple more cans of energy drinks – the Euroshopper ones, that tasted like rocket fuel, but were somehow addictive; it was a pre-session ritual; whoever went out first had to buy a can for everyone in the crew, before they knew how many of us would be turning out. Being in a crew was about looking out for each other, taking care of each other, as much as it was about painting stuff up together.

I stretched out on the grass, ignoring the slight damp; it got into everything in Lothing, and those of us who lived here learnt not to worry about it. Charlie jumped onto the back of the bench. The four of us drank in silence, saying nothing; there was nothing that needed to be said. What future there was, wasn't worth talking about – it would happen whatever we did, or didn't do. Our responsibility was simply to enjoy the ride while it lasted.

"So," Adam swirled the dregs in his can. "What're we going to do now?"

"We should do something on the toilets down the prom – they need cheering up." Charlie leaned back, taking a long swallow.

I shook my head. "Not just the toilets. We should do the Pavilion – it looks crap. They shouldn't just leave it empty like that. It'd be a great place to have a market or something, with people who're trying to get their businesses up and running without a lot of cash. It could be a great club, somewhere for kids to hang out, somewhere they'd be safe. It could be a fucking studio – but they'll just leave it to rot, because they're obsessed with money.

So, let's make them spend some money, instead of trying to snatch it off everyone else.

"Yeah!" Ricky was already on his feet, Adam glanced around, and, seeing that we were all on board with the plan, grinned, and picked up his backpack, the signal for the rest of us to follow him. The beginning of getting to work.

PC Tony Raglan
LB 265

"Lima-Bravo One from Lima-Bravo, receiving?"

"Go ahead, Shona."

"Report of vandalism, East Point Pavilion. Informant a council worker, a Derek Sherrington. Everyone else is tucked up, so if you could pop over and have a look, it'd be appreciated. Over."

"Not really an Area Car job, is it?"

"No, but the Area Car's available. Other units aren't."

"Surely it's a neighbourhood team thing?"

"Two-six-five from seven-six-one, do you have something better to do, Tony?"

I sighed. "No, Sarge."

"Shona can show Lima-Bravo One attending then, yes? If it's not too much trouble?"

"Yes, sarge."

"Thank you *so* much, PC Raglan. The tax paying public *will* be pleased to know that you do care about what happens to the fabric of Lothing."

In the passenger seat, Feroc was trying not to laugh.

"What?"

"You – you really shouldn't have become a copper, should you?"

"What makes you think that?"

"You don't take orders very well – it seems that something as formal as the police possibly isn't the best fit for someone with authority issues."

"I don't have authority issues." I swung the car up alongside the yacht club, and swung the door open, rolling my shoulders and stretching as I got out of the car. I heard Feroc close the passenger door, and break into a light jog. I keyed the lock, pausing to listen for the hissing click of the latch that followed the bleep of the remote

A man in an orange hi-vis jacket was heading towards us. Our informant.

"Mr. Sherrington?"

"You took your time. Over here." He jerked his head towards the East Point Pavilion. I was half inclined not to follow him – I didn't get on too well with people who decided to get narky about response times. Especially when it was a mickey mouse call like this.

Early dawn on the seafront is cold. It's rarely dark – the sun rises early here – but it's almost always bloody cold.

Sherrington paused, pointing. "There."

I followed Sherrington's finger, as Feroc held the torch steady. A crab, a wad of fifty pound notes crumbled in one claw, the Grim Reaper's scythe in the other. On a diagonal, in bold green, contrasting with the red of the crab and the cash, the same words Feroc and I had seen on the youth centre; WE R CANCER.

"Maybe you're looking for someone born in June or July," Sherrington offered. I gave him a look which stopped just short of being a glare. I didn't need another complaint, but people like Sherrington needed to be put in their place. They needed to know that people like me weren't here to put up with crap from people like them.

Feroc glanced at me. I raised an eyebrow. We were both on the same page. Whoever was responsible for this, was also responsible for the graffiti on the youth centre. Bloody vandals.

"Tony." Feroc had spotted something, had taken a couple of steps forward. There was a tone in his voice that instantly got my hackles up. I crossed the space between us in a single stride, following Feroc's gaze.

Blood. Only a couple of spots, but the colour and texture looked like the sanguine equivalent of the paint that was all over the Pavilion. I wasn't CID, but I'd say the blood and the paint fell at the same time, or very close to it. Whoever did the graffiti either injured themselves – unlikely, given the lack of blood anywhere closer to, or on, the Pavilion itself, or they saw someone bleeding. They saw someone bleeding, and they didn't call us. That, to me, sent up all kinds of flags.

It would have to have been full dark for our graffiti tykes to have pulled this off – people tended to linger on the seafront until the light was definitely and completely gone. I might be unusual, but if I saw someone bleeding, even a little, in a public place, after dark, I'd call for an ambulance, at the very least.

We would've been called for a shout like that, and there was nothing on the system that suggested we had been. I'd have to check to be sure, but I'd put money on the fact that I was right, and that our vandals hadn't reported what they'd seen.

"Should we get CID out here?"

I shook my head. "For that? Could be a nosebleed, or someone stubbed their toe on a sharp stone, coming off the beach." I grinned at him. "Take a photo, though, yeah?"

"Of course." Feroc pulled out his phone, and took a single shot. Sherrington was pacing by the Pavilion. I sighed, glancing back at him. "Go and reassure our prime witness, will you? I don't think I could keep from punching him."

"Sure." Feroc looked at me, something unreadable in his eyes. "Tony -"

"I'm fine. I just don't have time for the likes of Sherrington, that's all."

We stared at one another for a moment. Feroc gave a tight, curt nod, and headed over to speak to Sherrington. I looked down at the blood stain again, then turned, and stared out to sea.

Suddenly, without really knowing why, I went over to the sea wall, and leaned over.

"FEROC!"

Nicole

"D'you think we should have told someone about that guy, Char?"

"What guy?" Charlie was still half asleep. She'd never been any good in the morning – it was just as well she didn't have to be at work until this afternoon.

"The guy we saw last night."

"The drunk guy?"

"I don't think he was drunk. He looked ill, or injured – like he'd been attacked."

"He was drunk, Nic. He's probably sleeping it off at home right now." Charlie yawned. "I wish I was."

"I'm not happy about it, Char. I wish we'd called an ambulance, or something."

She sat up in bed. "He was just pissed, Nic. It happens. People stagger about for a bit, they eventually make their way home, pass out, and wake up with a blinding hangover. They don't need an ambulance, they don't need anyone bothering them. He'll be fine." Charlie got up, stretching slowly, almost sensuously. I watched her, wondering whether I could justify telling her to take a day off. I had some work she could be getting on with, after all.

"What are you thinking?" Charlie was pulling on a dressing gown – I'd literally never known anyone who wore dressing gowns before I'd met her – and padding across to where I was trying to get just the right amount of scruff going on with my hair. In the heavy, chain-hung pub mirror, my reflection grinned at hers. "Wondering if either of us would be missed if we didn't turn up at our respective employment prisons."

Charlie's reflection smiled back at mine. "We probably wouldn't be missed, but I think the landlord might miss his rent."

"Mmm." I turned to face Charlie. "I wish we didn't have to slog ourselves for someone else."

"I know. We'll get there, though."

"You will. I don't have the jazz to make it."

"Don't be ridiculous."

"I'm not – I'm just aware of my limitations, and making it in any kind of self employment is one of those. I just don't have what it takes to bring it through."

"I could look into getting some marketing -"

I put a finger on Charlie's lips. "It's okay. I'm okay with it. You're the one who's going to be a household name – if everyone had the same amount of talent, the world would be pretty boring."

Charlie shook her head. "I believe everyone does have the same amount of talent, but I sense we're going to have to agree to disagree on that."

My heart broke a little bit. Charlie was always trying to make everything better, and I got the feeling she actually felt physical pain when she couldn't change the way things were for other people. I wished I wasn't such a disappointment to her, wished I had her drive and natural talent.

But I didn't. I'd come to terms with that; it was time that Charlie did, too.

PC Feroc Hanson
LB 599

"Bloody hell." I looked up at Tony, who was already turning away, radioing our unexpected find back to base.

"What's going on? What is it?"

"If you could just wait over there, Mr. Sherrington. Please?"

"Is someone dead? Who is it? Is it one of them as done this?"

"Mr. Sherrington, just wait there, please."

"I'd do as he says, If I were you."

I hadn't heard Tony passing behind me; by the time I turned around he was already halfway down the ramp to the beach. "Go and get the tape out of the car. CID are on their way, with the FME and SOCO. Not sure what they're going to get from here, to be honest, but they might as well have a run at it."

"You can't tell me we're going to try and close the entire beach?" Tony shrugged. "I'm not telling anyone anything. That'll be down to SOCO. We just need to get it taped off. So, if you could hurry up?"

"Alright...calm down." I heard the soft yelp as Tony clicked to unlock the boot of the Area Car. Opening the boot, grabbing the barrier tape, my mind was whirling. The mess of the body on the beach seemed too intense to be related to the drops of blood on the esplanade, suggesting that something had happened between the blood drops and the body. And, being uniform, we'd probably never get to find out what.

Ricky

"D'you reckon we should've told someone about that guy? He didn't seem to be in a good way, did he?"

Adam glanced up from chopping courgettes into cous cous. "He didn't look too bad. I mean, yeah, he was bleeding, but it didn't seem like much. A nose bleed, or something like that. Maybe he'd been punched, or something. I doubt he'd've thanked us for getting involved."

I couldn't stop thinking about the man I'd seen as I caught up to the others after having had to nip behind one of the weary-looking palm trees that seemed to have been dying for the past ten years for a pee. A smartly dressed man, following the guy we'd all seen staggering along the seafront. He hadn't looked like he was just out for a walk; the energy was all business, all threat.

Adam and the girls had been well ahead of me; I guessed they either hadn't seen the group of three, or hadn't noticed them. I couldn't help wondering if they'd been after the bloke we'd seen staggering through the fountains. Although, thinking back, Nicole had looked as though she'd seen something that had worried her. Maybe she'd seen the man, too.

Adam turned away from the counter, carrying two bowls of cous cous salad. It'd made us laugh when the Sunday papers got all excited about how Prince Harry's wedding had "created a new trend" with "bowl food"; when you live in a tiny bedsit, pretty much every meal was eaten from bowls; there simply isn't the space for a dining table. Of course, the next thing we'd have to cope with would be the inevitable "contrarian" commentator sneering at how unhealthy and chavvy eating out of bowls was – we'd already had the comment, in the local rag, that "only dogs eat out of bowls" - that particular paper had never really come to terms with the fact that people other than wealthy retirees and second home owners lived in Norfolk and Suffolk, and its columnists took every opportunity to remind those of us who weren't well off that we weren't quite human. Being poor in

Britain was certainly an experience.

 I hoped that the guy we'd seen last night hadn't had a bad experience – but I had a feeling he had, despite my hopes.

PC Tony Raglan
LB 265

"So, what do you reckon?" I was leaning against the sea wall, eyes narrowed against the sun as I watched the turning tide. Feroc was shepherding the ghouls away on the promenade side. People; the world would be a better place without them.

The pathologist looked up, shaking her head. "Hard to say until I get a proper look at him, but I can be fairly certain he died between 8pm and midnight, and I'd put it towards the later end of that time span; high tide was 7.30pm, and the body's not wet, so he fell onto the beach well after that."

"Fell? Or was pushed?"

"Can't say for sure, but I'd say he was pushed – there's no sign that he tried to grab the wall, or put out a hand to break his fall on the rocks – both things you'd expect someone to do if they were drunk and fell. Also, he had a nosebleed before he died – that's what the blood stains by the fountains were from. From the splatter pattern, though, he had to have been punched – a spontaneous nosebleed wouldn't have had that much force behind it."

"The same person who punched him threw him over the wall?"

Claire straightened up. "You do the who, I just tell you what and how. Sometimes when, if you're lucky, and where on very rare occasions, when the moon is full and brilliantly blue."

"Not quite accurate – my team do the who, now. Thanks." DI Roscoe was leaning over the sea wall. Tam Freud was talking to Feroc.

"We'll leave you to it, then, guv. Are we alright to get back on patrol, or do you need us here?"

"I think DC Freud and I can manage, Tony." Roscoe turned to Claire. "Let me come down there and have a look at him, then we can get him off the beach."

"Sir."

Roscoe and Freud came down the ramp onto the beach. I headed up the ramp, onto the promenade. Feroc was already walking towards the Area Car.

"What's going on down there, mate?"

I glared at the bloke, all tattoos and beer gut. "Nothing that's going to affect your life, pal. Now – move along."

"Someone top themselves, did they? Walk out into the waves job?"

"If they did, it's nothing to do with you, is it, sir?"

"I might know them."

"Late twenties, short, dark brown hair, cut for a floppy fringe. Skinny bloke. Tartan shirt, blue jeans, Doc Marten boots, purple. Sound like someone you know, does it?"

A look of disgust crossed Ugly's face. "A bloke wearing purple boots? What was he, some kind of faggot? One of them trannies?"

"If you don't move along, I'm going to arrest you." Beside me, I felt Feroc stiffen.

"What for? What'm I doing? Eh? Tell me that – what law am I breaking?"

"Obstruction. Impeding a police investigation. Wasting police time." I stared at the guy, making him uncomfortably aware of my uniform, my height, my strength. The power I had to royally fuck up his life.

"Alright, alright. I'm going. Bloody bleeding hearts – where d'you reckon we'll end up, if everyone chops their bits off? When blokes stop behaving normal? There won't be any kids, no future generations. We'll die out, and them Muslims'll take over, that's what'll happen. Mark my words, mate. And it started with you."

I stepped in front of Ugly as he went to lumber off. "What's your name, fella?"

"What's yours?"

"PC Raglan. Now – name."

"John Grainger."

I raised an eyebrow. "Grainger. Not a very English name, that – sounds Scottish to me."

"You want a slap, do you, PC Raglan?"

"Go on – I'd love to add assault on police to your charge sheet."

"I can't believe people like you are defending people like that. Makes me sick."

"No one said the victim was a homosexual, sir." Feroc had stepped up, drawing level with me. Two people didn't make a line, but two uniforms were a lot more intimidating to one mouthy gobshite. "In fact, all we know about him is he's dead. Doesn't that bother you a little bit more than what colour he preferred his footwear?"

"Sod it. What's is matter, anyway? Are you going to let me leave?"

I held Grainger's gaze, deliberately waiting for him to look away, then stepped slowly to one side. Feroc and I both watched him leave, then turned and walked back to the car.

"You alright?"

"Why wouldn't I be?"

"Well, the stuff he was saying... didn't it bother you?"

"Feroc, if I got rattled every time someone starts being shady about gay people, I'd never get anything else done."

"Yeah, but -"

"Doesn't it bother you? If it's supposed to bother me, surely it should bother you, too?"

"It's different for me – I'm younger, I grew up with the community. I've got people I can talk to."

"And you think I haven't?"

"Have you, then? Other than me and Aimee Gardner?"

I felt my face twitch as I opened the driver's door of the Area Car and climbed behind the wheel.

"I get by."

Feroc got in beside me, closing the passenger door softly. "I'll take that as a no, then, eh?"

"I'm fine. I don't need some so-called community, I don't need to talk to anyone, and I don't get bothered by people like Grainger. Alright?"

"Whatever you say. So – the bloke on the beach? No ID, just twenty-seven pounds fifteen pence loose in his pocket. Not even a mobile phone – who goes out without a mobile phone?"

"Maybe he wanted a bit of peace and quiet. Was sick of people yapping all the time."

"Or maybe someone took the phone, and his wallet, so we wouldn't know who he was."

"Or maybe he decided to go out on the spur of the moment, and just snatched up some cash on the way out. Plenty of people don't take their entire world with them every time they step out the door."

"Do they?"

"I don't take my mobile with me if I'm just going for a drive."

"But you'd take your wallet, wouldn't you? I mean, if you were bothered about taking cash, you'd take your wallet?"

"Maybe. Maybe not. I've gone out with just a couple of notes before."

"A couple of notes is one thing; twenty-seven pounds fifteen pence is awfully specific."

"Is it? Sounds to me like he took thirty quid, and spent a couple of quid somewhere – maybe he had a pint in a pub or something." I pulled the car over. "Heart of Darkness is the cheapest pub round here – if he had thirty quid, and he's got twenty-seven fifteen now, then he spent two eighty-five, the Heart of Darkness is the only place he could've got a pint that cheap."

"So..."

I got out of the car, keys in hand. "So, I think it'd be worth having a chat."

I felt Feroc's eyes on me. "Sure?"

I sighed. "Feroc, I've been in the Heart of Darkness plenty of times in the past five years. I'll manage."

"Yeah, but you've not been back socially. The other shouts, you had action to keep your mind off the setting. It's not going to be like that now, is it?"

"I'll cope, Feroc. I always do. It's what I'm good at."

I shouldered open the door of the Heart of Darkness, a wash of remembered scent flooding over me. The antiseptic tang of the floor, sickly sweet over layers of saltwater and shit. A smell of burning, bitter and hot. The moist, wheaty smell of beer, the sharpness of spirits. Something sweet, sickly, and metallic. I closed my eyes, took a breath, and stepped forward. "Afternoon. PCs Raglan and Hanson. We're wondering if you could help us."

A couple of women, late teens or early twenties, got up with a show of fuss over coats and bags, and several backward glances at us. Exaggerated unhurriedness. An older man nudged his companion, who turned, and looked us up and down. Both men downed their pints too quickly, feet already moving towards the opposite door to the one we'd come in. Everyone else was either suddenly very quiet, or having some very animated, very banal conversations about the weather, jobs they may or may not have actually had, and how their football teams were doing.

An early-thirties male in a white shirt and tie, sleeves rolled up to the elbows, glint of fake gold tie clip.

"Finlay Harris; I'm the manager. What seems to be the problem, officers?"

"Were you working last night?"

"No, I wasn't; that would've been Gary Finch. He didn't mention that anything had happened."

"We don't think it did. Not here, at least. Don't suppose you know a bloke who wears purple boots, do you?"

Harris smiled. "You must mean Brewer – I don't have any other name for him. He works in the tattoo shop around the corner. He's always wearing something purple – it's a kind of trademark of his. The boots sound right up his alley."

"Cheers. We'll go and see what the tattoo place has to say."

"Is he alright? Brewer – or whoever this lad is?"

I turned back, meeting Harris' gaze with all the frustrated sorrow I felt, for all the lives I'd seen wasted over the years. "Not really, no. I'm sorry."

Harris shook his head. "Ah, shit. It's got rough round here."

I raised an eyebrow. "How long you been here, Mr. Harris?"
"Moved out from London three years ago. I thought it'd be nice, little seaside town, old folk, few office girls on a lunch break."
I shook my head. "Should've come a couple of years earlier. You might not've hung around for this."
"What happened five years ago, then?"
"I was shot. Nearly died. Right where you're standing."

PC Feroc Hanson
LB 599

"Was there really any need to creep Harris out like that? Tony? Tony – are you with us?"

Tony blinked, and turned, slowly, to face me. "Yeah. I'm fine."

"Harris?"

"He annoyed me. Smug git."

"Tony..."

"Don't start, Feroc. I'm so far from being in the mood, you wouldn't believe it."

I turned to face Tony, angry, and afraid.

"I'm going to start, Tony, because I need to stop this before it goes anywhere. I need you to level with me. What's going on, big man?"

Tony turned away. That was a knife to the gut – I loved Tony's eyes. They were the kind of soulful eyes you wanted to jump into and drown in. The times he turned away from me were the times I most wanted to break down.

"Tony."

"Nothing's going on, Feroc. Nothing's wrong. Just..." he shook his head, as though he had something in his ear, and carried on walking towards the car. "...Just leave me alone, okay?"

I let the silence hang between us; it seemed more effective, somehow, than breaking it.

As we drove back to the station, the silence remained unbroken. Either nothing was happening, or those it was happening to felt it was none of our business. Either way, the only radio traffic was chatter; everyone sounded restless and bored.

When we got back to the station, everyone who was in was, inevitably, eager to know about the body on the beach. Tony ignored them all, heading for DIU. I followed him, making apologetic faces at colleagues I might otherwise have stopped and spoken to. A murder find shared is a murder find halved by giving twice the number of people nightmares, after all.

In the DIU, Tony's fingers moved slowly over the computer keyboard, like a composer playing out a particularly tricky piece. "Brewer...Brewer... " He glanced to his right, nodded once. "Yep, got you." He looked up, frowning a little, as though he hadn't expected to see me standing there.

"It's Brewer, then? The body on the beach?" I'd never picked up the habit of treating the dead as inanimate objects, absent personalities whose sensitivities and preferences no longer had to be considered. I could understand where the habit came from, though; if you didn't think of the body as a person, it wasn't quite as crushing, as soul-destroying, if justice evaded efforts that went far beyond your best, if a conviction failed to materialise in spite of nights without sleep, and days with little patience for anything other than the murder.

I wondered how many bodies Tony had seen. Wondered, too, how many he'd known. I wondered if his reluctance to be a brute came from close calls, and the inescapable awareness that he could so easily, on so many occasions, have been that ragged assortment of skin and bones on a mortuary slab.

He nodded. "Yeah. Val Brewer – short for Valiant. No wonder the poor sod only used his surname. What the hell some parents are thinking, sometimes, I'll never know."

I smiled to myself at Tony's utter obliviousness – it wasn't as though "Feroc" was the most normal thing you could name your child, after all. But, like so many other people with opinions, Tony didn't mean me – no one ever did, and they were always shocked you could think that they might have done.

I went over to the computer terminal, and studied the screen. The image was a match for the body we'd found that morning. Val Brewer was twenty-nine, one caution for speeding, a couple of arrests for possession of cannabis.

I recognised the address; a block of flats only about two minutes from Excelsior Street.

My heart lurched when I saw the notes for next of kin; we would be telling a twenty-seven year old woman, whose child, just six months old at the time of her father's last contact with police, would now be almost two, and old enough to understand, that her husband, the father of her child, the man she'd believed would be there and provide for her, had been brutally murdered.

Tony stood up, stretching slowly. "Come on. Let's get this over with."

As we headed down the corridor that led to the rear yard, we passed the double doors that led out to the main entrance. I paused, glancing through to the front desk, a habit I'd had from my first day at Lothing.

"Tony – wait."

"What?" He followed my gaze. A young woman, clearly agitated, purple streaks through blonde hair, tugged a toddler close to her with one hand, and pushed a strand of hair out of her eyes with the other.

"You reckon it's her? The wife?"

"We may as well find out."

I pushed the doors open, stepping into a conversation that was already well under way.

"- yesterday. He went to work like normal – he's got the Skin In The Game tattoo studio, on Parade Road? He left about half nine; he opens up at ten, it only takes a few minutes to walk there from ours, but he likes to give himself plenty of time. I was expecting him home around six, six-thirty. He closes up at six, unless he's got an evening booking, but, in that case, he'll go in later. When he hadn't come home by seven, I assumed he'd gone for a drink. I tried his mobile, but he didn't answer – he sometimes forgets to take it off silent when he's finished at the studio. He's not really into technology the way a lot of people are – I don't mean he hates it, just..." The young woman took a deep breath, and hugged her child, kissing the top of its head. "Sorry. I'm rambling. Anyway. When he hadn't come home by ten o'clock, I sent him an angry text – I was pretty annoyed, to be honest; I mean, I don't have a problem with him going out, but he *knows* to call me, so I can give my mum a ring to help out with Kat – she's at that awkward stage, asserting herself, finding her spirit, and sometimes I just need an extra pair of hands. So, I wasn't as polite as I might've been. When he wasn't home this morning, I assumed he'd got a strop on, and had slept in the studio, or on the sofa, and left before I woke up. I felt bad, so I went to the studio... I've just come from there... he'd never arrived that morning. His apprentice was there, Jared Searles; he'd tried to call Val, but couldn't get an answer."

"Excuse me," I stepped forward, trying to settle my face into pleasantly neutral. "Are you talking about Valiant Brewer? Are you Rachel?"

"Rae. Everyone calls me Rae. And yes – oh, god, don't tell me he's got himself arrested again. It's medicinal, why he takes cannabis – he was in a car crash when he was a teenager, and it's left him with a lot of pain in his legs and back; the cannabis helps, a lot, but I've told him over and over not to smoke it in public. I don't let him smoke in the flat, because of Kat – he made us a bit of a balcony, so he'll go out there -"

"I'm sorry to have to tell you this," Tony's deep, rough-around-the-edges voice was smoother, softer. "But a man we believe to be your husband was involved in an incident last night, sometime between eight pm and midnight. I'm afraid the incident was fatal."

Rae Brewer stared at Tony like a deer in the headlights, then looked to me, as though I might be able to undo the pain of Tony's words.

"You mean...dead? Val's dead?"

"We don't know. We're fairly certain, but we can't be a hundred percent. Not until someone who knew him has formally identified the body we found." Tony's voice was gentle, offering a comfort that could never do as a verb any of what it promised as a noun. "Oh, god..."

I stepped forward quickly, putting an arm around the young woman's shoulders, steering her towards the double doors we'd stepped through, just before we ruined her life. Tony swung little

Kat up into the air, peering at her.

"Well, now – what's your name, eh?"

"Kitty-Kat."

"Really? That's a lovely name. I'm Tony."

"Like tiger?"

"Exactly like the tiger. So, we've got a kitty-cat and a tiger – that's a pretty good start, isn't it?"

A head of auburn hair bobbed up and down, bright eyes taking everything in.

"Her name's Kat-Yvonne. We call her Kitty-Kat, because she can't say her whole name yet. Her middle name's Dee. Val named her – I wanted him to." Rae Brewer gave a mewling, gulping sob. "He can't be dead. He just *can't* be. When can I see the... the body you found? You said I'd need to tell you, if it was him?"

"Soon." Tony was still in his soothing mode. "We just need to ask you a few questions, first." I glanced into the soft interview room; no one else was using it. I opened the door.

"Let's go in here – it's nicer than the standard interview rooms, and there's some toys Kat can play with."

"Horsies!" It wasn't a question; the little girl was already wriggling strongly against Tony's grip. He set her down, and she made a beeline for the toybox at the end of the room, crouching down, and being surprisingly careful as she sorted through.

"Oh – a *princess* horsie!" Kat's voice was pure wonder as she turned around, holding a plastic horse, champagne coloured, with a pale pink mane and tail, and gold hooves, saddle, and bridle. "A *princess.*"

Tony smiled. "She seems happy."

"Yeah. She loves horses. And princesses. So..."

"Firstly, it's probably going to be best if you found someone to look after Kat when we go for the identification. It's not really the sort of thing kids should go through."

"Of course. I didn't think...Can I call my Mum?"

"Of course."

"Thanks. I didn't know whether I could use my phone in here. It's okay, yeah?"

Tony nodded. "Go ahead. I'll go and see what the princess horse is up to."

I smiled as he settled down beside Kat, seemingly completely absorbed in the life and times of princess horses. Rae followed my gaze as she scrolled through her phone. "He's good with kids, isn't he? You don't expect it from a bloke like him, really, do you? Mum? Hi, it's Rae. Look...something's happened... I'm at the police station – no, I'm not in trouble – they think that... they think... I've got to go and see a... a body. They think it might be Val, that he's had an accident... I need you to come and pick Kat-Yvonne up. I... I don't want her... if it is Val. I know...I know... I don't know... Yeah, yeah, Lothing. Thanks. I'll tell you what's going on once... yeah. Yeah. Love you too, Mum. See you soon."

She switched off the phone, and looked at me with that hopeless, desperate expression, one I'd become increasingly familiar with over the years.

I took a deep breath. "Okay, so we need a few details first..."

PC Tony Raglan
LB 265

I glanced at Rae. She looked surprisingly calm, if I pretended not to notice the way she was biting the inside of her top lip, and the way her fingers were wound around the strap of her handbag.

 Maureen Gale, Rae Brewer's mother, had arrived about twenty minutes ago. Kat-Yvonne had been delighted to see her "gammama", but disconcerted about the possibility of leaving the "princess horsie" behind; that was easily solved by an offer to let Kat-Yvonne keep the toy; Maureen offered to pay for it; I shook my head.

"It's okay – these are things we pick up cheaply. I'm sure one horse won't be missed." I smiled at Kat-Yvonne. "You're going to take care of your princess horsie, aren't you? Give her a very special home?"

Kat-Yvonne nodded furiously, clutching the horse to her chest. Feroc and I had watched Maureen Gale lead her granddaughter out of the room. Rae Brewer took several shaky breaths as her daughter waved goodbye, trotting happily alongside her nan.

 I'd turned to Rae. "Are you ready?"

She'd nodded. "Okay."

 In the mortuary, as Rae tried to convey an appearance of bravery in the face of possibly the worst situation anyone could be put in; the moment where they might have to admit, out loud, to strangers, that someone they loved was dead.

 Feroc nodded to the mortuary assistant, who slowly pulled back the sheet covering our victim's head.

"Oh god! No!" Rae stepped forward, fingertips on the glass viewing window, tears already welling up.

"Val... what happened, Val? Oh, god, Val..."

Feroc spoke quietly. "Can you confirm that this man is your husband, Valiant Brewer?"

 Rae nodded, a soft, mewing noise rising from the back of her throat. "Val. Oh, god... what am I going to tell my Kitty-Kat?"

DI Mark Roscoe

"So... what do we know about Valiant Brewer?"

Tony Raglan shrugged. "Not much. We've had him in a couple of times, possession of cannabis. Eighteen months ago, the last time. He ran his own tattoo studio – Skin In The Game. Local place, Parade Road. They're pretty busy, from what I've seen, and apparently he owned his flat, so he can't've been doing too badly. Wife and a little girl." Tony shook his head. "I really hope she doesn't end up losing the place. The wife, I mean."

"If he's had any sense, he'll've set the mortgage up to end on his death."

"Yeah, if he can, boss – I wasn't able to."

I laughed. "Yeah, but tattooists aren't as likely to die young as coppers, are they?" I realised what I'd said, and shook my head. "Sorry – that was in poor taste." I suddenly processed something Tony had said. "How would you know how busy his tattoo studio was? There been trouble there?"

"Not at all – I've thought about getting a tattoo, a few times – never quite been brave enough. Or committed enough. But I've been in and out, having a look around... I must have seen Val Brewer, maybe even spoken to him." He shook his head again. "I don't remember him, though."

I studied the photo. "To be honest, other than those purple boots, he doesn't look particularly memorable, does he?" I looked up. "You said he had a wife and kid?"

Tony nodded. "Yeah. Rae. Rachel. And Kat-Yvonne. That's the little girl. She likes horses. Why?"

"Well, the purple boots...not what you'd expect a bloke to wear, is it?"

Tony's laugh came as a bark of pure amusement. "You think only gay blokes'd wear purple boots? Can you imagine me or Feroc in purple anything?"

I laughed, shaking my head. "No. Sorry, I shouldn't've even been thinking that, should I?"

"As far as I'm concerned, boss, there's nothing you shouldn't think about. When we tell people they can't think things, we make them resent the people they've been told not to think about. That's where everything's gone wrong, people being told they can't think this and they can't say that. No one's as fragile as the social justice brigade want us to believe. Say what you want, think whatever passes through your mind. Ask the awkward questions. It's the only way difference will ever be understood. I'd rather people get everything out in the open than there be all these shadows and half-truths that lead people to make wild assumptions and behave like animals to their fellow man."

"That makes a lot of sense." I glanced back at the photograph. "Poor sod. So, no idea who'd want to take him out like that? It's particularly vicious, isn't it? I'd say that kind of violence was personal, wouldn't you?"

"Definitely. We think he'd been punched earlier in the evening – there were blood stains on the promenade – we got photos of them, too."

I flicked through the crime scene photos until I found the two tiny specks of blood on concrete, the fountains splashing in the background.

 "Ah, yes. Here we go...nosebleed?"

"Yeah – the kind that's caused by force, rather than by accident. Someone made his nose bleed, either because they were angry at the world in general, or at Brewer in particular. My money's on the latter."

"Mine too. People don't typically just punch other people in the face because they hate the world. They punch other people because they hate those individuals, specifically. Our first question has to be why someone hated Val Brewer – because that's going to tell us why he died."

"Yeah... but it won't help his missus, will it? Or his little girl."

I studied the big man, taking in the set of his shoulders, the soft sadness in his eyes, the weariness etched in lines across his face. I felt my heart break a little. Tony Raglan was a gentle copper, dedicated to getting his man, but getting them in the right way. Making it stick. Making it right – for those left behind as well as those we came into direct contact with. And when it came to women and kids, he'd always been conscientious when it came to protection. He was a dedicated guard dog, a shepherd, rounding up life's waifs and strays, widows and orphans, and leading them to the closest thing to safety he could find. I didn't like to think of how he'd feel if we couldn't make it right for Rachel Brewer and her daughter.

I reached out a hand, lightly touching Tony's shoulder. "We'll do everything we can, okay? We'll make it right. I promise."
Tony shook his head. "No, you won't. You can't." He turned away, shoulders squared, pulling back on the mask he needed to face the world. "None of us can."

As I watched Tony Raglan walk away, I felt a chill settle in the pit of my stomach. I'd bring right from this, even if it destroyed me. I didn't like seeing relatively innocent young people killed for no apparent reason, and I certainly didn't like the idea that the people who were responsible for an innocent young man's death were still wandering around somewhere, feeling like they were invincible, because they thought they'd literally got away with murder.

DC Tam Freud

"So, Tony and Feroc were investigating reports of graffiti, and they stumbled over the body while they were out there? That's pretty rough."

Roscoe nodded. "Yeah. Tony seems really cut up about it – I think the fact that the guy had a wife and a young kid really got to him; he feels like he's got to look out for them, and part of that is getting a resolution on Brewer's murder."

"We're sure it was murder? I mean, obviously, this looks pretty bad, but we're sure he couldn't have got those injuries falling over the sea wall onto the rocks?"

"Pathologist's pretty sure. He was attacked, violently, with fists and feet. And then thrown over the sea wall, when he was already dead."

I studied the pictures, thoughts chasing one another across my mind. "The problem with attacks like this, guv, is they take place at night. No one sees anything, those who might see something were somewhere they shouldn't have been, doing something they shouldn't have been, nine times out of ten. They don't come forward, not even anonymously. So, we never really get the answers."

"I know that. We all know that. It's a pain, but there's no way round it. Even when we do get someone who's willing to come forward, they're so dodgy, any defence brief worth their salt wouldn't give them five minutes. I don't know what the answer is, you don't know what the answer is, no one knows what the answer is."

I looked up. "I might have an idea on that, actually, guv."

"Yeah?"

"Well...it occurred to me when you mentioned that Tony and Feroc had been called out to graffiti. Graffiti crews go out at night...if we were to set up a crew of our own, get the right kind of coppers, we wouldn't stand out like sore thumbs, and we also wouldn't be noticed. The point of being a graffiti crew is that you're not seen – your work is."

"So, what are you thinking, Tam? A full operation?"

"If we've got the budget." I took a deep breath. "And we might need to bring in officers from other stations. We need young looking faces. And that's likely to mean probies. I mean, this job isn't exactly known for its anti-ageing properties, is it?"

"I suppose not, no. Feroc doesn't look too old – he could pass for very early twenties, a little bit immature, hasn't quite grown up yet."

"Definitely. And I'd like Aimee Gardner on board, too. I don't know that we have anyone else, do we? Seamus Hanratty, he's not been around too long."

"That's three of you, but they're all from uniform. I'm fairly certain Bill Wyckham'll give you the nod, but, if you're recruiting from other nicks, I want CID – I can square it with their guv'nors."

"Colt Devereux – the guy who was on Killjoy with Tony. He's got that ageless quality."

"Devereux I know I can do – me and his DI go back a long way, and I know Devereux's keen to do some more work with us; I get the feeling he wants to come on board. Do you need anyone else?"

I shook my head. "No. I can probably pull off mid-twenties; baseball cap and a baggy coat, I might look younger."

"Right. I'll talk to Bill Wyckham, and Devereux's DI. You start getting a plan of action together."

"You're sure we can run with this?"

"I'll make sure. It's a good idea, and I want you to have experience running your own operation. It'll serve you well when you put in for your sergeant's exams."

I felt myself blush. "The thing is, guv, I -"

"Don't tell me you don't think you're ready, Tam, because I know you are. And this operation's going to prove it. So; what's the moniker going to be?"

"Guv?"

Roscoe walked away. Over his shoulder, he called back;
"Your op, your name. Go for it. Make it good."
A broad smile began to spread across my face. "Will do, guv."

PC Feroc Hanson
LB 599

"Nightshade? What's it about, then?"

"Well, a lot of crime, we miss because it happens after dark, out of sight – we don't see it, and those who do see it, don't tell us about it. We might as well be separate species, the police and the kind of people who live for the night. Different language, different culture. And it's becoming harder for us to go incognito at night – we're awkward and uncomfortable in clubs, the internet's made it unusual to find toms prowling their patch; those who are out on the street are junkies, and we can't pass for anyone far enough along to have lost access to the internet. One of the things we could make work for us, with the right officers on board, is posing as a graffiti crew. There are some legitimate sites around Lothing, we could easily hang around there, get our faces known a little. The good thing with graffiti is you don't have to actively be doing it to pass as an artist of crew; you can hang around, act like you're scouting potential spots. We need young-looking coppers; as well as yourself, Feroc, I'll be asking Sergeant Gardner and Seamus Hanratty. I've also been given the green light to approach Bethel Street, in Norwich; I think Colt Devereux looks the part, and it's never a good idea to let you lot outnumber CID by too many, is it?"

Tam Freud grinned. I laughed. "Count me in. Sounds just what we need, to be honest, and the great thing is, no one'll think it's weird if we have cameras with us; it'll just look like we're taking shots of potential sites, work we like. No one'll notice."

"Good. So, that's two of us sorted – just got to get the others on board, then I can have the all-important conversation about whether there're enough coins in the piggy bank to pay everyone for everything."

I rolled my eyes. "Yeah – or whether we're going to end up trading rest days, swapping shifts, and scratching around at the frayed edges of the spirit of our contracts to make it work."

"Exactly."

I shrugged. "Nothing we're not used to in uniform, and it's in aid of a good cause."

"Thanks for the vote of confidence, Feroc. To be honest, I wish the DI'd pulled rank and taken this one off me. Whenever we used to have sponsored anythings at school, I always just used to hand over money from my paper rounds – I hated asking people for money then, and I haven't aged into it."

"You think you have it tough – I've got to explain to Tony that I'm going under."

"Oh dear."

"Yeah. One of the first things he did, when we got back off honeymoon, was to make it clear to the brass that he didn't want to go under again, and now here I am, doing exactly what he feels it's too dangerous for him to do."

"But Tony Raglan's been a copper a long time. He's had plenty of time to go under. You haven't even got out of the blocks, yet. You need to be allowed to feel your oats a bit."

I pulled a face. "And you can see Tony being relaxed about that, can you?"

"No – but he doesn't have to be relaxed about it. He just has to accept it."

"Tony Raglan's never been good at accepting things, has he?" My eyes met Tam Freud's. "After all, you've been here longer than I have. What do you know about him, about the way he sees things?"

She shook her head. "Tony Raglan's always been...complicated."

"Complicated?! That doesn't even begin to get the half of it across, does it?"

Tam laughed. "I suppose not. So – you're keen for this, yeah?"

I nodded. "Yeah. From what I saw of Colt Devereux – which wasn't a lot, granted – he's someone I'd like to work with, get to know better."

"You know he's -"

"Yeah. I think the whole Force does. Poor sod."

"Surely he'd rather everyone knew? That it was out in the open?" I gave looked at Detective Constable Tam Freud, letting the seconds pass.

"Really? I know it wasn't easy when people found out about Tony and me the way they did – I mean, I'd barely accepted that I felt like that about him, and suddenly it was all round the nick. And given how quiet he kept things with Max, I get the feeling Tony would've preferred to keep things on the down low, let them take their course without everyone being up in our faces about it. Some people still haven't realised they don't have to vocalise every thought that crosses what passes for their mind. It gets..." I sighed. "It's exhausting, sometimes. I can only imagine how much worse it's going to be for someone like Colt."

"I suppose you're right. But, if you rate him, and Tony does -"

"He does. He told me that himself."

"Well, then – he's always going to have family here, isn't he? Perhaps Nightshade will help him make the right decision. God knows, we need a few more DCs."

"It'd be good to have him here; we need to send out a message that being gay, or trans, or queer, isn't just some trendy city thing they only do in London, Manchester, Brighton, Norwich. That there are people 'like that' in every town, every village. That they can't just ignore us any more."

"You think he'll want to leave Norwich?"

I paused, thinking about it. "I don't think he's had the easiest time of it out there, anyway. At least here, he'd have a couple of ready made friends."

"Three. He'd have three friends. And Aimee Gardner – I'm sure she'd be up for running with him."

I nodded. "It's not going to be easy, whatever he decides – but I think he'd fit in alright here. He's got the right attitude, the right mindset. The way Tony tells it, he was completely on the ball with Killjoy; like he'd done it a hundred times before. He's only a year or so older than me, but Tony says he felt like Colt could take care of him, like he'd look after him. That's an incredible skill to have, the ability to make someone feel that relaxed, that trusting."

"Especially someone like Tony – he's never been good at trust, not really. You were one of the first people he ever really had complete faith in here."

I felt the heat rise through my cheeks. I glanced away. "I didn't know that. He's always been really hot on how I should trust the team, like it was something he'd got sorted."

Tam shook her head. "Watch him sometime, Feroc – don't just look at him; *see* him. Listen to him. Listen to everything he doesn't say, as well as what he does. And I think you'll realise how wrong you were about how much trust he has in his colleagues. He's wary, Feroc – warier than he has any right or need to be. He hides it well, but it takes him a long time to let his guard down, and I'm not sure he ever completely manages to. He puts a brave face on it, but he's hurting. He needs you, Feroc..." Tam looked awkward.

"What?"

"Look...if Colt does come on board, as a result of Nightshade... he's around your age...and..."

"Woah! We don't even know which team Colt plays for! And I wouldn't do that to Tony."

"You might not mean to, but these things happen, you know how it is."

"Not with me, they don't. Not if it means Tony getting hurt."

"Right."

"I wouldn't hurt him, Tam. We've been through too much together for me to do that to him."

Tam nodded. "I know it's been rough for the two of you." She laughed, shaking her head playfully. "I mean, accident prone doesn't even begin to describe Tony Raglan, really. He should've died at least a thousand times over by now, and you along with him; I can understand the kind of bonds that sort of fire forges."

"Yeah. Steel chains." I frowned, and gave a long exhale of breath."Sometimes -"

"What?" Tam looked at me, concern in her eyes.
I shook my head. "Nothing."

DC Colt Devereux

"You doing okay, being back to reality, after Killjoy?"

I nodded. "Yeah. It gave me the confidence I needed to handle the everyday, you know?"

Tam Freud nodded. "I can understand that. So... you wouldn't be averse to going under again?"

"Is that why you're here?"

"Yeah... we – I... there's something a bit different going down, and I need some young-looking blood on the team."

I laughed. "I'm glad I count as young-looking. So, who else is on board?"

"One of our uniform sergeants, Aimee Gardner. A uniform PC, Seamus Hanratty, and Feroc Hanson; you remember him, I assume?"

I felt my stomach lurch. "Of course. Tony Raglan's partner."

"That's the one. And I'll be dressing myself up as lamb, trying to look young enough to be out painting the town – quite literally. Nightshade is going to involve setting up a graffiti crew – or as close an approximation of one as we can pull off without actually getting involved in anti social behaviour. We realised that the kinds of folk who go out tagging are essentially invisible to anyone else out at night who's up to no good, so we – I – thought it might be a good opportunity to dredge up the kind of pond life that usually manages to avoid us by staying in the shadows."

"Sounds spot on to me." I wanted to ask Tam something, to get an idea out of my head and into a spoken reality... but, at the same time, I didn't want to risk being shot down; it mattered too much for that.

"Is there anything else you want to ask?"

"It's just... I mean... I'm the only officer from outside Lothing...."

Tam got to her feet, smiling. "If you wanted to put in for a transfer, Colt, your presence as part of Nightshade would absolutely be taken into consideration."

"Right." That was what I'd been afraid of.

As I watched Tam Freud leave, I wondered what the hell I was playing at – did I really want to step back inside Tony Raglan's circle? What had happened between us had been insane, from anyone's perspective. Turning up at his wedding like that, lurking in the shadows, had been madness. And getting reacquainted with him, working in the same nick...

It was foolishness. The most extreme kind of stupidity anyone could be guilty of. I shouldn't be that stupid.

But, from the moment my DI had told me there'd been an approach from Lothing to have me go undercover for them, I'd known I'd use it as a way to get out of Norwich, and back into Tony Raglan's orbit. He was like a drug I couldn't give up, A drug I didn't *want* to give up.

PC Tony Raglan
LB 265

"Colt Devereux's coming out here?"

"Apparently." Feroc took a long gulp of orange juice. "They want young faces for Nightshade, and they'd run out of them in Lothing."

"Don't know why they didn't ask me."

Feroc laughed. "Yeah, me neither." He looked at me. "You'll be looking forward to catching up with him, I expect? You seemed to rate him on Killjoy."

I put my coffee down. "He pretty much saved my life on Killjoy."

Feroc and I stared at one another in silence. Too many memories. Too much pain. Too many times we'd both come too close. Too many times I'd brought Feroc too close to never coming back. That was always the problem with falling in love with someone, you inevitably ended up leading them into the mess that passed for your life, and, because you'd never learnt to cope with it, they got trapped there. The blind abandoning the blind, because they couldn't even begin to imagine leading them.

I wasn't a leader. I'd realised that early on, but it had taken me a little longer to realise I shouldn't tell people that. In Britain, we like leaders, and we believe everyone should aspire to be a leader. When the world encounters people like me, who have neither the ability nor the skill to cope with the challenges of leadership, they look down on us, because it's human nature to want to consider someone else lesser, to find someone you can cite as "at least I'm not like that." To judge is human, and an inherent flaw in the design of an apex predator with the capacity for high-level abstract thought; abstract thought eventually leads to insecurity, insecurity leads to anxiety, and anxiety leads to cruelty, as we identify what we are by punishing and destroying everything we're not.

Of course, we only really became apex predators by accident; our abstraction lead us beyond our level of competence, dashing us against the rocks of responsibility and a search for purpose. Seagulls don't search for a purpose. Sharks don't claim their lives have no meaning. Wolves don't seek the approval of others, although they will drive non-conformers out of the pack, just as we try to. Some wolves, however, flourish as lone wolves, and even go on to become the alphas of their own packs, formed of other lones, wolves who learned the value of community in the splendour of isolation.

Humans, though... we care very deeply why we're here, whether we're happy while we're here, and what people think of us while we're here, being happy, or not. It's ridiculous, when you think about it – which you probably shouldn't do, because thinking about things you can't change is a pretty surefire route to madness.

I can see Feroc going all the way, and I think he wants to give himself that chance; I don't think he understands that I don't want what he wants, that I wouldn't be any good at it, even if I did want it. That's the hardest thing about being me; the weight of awareness of all the things I couldn't do, even if I wanted to. If I could give up one part of being human, it'd be an awareness of limitations. That's what's ruined the world – all the freaks and weirdos we complain about are just kicking against the traces of their limitations. We always have been.

"Are you alright?"

"Yeah. Just thinking."

"What about?"

"About you. All the times I've nearly got you killed."

"None of that was your fault. And we both came through. You brought us through. You kept me safe, Tony, and that's what matters. Not what happened, but how you handled it – and you handled it like a pro, Tony. Okay?"

Feroc's fingertips stroked my shoulder, and there was something soft and kind in his eyes. I wanted to weep; kindness was still an unfamiliar visitor to my world, and encountering it still shook me up.

"It's not okay, though – I'm supposed to protect you, and I screwed that up. I keep letting you down."

"No, you don't." Feroc tilted his head. "What's this about, Tony?"

It's about the fact that I slept with Colt Devereux. It's about the fact that I still want to. It's about the fact that I don't know what that means about me, or us, or him.

"I don't know. Things just feel a bit... strange, right now. I don't like the idea of you going undercover. It doesn't seem safe."

"And Killjoy was?"

"That was different."

"Why? Because you were the one undercover?"

"I have had a little bit more experience than you, Feroc."

"I've been in the Job five years, Tony. Everyone has to start somewhere, and this is my start." Feroc gave a wry grin. "I'll be alright, Tony. And it's not like I'll be completely gone; I'll just be meeting the rest of the crew in the late evening. You'll see me; it wasn't like that when you were on Killjoy."

 He was right; of course he was right. But I really, really didn't want to accept that. Stubborn? Yes – but with reason. It was a dangerous world out there, and I'd been under away from home; there had been very little chance I'd be recognised.

 I was being ridiculous. Feroc wasn't a probationer any more; he'd grown up in the five years since we'd met, become a man. I sighed, closing my eyes against the recognition of the fact that it was time for Feroc to earn his spurs – and I had to let him do that.

DC Tam Freud

"Okay... for those of you who haven't met him before, this is Colt Devereux; he's over from the wilds of Norwich, making up the numbers of the young and beautiful, getting some good sea air. Colt; you know Feroc Hanson, that's Aimee Gardner, a uniform sergeant here, and your red-headed lad is Seamus Hanratty."
 Seamus nodded a greeting to Colt. "Aright, fella? Lookin' forward to a new run, eh?"
"Yeah; sounds like a good idea."
"Yer arty, at all, then?"
Colt laughed. "Not really. You?"
"Ah, sure, I dabble. The sergeant, now, she's yer man for that sort of thing."
"I'm not – not really." Aimee Gardner glared at Seamus. I was tempted to, too; his accent was never as thick as he played it whenever he met a new face. Seamus Hanratty had the softest hint of Ireland beneath a light, bland voice – except for times like this, when he sounded as though he'd just got off the boat.
Colt smiled. "I'm sure you're a lot better than you give yourself credit for, Sarge." He turned to Feroc. "What about you, Feroc?"
Feroc shrugged. "I write. Sometimes I doodle. This is graffiti, though. It's different – easier and harder at the same time."
I raised an eyebrow. "You know more about this than you let on, don't you, Feroc?"
He gave a bashful nod. "I read about ... well, I read. Graffiti interests me, especially the more artistic styles."
"And what does Tony think about this?"
Feroc gave a snort of laughter. "Tony thinks all graffiti's vandalism. He's got no time for it. Shame, really – he misses out on a lot by being so prejudiced."
"Are you allowed to say that? I mean, he's... well, he plays for the other team, doesn't he? I didn't think youse lot could be called prejudiced, like."
"Your accent's slipping, Seamus – lot more London than

Londonderry, boyo. And trust me, Tony's as prejudiced, in his own ways, as any of the idiots on Facebook."

"That wasn't the impression I got when we worked together on Killjoy. He seemed very open minded."

I noticed a faint flush on Colt's cheeks. I wondered what he had to be embarrassed about; the statement seemed innocuous enough to me. I decided it wasn't something I needed to worry about just now; I had enough to be getting on with working out how I was going to survive running my first solo operation.

"Right; let's get down to business on this, people. Feroc, Aimee; you know a bit about this scene, so why don't you talk the rest of us through it? Graffiti culture 101, please."

Beck

When Tam had asked me about setting up a sham crew, I'd been worried. Not because I thought she couldn't pull it off; Tam was the kind of woman who could achieve anything. It seemed, sometimes, that she just had to click her fingers, and things would fall into place for her. I often felt she could walk through fire and not get burnt. Although maybe that was her red hair, making it seem that she was born of fire, and that all the blazes of Hell would simply bow before one of their own.

 I'd been worried that it meant she was moving on with her life, that she would eventually move on from me. When I'd met Tam, I'd spent years being left behind. It started with my dad, before I was even born, moved on to friends, primary school, high school. My mum walked out when I dropped out of University, the front door slamming against an echo of her fury that I'd let her down, thrown everything away, an echo of her final, damning comment, the judgement I'd carried with me for the past ten years; "You've just ruined any chance other people like you have of achieving! You've confirmed what the rest of us know – that people like you can't stick to anything, that you're lazy and feckless." Employers had slammed further doors in my face. Even the Job Centre had given up – an argument between departments, over whether I was or was not fit enough to work, had resulted in me being told I couldn't have anything. No money, no support – nothing. I ended up doing things no one should ever have to do, just to make sure I didn't starve. Sometimes, it wasn't so bad; sometimes, people bought my paintings. Sometimes, I had enough money to enter painting competitions, with the chance – which sometimes came through – to win more money, enough money to rent a caravan for two, sometimes three, weeks. I got a grand, a couple of times – that paid for a month's rental on a holiday villa, plus all the food I needed, with a bit left over. The first win got me a villa for May; I had to wait until October for the second four-figure win.

 That was when I met Tam. She part-owned a villa with her

parents, sister, and her aunt and uncle. I was struggling in the pool, she was gliding through the water like she was born to it, and took time out of looking sleekly fabulous to rescue me. I got embarrassed about having to be saved by a girl, and, like too many people, when I'm embarrassed, I get angry.

I got angry with Tam. Looking back, I caused a bit of a scene. She just stood there, calm, cool, and then finally, as I struggled to get my rage under control, asked simply, blandly; "Is that it? We done now?"

I was done - "we", it turned out, were just getting started, taking our first steps into the complex arrangement that would prove to be our life.

It was rare for people to meet me and Tam together; we didn't want to deal with explaining that their assumptions were never accurate. Correcting people was exhausting, when you had to do it all the time. It ended up being easier to simply ensure that we weren't in a position where people would be asking those questions in the first place.

Tam had taken care of me for two years, now, and I'd spent the last eighteen months expecting her to walk out. She probably needed to – I wasn't great for anyone's social life, and it had to be a chore for Tam to be around for me; I wasn't great company at the best of times, and there weren't many "best" times. Something I saw on Facebook summed it up; "Other people have good days and bad days; for me, it's more like good moments and bad years." That's how it was for me. Good moments, bad years. The one thing that had held Tam back, kept her yoked to a loser like me, was the thread of insecurity that ran through her psyche, and compromised her self-belief.

But now? Now, she was being given sole charge, more or less, or a complete undercover operation. If she pulled this off, it would give her the confidence boost she needed to walk away from me, to leave me behind, just like everyone else had. Just like people always would. As Tam's friend, I should want her to succeed. As someone who finally felt appreciated, valued, and wanted, I was determined to do everything I could to sabotage this op. Destroy Tam's faith in herself, and keep her with me.

Chris

I watched the shadow shape of a hooded figure as it limped along in front of a wall, one hand gripping a crutch, which reflected sharp, wicked slivers in the moonlight, the other spraying silver sparkles in careful arcs along the brickwork. Lamplight pooled, revealing that the figure was wearing a red hoodie, but shrouding everything else in deeper shadow.

I wasn't surprised that the artist was disabled – I knew a guy in a wheelchair who created truly epic pieces; I'd met him online, and gone out tagging with him in Brighton, where he lived, on a couple of occasions, and I knew of plenty of other artists with disabilities. It wasn't easy for disabled people to succeed in the mainstream art scene. Graffiti had always been a levelling, where people succeeded because they were talented, or daring, or stunningly creative in their methods or pieces, and it had a lot in common with the emerging movement of cripplepunk, which celebrated the fact of disability, giving a community to those for whom recovery wasn't an option, and encouraging them to be present, and be proud.

So, a disabled artist wasn't noteworthy. The glitter element of the spray can was different, as was the fact that this individual didn't seem to be too worried about being seen. They moved slowly by necessity, but they worked close to the streetlight through choice. That was unusual, and suggested they were new on the scene, and looking for a crew. Or, at least, for the approval of others like them.

I watched for a few minutes longer, then headed over, making sure to walk in a straight line, towards the glow of the streetlight, giving them the best chance to see me.

They turned when I was about four feet away, resting heavily on their crutch. Sharp, slender face, wide-set eyes. A black knit cap hiding any trace of hair. A slender broadness to their build. All androgyny, which, again, wasn't all that uncommon in the graffiti world.

"Hey."

They regarded me, slowly. "Alright."

"I'm Chris."

"Nice for you. They just call me Beck."

I wondered who "they" were. Beck's voice was bland, a pitch that could be either male or female. They looked and sounded older than most people on the scene. There were enough older artists, though, for that in itself to not be surprising. "I've not seen you around before."

"No... I haven't been out in a while. I used to be into this sort of thing, and started to feel I wanted to get back to it."

"Right – well, I've got a solid crew, the Cancer Crew; you're welcome to hang with us, if you ever feel like a bit of company, shared inspiration, that sort of thing. Or, if you're happy to do your own thing, we'll leave your pieces alone." I studied the wall, simple lines of spray paint telling a story; swirling forces, a dreamer and their dreams, a sun, suffocating under dark blanket of cloud. That – that wasn't usual, at all. A single colour. Striking lines. This was art, in every sense of the word. I could imagine Beck going all the way with this. I wondered why they'd come back to the streets.

"What brought you back? You said you'd been away from the scene."

"I just felt the itch. You must know how it is."

"My crew's out most nights. But, yeah... I get it sometimes in the daylight hours. You see a nice, blank wall, and you start picturing what you'd paint there, how it would look. You wonder how long it would last, how many people would see it, before the council washed it off."

Beck was nodding. "That's about the way of it. I've been keeping a clean slate for years, and then, one day, I was walking through town, thinking how much of a dump this place is, how much better it'd look if I got to have a go at it. Then I saw the silver spray paint in one of the shops – that was it, sorted."

That was always how it was; you saw the surfaces first, started thinking about how to make it look better. Once you saw a paint colour that sparked your interest, that was it – you were just counting the hours, or the days, until you could get out there and make your mark. It was as natural and as essential as breathing. Paint and life weren't just synonymous – they actually were the same thing.

"Your work's not bad."

Beck gave a wry smile. "Thanks." The spray can was held out. "What do you do?"

I grinned, shook up the can, and stepped closer to the wall.

PC Tony Raglan
LB 265

"Tam Freud's never even run an op before. What does she know about keeping a team safe?"

Ryan Hartley rolled his eyes. "Give it a rest, yeah? Feroc's not your puppy any more. He's a big boy – let him look after himself for once. If you've taught him proper, he'll come through alright. Just let him be. Give him a chance."

"A chance to do what?"

"To prove himself."

"He doesn't need to prove himself!" I heard myself shout, felt my knuckles tense on the steering wheel. I needed to rein myself in. Needed to. Didn't.

"He does, though." Ryan spoke softly, with an edge to his voice. "He needs to prove that he's not just your other half. Not just Tony Raglan's crew. You've been given a lot of rope, Tony – it's not fair to keep Feroc leashed up."

I drove in silence. The worst thing was, I knew Ryan was right. "It's still true about Tam, though."

"Yeah? So what? Everyone has a first time, most of us more than once. You find your feet, you prove yourself, you get better." He met my eyes in the rearview mirror. "Once, you were getting behind the wheel of an Area Car for the first time. No one tried to stop you, did they?"

"That's not the point – I'd been trained to handle an Area Car. Feroc hasn't been trained for this."

"He has, though. You ran interference for Connor Greaves, all those years, right? You'd gone under before Killjoy, yeah?"

"Yeah – and look how things worked out with Connor."

"Worked out alright from where I'm sitting – last postcard we had, he seems to be perfectly happy up there."

"Someone died. I killed them. Connor could've been killed. No one was in control of that op. No one was keeping Connor safe – why should they suddenly keep Feroc safe?"

"They kept you safe, didn't they?"

"They forgot about Connor."

"Connor was under for fifteen years, Tony. That's a long time. Things..."

"People forgot. They couldn't be bothered to care about what happened to him. Clever dealers, a job that took too long to bring a result... they weren't interested, in the end."

"They were, Tony – you should know that; you made it possible for him to get word back, you got him what he needed, info, warnings..."

"And he had to stand there, watching, not knowing if I'd live or die. He could've been killed himself. I don't want Feroc in a situation like that."

Ryan sighed. "He'll have back up, Tony. Trust the process, yeah?"

"No. The process isn't trustworthy. When it comes through, it's more by luck than judgement. I don't want Feroc's life left up to luck."

"And maybe he doesn't want it left up to you." Ryan spoke quietly, but his words had a deafening echo. I drove, staring at the road ahead as though it could block out the thousand other images falling through my mind.

What would I do without Feroc? If he was killed, that would be bad enough, but at least there would be a ritual. People would care. I could work through a process, step by step. If he found the courage to leave me, though? I didn't have the first idea what I'd do then.

Sergeant Aimee Gardner
LB 761

There was something going on between Feroc and Colt
Devereux; it was obvious from the way Colt blushed, the way he
wouldn't look directly at Feroc.

 Someone should tell Tony; I knew he'd kept in touch with Colt,
after Killjoy; I imagined they'd become friends, he'd invited Colt
over to his place a few times, just hanging out, chatting... Feroc
coming to realise he had more in common with Colt than Tony...

 I didn't blame Feroc for falling in love with someone else; it
happened, humans, like the majority of animal species on the
planet, probably weren't intended for monogamy. What was
wrong, what I did blame Feroc for, was not being honest with
Tony, the man who would walk through fire just to be able to
offer warmth when Feroc complained about the cold. Tony
Raglan was a good man, and he didn't deserve to be treated like
this.

 I sighed. The echoes of Killjoy were being felt in more ways
than one, then. I was glad that Nightshade had come along,
actually; the horizon contained strong hints of extreme left-wing
violence. It might not reach Lothing – the town wasn't known for
its modern outlook and tolerant nature, after all – but, all the
same, it was something to keep an eye on, and a reason to be glad
of a more involving occupation. If a couple of strays did wash up
here, I'd rather not be responsible for mopping their blood off the
pavement after the natives were done with them.

 I covered a yawn as I headed back to my office. It must have
been nice to have been a sergeant in the days when that rank still
meant you could justifiably spend most of the day in the station,
out of harm's way. Nowadays, I didn't even book in prisoners
unless one of the civvies who handled the desk had called in sick.
I say I *didn't*; I mean I wasn't *supposed* to – I still did, when I
thought I could get away with it. The Job was being taken over by
civvies, and half-civvies, with three months' training; they were

somehow worse, the twelve-week 'tecs, as Tony Raglan had called them, when the first two had somehow found their way out here.

They didn't last long; theory never does when it clashes with reality.

I'd seen the fear in Tony Raglan's eyes then. What would happen to him, how would he react, if Feroc and the Job were both taken away from him?

Reaching my office, I opened the door, standing on the threshold. I felt as though I was doing that in my life, too; standing on the threshold between what was possible, and what I wanted. I had a decision to make, but I had the sense that Nightshade might just make it for me. Wait and see – but go with whatever answer was given, when the time came.

I sighed, and started to close my eyes -

- "Lima Bravo One to all units, urgent assistance required, Lakeside Avenues; vehicle and officers under attack; about fifteen youths, armed with bottles and baseball -" the sound of breaking glass was so loud, so sudden, I caught myself jumping back. Along the corridor, the sound of heavy boots moving at speed echoed like a herald of the End Times.

I joined the flow of officers, most of whom would have had their refs interrupted, surging ahead of the pack, shouting directions, sending people to vehicles, vans, points along the route, calling out instructions for someone to get CAD to radio for an armed unit to assist. Not for the first time, I wondered how the civilians kept so calm, what they thought about the chaos that people like me took for granted. That was another reason I tried to ensure I was visibly present, even when the rule was we let the civvies get on with it; this wasn't civvy street. It was never going to be a normal office job, never going to be a nine-til-five, even if that did happen to be when the civvies went home. No public enquiries after dark, no lights at the front of Lothing nick. Units would be out on the prowl, a skeleton CID would be present. When darkness rose over Lothing, Lothing police station became all about business. The shutters were down, and the gloves were off.

As I ran, I saw Colt and Feroc exchanging terrified glances, and wondered if I'd got it wrong about who loved whom in that triangle.

PC Feroc Hanson
LB 599

"I've got to go."

"I'll come with you."

"No, you won't – your boss would never forgive us if we sent you back in a box."

"I can't just -"

"Yes, you can. I'll wait it out with you. The others know what they're doing, Colt. Let them get on with it. They're trained for this, it's not the first time it's happened, it won't be the last." Tam Freud's voice was calm, but stern. Colt sank back down, hanging his head as he gulped shaky breaths. I let my gaze linger, then took off, catching up to the tail end of a pack that was running for their lives.

We were a unit, a whole, a hive mind; if one of us got cut, everyone bled. The fear and rage were bad enough when you could see what was going down, and knew you'd get there in time to stop it. When you were at least ten minutes away? The agony of the knowledge of all that time and ground between you and your colleagues could send you mad. It *had* sent coppers mad, when they didn't make it in time.

If I didn't make it to Tony and Ryan, I knew I'd be lost to madness.

I surged ahead as corridors yielded to the soft light of the rear yard.

"Sarge!"

She turned, a single, sharp nod; nothing more to say, nothing more needing to be said, by either of us. I jogged over to the car she was getting into, dropping into the passenger seat, and cursing all the gods I believed in, and several I didn't, for letting this happen.

As we swung out onto the road, the car picking up speed on the slight incline, I wondered whether anyone had come up with a collective noun for multiple police sirens. A discordance,

perhaps? An atonality? It always struck me as odd, the way no
two sirens ever sounded quite the same. There'd been times, when
we'd been off duty, walking through town, or relaxing on the
beach, or in one of the parks, that Tony had been able to identify
one of the Lothing cars purely from the sound of its distant siren.
I felt the heat of tears behind my eyes; Tony was so talented, so
competent, so genuinely good at what he did; he couldn't die. The
gods wouldn't be that cruel, surely, to let him survive the very
obvious dangers of Killjoy, only to die at the hands of some basic
street scum, the kind of people we dealt with every day?
"Feroc? Are you okay?"
"Yes, sarge."
Aimee Gardner gave me a look. "I'll pretend I believe that." She
swung the car round a corner, just as the howl of a siren a little
higher than any of ours met us, coming into Lakeside Avenue
from the opposite end.
 I caught the stench of petrol a second before I saw the flames.
The car lurched forward as Aimee Gardner slammed on the
brakes. We were both out and running, my feet half a pace ahead
of hers. I could feel the wind in my hair. Someone was
screaming, a single name, over and over and over again.
"Tony! Tony!! TONY!!!"
 The voice was my own, but I didn't recognise the sheer terror, the
agony of loss, vividly imagined, that rang through it like church
bells through Sunday sleep.
 No one answered. That was the worst part, the memory I knew
would always haunt me – the sound of absence.
 Another voice cut through my screams, the whoosh of high
pressure hoses, seeking to subdue the flames, and reveal the
terrible reality that lay beneath. Over it all, I could still hear the
echoes of my screams. I wasn't screaming, though; my throat was
too raw.
"FEROC."
I spun round, away from the water and flames, still deafened, but
hearing my name. I stared at the person I saw for a long moment.

Blood streaking silver hair, crushed rose petals on ash and embers. Oil-slick tears, eyes still heavy with shock. It could have been a flashback, except for the fact that, this time, we were wearing close-fitting, soft-feel t-shirts, dark enough to disguise stains, dark enough to make the man in front of me look handsomely burly, rather than overweight. Not dark enough, though to stop the thudding echoes of remembrance. Not dark enough to keep me from seeing the torn white shirt, stained with blood, of the moment I first realised that Tony Raglan affected me more than someone who was simply and solely a colleague should do.

It was happening again. I was seeing Tony Raglan bloodied and wounded, again. It hit me, then, that this was going to be my life; the eternal return of the same scene, the same terror, the same sickening anxiety.

"Feroc...look at me?"

I lifted my head, trying to ignore the agony of the reality that was relevant to me by focusing on another, equal part of it, that didn't concern me so much, but should have done.

"Where's Ryan? What happened?"

Tony swayed; rushing forward, I wrapped my arms around him, guiding him down. Sitting there, on the kerb, uniform stark against the grey tarmac, and his ashen face, Tony took a shaky breath, licked his lips.

"I don't know. He got out of the car, took on one of the gang. The others turned on him. That's when I was able to get out...we were getting stuck in, trying to bring them down... a group of them made a run for it. Ryan went after them... I don't remember much after that."

"When did he get out of the car? You called in the urgent assist from the car." Aimee Gardner, sergeant's hat fully on.

"When the windscreen broke... they'd pulled back, after the brick was thrown."

"First units were on scene within four minutes. We arrived three minutes later. He can't have got far, not on foot, not in that time."

"Sarge! Over here! It's Ryan – he's okay! He's taken a kicking, but he's alive!"

A ragged cheer went up. Aimee Gardner laid a hand on Tony's shoulder, briefly, then headed in the direction of the shout, others following her. I stayed there, sitting in the dirt and the dust beside Tony, my head reeling, and my heart breaking.

"Fer?"

I looked at Tony, letting him see the depths of my pain, a punishment, of sorts, for his inability to hide his own from me.

"I don't think I want this, Tony."

"What do you mean?"

I sighed, and looked away, ashamed of what I was about to say. "I don't want to be part of a community that thinks someone who's been beaten up is 'okay' simply because they're not dead. I don't want the new normal to be 'it's alright – they're badly hurt, but alive.'" I shook my head. "I don't think I want to be part of your world, Tony."

A moment of silence stretched between us. I felt my heart begin to race. I forced myself to look back – and saw the blood, frothing at Tony's lips. Noticed, for the first time, the flash of paleness, skin showing around a wound his shirt had kept hidden.

A slow, yawning siren had me on my feet, frantically waving down the approaching ambulance.

"Please – help him. I think he's been stabbed."

"Feroc – oh my god; what the hell's happened?"

The paramedics, oblivious to Aimee Gardner, were speaking a language I couldn't follow, a jumbled stream of words and numbers. From the corner of my eye, I saw Ryan, on a stretcher, being hurried to a second ambulance. Beside me, around Tony, Velcro ripped, syringes glinted. A stretcher clattered down. Voices urged Tony to his feet.

I got to mine, slowly unbuckled my duty belt, unzipped my stab vest, and dropped both in the middle of the road.

"Feroc – what are you playing at? Feroc!" I kept walking. I heard the sound of my sergeant following me, then another voice, low, gentle, masculine.

"Leave him, Aimee. Give him a bit of space. He's had a shock."

"Sir -"

"Trust me. It's better this way."

Inspector Wyckham was wrong. This could never be 'better.'

DI Mark Roscoe

"Okay. Thanks. Yeah, that's helpful. No worries. Thanks again."
I put the phone down, and looked around a briefing room that
was too quiet, too still, too subdued. Everyone on my team was
struggling to come to terms with what had happened yesterday. In
the far corner, Colt Devereux was fighting hard to keep from
crying. He shouldn't be here, really, but he'd been adamant he
didn't want to go home. He'd slept on a sofa in the rec room,
crying himself to a fitful sleep, and then presented himself,
washed, but not shaved, in the morning briefing.
 I wasn't about to argue – or ask what was going on that he'd
taken the news of Tony Raglan's stabbing quite so badly.
"Right... some good news; Tony Raglan and Ryan Hartley are
both going to be fine. Ryan Hartley was knocked about a bit, he
took some pretty hefty blows from what were probably baseball
bats; he's got a broken arm, cracked ribs; he'll be off for a few
weeks. Tony Raglan was stabbed; the knife nicked one of his
lungs, but he's going to be okay. He'll be in St. Ralph's for a few
days, but he's out of danger. Our body on the beach, as most of
you already know, was also stabbed – those wounds weren't
immediately obvious, because the body had experienced severe,
repeated trauma; they were discovered at autopsy, and were
focused around the lower abdomen. Preliminary examinations
suggest that the knife used on Tony Raglan bore a very close
similarity to the one used in the attack on Valiant Brewer. Now,
obviously, the location of the injuries are different, so we may be
dealing with two separate attackers. The blade profile's fairly
common; long, slim, tapered blade, no serrated edge. The kind of
knife that probably everyone has in their kitchen at home. The
kind you can buy from bloody Poundland, probably. So, that's not
really helpful, but it's what we've got." I paused, waiting for the
ripples of frustration to die down.
"Okay... now, as some of you may have noticed, we have a new
face; DC Colt Devereux is joining us temporarily from Bethel

Street, out in the wilds of Norwich – don't worry, he has had his rabies shot."

A trickle of laughter glimmered through the room. I started to relax a little. If the team were laughing, we were on track. If they were laughing, they weren't going to end up so overwhelmed by emotion, and the desire to stick someone on for the assaults on Tony Raglan and Ryan Hartley, that they lost sight of the importance of doing it *right*, rather than just doing it. If my team were laughing, I could trust them to do a job whose result would go the distance. "DC Devereux is mainly here for Operation Nightshade, DC Freud's little escapade, that you reprobates all look far too world-weary to qualify for. But, since that's not going to go ahead until we have definite confirmation that Tony and Ryan are out of the woods and on their way to recovery, he's offered to hang around and help us out. Colt; do you want to say a few words?"

He looked startled, but covered it well. Getting effortlessly to his feet, he glanced around the room.

"Hi, everyone. Yeah, ah, there is something I need to say, and it's pretty important. Some of you, I know, won't like it, and some of you might well think I don't deserve to be in the Job..." he paused, looking worried. My heart sank. He didn't need to tell them. If they knew, fine. If they didn't – why rock the boat?

"The thing is... I make an absolutely lousy cup of tea."

The laughter that followed brightened the room, and my own relieved, exhausted amusement flowed and mingled with it. We were going to be okay. The good guys had this. Everything was going to be alright.

129

PC Feroc Hanson
LB 599

I stopped walking when I got to the sea. So much violence.
Lothing was a town soaked in blood, and we relied on the sea to
take it all away. But no amount of wave power could wash this
away.

I sat down in the sand, waiting for tide to take time away.
Waiting for the cleansing salt of this constant water to wash away
the sins of this town.

The sky was too blue, the sand too warm. People laughed too
loudly. Didn't they realise what had happened? Couldn't they hear
the chaotic howls as my mind fell apart? Couldn't they hear the
echo of violence?

I got to my feet, snatching up stones, hurling them at the useless,
callous, uncaring sea.

PC Tony Raglan
LB 265

The light was too soft and too bright at the same time. Everything sounded like it was happening underwater. I had a headache.

Feroc. He'd sounded scared, before. I needed to get to him, take care of him. I could smell petrol, feel the heat of flames – what the hell had happened out there? Where was Feroc?

"Hey! Hey – take it easy! Where do you think you're going, eh?" I blinked a couple of times, trying to process why a nurse was out on the street, in her uniform. Then I realised I knew her. "Sonia."

"Well done, Tony. How are you? Enjoying being a burden on the NHS?"

I tried for a smile. It didn't hurt, which was good – meant I hadn't been given a kicking, at least. And the burning in my chest didn't feel intense enough to have been a bullet. "Where's Feroc? What happened?"

"You weren't out with Feroc. You were with Ryan Hartley. He's taken a few knocks, but he'll be fine."

"This is St. Ralph's." It should've clicked sooner. Whatever had happened must've really taken it out of me; I'd always been on the ball, had a reputation for sussing out the lay of the land at a glance. What the hell was happening to me?

"The luxury, private hospital, with the spa and wine bar, was fully booked, I'm afraid, so you'll have to make do with stretched-to-the-limit facilities, dry sandwiches, and overworked, underpaid staff."

"I don't need to stay in – give me whatever form I've got to sign, and I'll be out of your hair. Home, warm bath, glass of Scotch – right as rain in a couple of days."

Talking hurt. I winced, and started coughing. That hurt even more. I closed my eyes, tried to keep my breathing shallow. My chest felt like it was on fire. I needed to breathe, but it hurt too much.

I felt tears brimming in my eyes.

"You'll stay here for a couple of days." Sonia's voice was rich, warm, comforting. Concern, compassion, and a genuine love of the hard, frustrating, difficult job that people like her didn't get paid nearly enough to do. "You were stabbed, Tony – the knife grazed your lung. It's not serious, but we'll need to keep you in here for a while. Okay?"

In an agonising crash of memory, I heard Feroc's voice, sound blending with the scent of burning rubber, the feel of rough tarmac, and the taste of blood in my mouth; "I don't think I want to be part of your world, Tony."

"Hey – what's wrong? Are you in pain? Let me get a doctor ..."

I was crying. Tears were streaming down my face, and I couldn't grab a breath long enough to tell Sonia that a doctor couldn't help. What was wrong with me wasn't anything that would heal in a hospital bed.

Machines beeped. Doors swung open, and slammed closed. Voices asked questions, urged compliance with instructions phrased as suggestions. Above it all, I was being torn apart and deafened by the sound of my heart breaking. I'd done everything to ensure Feroc could have whatever future he wanted in the Job, and it turned out he didn't want any kind of future with it at all. That was a kick in the teeth, and it hurt.

Sergeant Aimee Gardner
LB 761

"Feroc – a word, please?"

The briefing at the start of the afternoon shift had been understandably subdued, with a dangerous, simmering edge that threatened to boil over. I'd done my best to calm frayed tempers, and make it clear that revenge wasn't on the menu, and just had to hope my best was good enough. But I'd heard what Feroc had said to Tony, and I knew I needed to talk to him. If Feroc Hanson was thinking of leaving the Job, I needed to be the first to hear it for definite.

 He paused in the doorway, turning back with reluctance."Sarge?"

"Close the door."

"Is this about yesterday, Sarge? About what I said to Tony?"

"What do you think, Feroc?"

He closed the door softly, and took two steps into the room. "It was the heat of the moment, Sarge..."

"Sit down, Feroc."

"Sarge, I -"

"Feroc. Sit." There was bite in my bark. Feroc looked at me, then sat down, hands folded in his lap, head bowed.

"Look at me, Feroc."

He flinched as he listed his head, as though he was expecting to be hit.

"Right." I pulled my chair round, and sat down diagonally beside |Feroc, leaning forward, getting close without being threatening. "Let's start with what you said to Tony yesterday. I presume you remember what you said?"

Feroc nodded. "I was... I was upset. I hadn't been expecting... well, you know."

"So you didn't mean it? Is that what you're saying? You didn't mean what you said to Tony?"

"Yes. I mean, no. I don't know."

I took a deep breath. "Feroc, I need officers who are one hundred percent committed to the Job, to this team, and to their place in it. If you're feeling flakey, you need to go sick. Now." I paused. "Simple question, Feroc; do you still want to be a copper?" The sound of the clock ticking hurt like eternity.

"Yes. But I don't want to be the kind of copper who gets told that their mate's been battered. I don't want to be a copper who has to worry about what's going to happen every time he goes out. I don't want to have to see the man I love coughing up blood on some shit-stained pavement. Sorry."

Feroc flushed red. I almost laughed; I'd never heard him swear before, which was remarkable, in this job, and he seemed surprised at the words that had come out of his mouth – mild words, compared to some of the things I heard.

"Right. So, basically, you want to be an office poodle?" Feroc got to his feet. "Better than a dead wolf. Sarge."

"So you don't care what happens to Tony? Just as long as you don't suffer?"

"That's uncalled for, Sarge!"

I got to my feet, moving quickly to step in front of him. "I don't think it is, Feroc. I think it's entirely called for. Tony risks his life day after day. Everyone on this team does. And you're acting like you're the only one who's ever felt like the crap we get put through, the fear we feel, is too much. I mean, what the hell makes you so special? What makes you think you deserve to live more than Tony, or Ryan, or any of us?"

Feroc stared at me. "I don't -"

"Really? You think that your reaction yesterday was completely selfless? You think it didn't hurt Tony? You think he didn't hear you? That he didn't know exactly what you meant?"

Feroc looked away. "I didn't think..."

"No. You didn't think." I sighed, let some of the softness come back to my voice. "Look, Feroc, you're young. You've grown up with the default understanding, from just about everyone you've ever met, that there's nothing wrong with being gay, and that anyone who has a problem with it is out of order. I'm not all that much older than you – but I've got just enough years in head to remember a different reality. And I'm black, and female, which makes it worse. Gives me the kind of experience Tony is likely to have had – an experience where the best case scenario was people shaming you for what you were. Where that was the very least that would happen to you, every time you stepped out of your front door, if people knew. And you basically told a man who's been through all of that, a man you claim to love, who'd just been stabbed, that simply *seeing* brutality was too much for you, too hard, too upsetting. Can you imagine how that must have sounded? Can you imagine how it must have made Tony feel? Feroc?"

PC Feroc Hanson
LB 599

I could imagine it. I could hear the echo of my voice, see the look
in Tony's eyes as he turned away. I could remember it, imagine it
– but I couldn't take it back. The problem with the truth was, it
always hurt – and it usually hurt someone else. I wondered
whether I'd subconsciously been drawing away from the Job for a
while, if the stress and shock of yesterday had just triggered
something that was waiting for a more appropriate time.

"Feroc... look..." I glanced up, surprised; I'd assumed I'd be the
one expected to break the silence. Aimee Gardner rubbed a hand
over her face, and I saw, for the first time, just how tired she was.

"I can understand how you feel – believe me, I think we've all
been there, at one time or another. But give it a bit of time,
okay?" She got up, controlled pacing as she circled the room.
"Nightshade should be something a little bit different. It should
give you a break from the every day realities for a few nights. No
one's getting overtime on this – that was confirmed just before the
briefing – so I've told Tam Freud she can have us on those shifts
we'd be working nights anyway. Colt will have to square it with
his bosses. I don't know what CID's situation is as far as Tam is
concerned. You okay with that? It'll give you a change of scenery,
if nothing else."

I nodded. I felt suddenly exhausted, in a way that was more than
yesterday catching up with me.

"Feroc?"

"Yes, Sarge. That's fine."

Aimee Gardner shook her head. "If you still want to leave after
Nightshade, you can. I won't stop you. Whether it's a transfer you
want, or something completely different, I'll do everything I can
to bring it through for you. Okay?"

I nodded. "Sarge."

"I'm impressed you came in today; I wasn't expecting to see you."

"I didn't know whether I'd be welcomed... whether Tony would want to see me...."

Aimee Gardner nodded. "Well, I think you should face him sooner rather than later. There's a reason you're with me today, Feroc – I'll drop you at St. Ralph's just now. Go and see Tony – it will do you both good."

"Sarge -"

"Don't argue with me, Feroc. I can deal with a copper who's having doubts about the Job, but a copper who's trying to avoid another officer, whom they happen to be in a romantic relationship with? That, I don't need, and won't deal with. You'll go and see Tony, you'll sort things out with him, and you'll get your head in gear. Is that clear?"

I got to my feet, a sense of despair settling. "Yes, Sarge."

"Good. Let's go."

As I walked out, I realised I was on the verge of tears. I wished I was strong enough, bold enough, to simply throw down my warrant card, and walk away – from the Job, from Tony, from everything. I didn't really have a clear idea of the life I wanted, but I knew it wasn't this.

Did everyone feel like this? Was it only coppers who found reality impossible to cope with? Or was it just me? Was there something about me that meant I wasn't operating at the same level as everyone else. Maybe I was the one with the problem, rather than society, the realities of the Job, being at fault. I didn't want to see Tony. I hadn't wanted to be at work this morning. I wanted to pack a bag, walk out the front door, get into my car, and keep driving. Keep going until the tank was empty, and stop wherever I happened to end up. Make a life for myself there. New name, new start. Forget about the Job. Forget about Tony Raglan. Forget about the streets he taught me to roam, and was training me to own, in the years that I'd have once he was gone.

The streets of Lothing could never be my streets, however well I was trained. They would always be 'Raglan's streets', and I could never live up to that ownership, that image. That strength.

I didn't want to be Tony Raglan, or to inherit his streets. I wanted to be myself – and I felt that I lost something of that every time I put my uniform on.

Beck

"Where have you been?"

"Does it matter?"

Tam glared at me. "If it didn't, I wouldn't be asking, would I?"

My leg was hurting. I was finding it hard to breathe. Hot salt splashed the backs of my eyes. I was feeling it, but I wasn't going to talk about it. Not to Tam, anyway. She wouldn't understand.

I'd met up with the Cancer Crew for the first time. I'd been surprised to see an equal mix of girls and guys in the crew; not because it was so unusual to find females on the scene, but because they didn't usually run with crews. Girls usually worked solo, or acted as lookouts for their fellas. And that dynamic had seemed notably absent from Cancer.

It'd been a great night, low key, more saying than spraying, which suited me just fine; plenty of time sitting on benches, chilling. It reminded me of everything I'd liked about the scene the first time round; the social aspect, the sense that it was you, or you and your crew, against the world.

Tam took in my rucksack, saw how heavily I was leaning on my cane. "Have you been out spray painting?"

She sounded panicked. That wasn't normal for Tam. Nothing fazed Tam.

"Graffiti. And maybe. A little. Mostly chatting to some other guys. And girls. A crew, a graffiti crew. Like the old days."

"When I used to worry myself sick about you."

"When you didn't have to. When I told you, over and over, that I was fine. The old days, Tam – when I felt free. When I was good at something for once. When people didn't notice that I was a cripple."

"Beck!"

"No! You don't get to tell me what to call myself. You don't get to tell me I can't use certain words. My disability is my business, not yours. I get to use my own words. Tell it my way. I already live in a world that tries to deny my existence – I won't have my words taken away from me, too."

"I don't want you to spend your life hating yourself, Beck. I don't want you to resent your situation."

"I don't. No hatred, no resentment. Not on my part, anyway." I raised my head, challenge blazing in my eyes. "How about you?"

"Beck -"

"Forget it." I lurched forward, barging past Tam as I made my way to the sofa. "You want to get me a beer?"

"You can have a coffee. We're out of beer." She paused. "You do realise it's almost midnight?"

"So?"

"Beck... if you're spraying again, we need to talk."

"Coffee. Then we talk." I picked up the remote, and clicked the TV on.

"Fine. Because nothing matters, does it? As long as your life's sorted."

"I'm tired, Tam. I hurt. Okay?"

She switched the TV off at the wall. "No, Beck. It's not okay. We need to talk. It's about my work. And your...hobby."

I looked up. "I know. You're setting up a sham crew. I'm not stupid, Tam – I'm not going to blow it. Or is it more than that? Is it that you don't want to risk me getting nicked, risk me being an embarrassment?"

"Beck, I've told you – this op isn't about nicking people on the scene. I shouldn't even be talking to you about it."

"Then why are you?"

"Because I've always looked after you, Beck. Ever since we first met. I've looked after you from that day forward. Almost as though we were married."

"Until looking after me, in the way that would have allowed me to be who and what I am, to feel normal for the first time in my life, became a risk to you, to your precious reputation." I was angry, could feel it, burning at the back of my throat. Coursing through my veins. Tightening in the cords of my muscles. Firming in the set of my jaw. It was beginning to take me over, and I didn't want that. Not with Tam.

Or did I? If I pushed her away, there was still the crew. I could have a life beyond her limitations.

"Beck...Beck... I do understand. I honestly do... it's just...I can't have anything that could be used against me. You must understand that?"

The rage won. I got up, unsteady, my anger lethally quiet, deadly cold on my lips. "I'm not a 'thing', Tam – I'm a human being. A person. Part of you."

"Beck!"

I was already at the door, my leg and lower back on fire, the anger rising over the pain. The night air was cold. The door sounded too loud as it slammed shut behind me. I limped, fast and furious, breath catching in my chest.

That had been last night, the early hours of this morning. I'd spent the night on the sea front, moving between benches, sitting on the steps outside the faded elegance of the pavilion. I'd watched ships pass in the night, no traffic on the bascule bridge, no drivers to be outraged at a need for patience. I'd been ignored by the crowds piling out of Faith, and had wondered why it was that such dens of iniquity always had an angelic moniker. Faith. Heaven. Angels. Mantra. Prayer. Zen. I'd watched orange hi-vis jackets greet a blood red sun, seen the sky turn from Mondrian to Monet. Dogs and joggers had come and gone. The relentless flow of traffic had started.

Now, at eight a.m, Lothing was awake. It was time to mingle with the crowds that commerce brought, time to pretend I wasn't falling apart.

Time to imagine a life without Tam.

I got up, struggling, swearing, sweating. Steadied myself. I turned to face the sea, and ran a hand through my thick, red hair. Fingers snagged on tangles. I needed a haircut. New clothes. I needed a life.

I could hear the sound of a bus, labouring up the hill. I checked my wallet. Just about enough. I hobbled over to the stop, waving the arm that wasn't attached to a cane.

Time to go out, and start getting what I wanted.

PC Tony Raglan
LB 265

"Who died?"

"What?"

"You look like you're at a funeral." I swallowed water, wincing. For once, I didn't try and hide it from Feroc. He didn't deserve that courtesy. "Or maybe you are. Left the Job, have you, Feroc? Cleared your stuff out?"

The cruelty in my voice surprised me. I hadn't meant to give Feroc the same taste of the whip he'd given me. Although perhaps I had, without realising it. Subconscious desires – that was the term the shrinks used, wasn't it? Where you did something you didn't think you meant to because some other part of your brain actually wanted to? All a load of tosh, like that idea everyone wants to bang their mum and bash their dad. Not a chance, the mother I'd had. Probably still *did* have – I hadn't seen her obituary yet, though I lived in hope. I wondered how Dad was coping.

Strange – I hadn't thought about them in years.

"I'm not leaving you, Tony."

"Just the Job. Just the sole reason we even met in the first place."

"Maybe not even that. I don't know, yet. Sergeant Gardner wants me to think about it."

"Oh, that's nice. You'll do what Sergeant Gardner wants, then?"

"Tony -"

"No. Don't try and get me to back down, Feroc. I've always kept the darker side of my feelings from you. Always protected you from the worst of myself. For once, you're going to listen to that darkness, to the pain, and the rage, and the jealousy, and insecurity -"

I started coughing, panting, my chest feeling like someone was dragging razor blades through it. I was too hot and too cold all at once. I closed my eyes, as though the agony were some physical creature, standing in the room with me. As though I could see it.

"Easy – take it easy. Here..." Tightness and plastic, something

sickly cold. My heart rate dropping. Razor blades being pulled
out. I could breathe, just. I opened my eyes. An oxygen mask.
Someone – one of the crowd of people in identical white coats –
had put an oxygen mask over my face. I raised a hand, batting at
the plastic, scratching at the edges. Someone took my hand.
Damp heat touched my forehead.

"It's okay, Tony. Rest, okay? I've got to go – I'll come and see
you after shift, okay?"

I was too tired to argue. Everything hurt too much. I made a small
sound that could have been taken as agreement, or could have
gone completely unheard. I closed my eyes, finding the light too
bright. Everything was too loud, too close. Closing my eyes
helped.

"I love you." It was a whisper, and, perhaps because of that, it got
through. I opened my eyes, summoned what felt like the last
shreds of tattered energy I had left, and pulled off the mask.

"I love you too, Fer."

As he walked away, I let the tears fall in silence.

PC Feroc Hanson
LB 599

"Well?"

"He's angry, Sarge. And hurt. I never meant to hurt him."

"He's probably angry *because* he's hurt. That's the problem with being human – we're very good at hurting people without meaning to."

"I think that's always been the problem – Tony's never really seemed fully human to me. He's always been something more vital, less vulnerable." I couldn't take my eyes off Aimee Gardner's fingers on the steering wheel; so different from Tony Raglan's, yet so similar, in a strange sort of way. It was almost a bizarre kind of hypnotism.

"But he is human, Feroc. Human, and vulnerable – however much he may prefer to pretend otherwise. He can be hurt, and I think he has been, quite badly, somewhere along the line."

"I know, Sarge."

"And does he?"

"Sarge?"

"Does he know he's carrying open wounds? That things said without any intention of harm can take their poison straight to all that's vital?"

I hadn't thought of it like that. Hadn't thought that Tony might have as little control over how he reacted, as I did over the feelings I expressed. Just as it hadn't occurred to me that Tony might be keeping his feelings from me, a deliberate act of protection that was slowly destroying him, until he'd told me.

I wondered what else he'd kept from me.

"Sarge...What do you think I should do?"

"About what?" Aimee Gardner hadn't quite mastered the trick of looking at her passenger and the road at the same time. Mind you, I wasn't sure anyone other than Tony Raglan had got that one down.

"About .... everything?"

She shook her head. "That's for you to answer, Feroc. It's your life. It has to be your decision. Not mine, not Inspector Wyckham's, not Tony Raglan's." She suddenly started laughing. "Sarge?" Her laughter was infectious. I found myself smiling, even though I had no idea what was funny.

"I've just realised – the fitness test is tomorrow. Tony's excelled himself in getting out of that."

"Typical." My laughter mingled with hers. Beneath it, though, was the suspicion that, given his current state of mind, Tony wouldn't be as relieved as Sergeant Gardner seemed to assume.

Beck

I'd calmed down by the time the bus finally arrived in Norwich –
over an hour to manage a journey of forty miles. I felt tired,
hungry, and generally sorry for myself. I checked my phone,
which had been on silent since I'd stropped out last night. Three
missed calls, ten texts. All from Tam.

 I missed her, suddenly and intensely. I'd been an idiot last night.
Half battery – just about enough.

 Listening to the phone ringing, waiting for Tam to pick up on the
other end, I started to feel calmer. Maybe things weren't so bad,
this way. Maybe they didn't need to change. Maybe I didn't need
to change,

 "Tam? Look – I know. I'm sorry about last night, this morning,
whatever. I was stupid. I'd been feeling really good, really
enjoyed being out on the scene again, and then it just felt like you
were trying to take that away from me. I overreacted, storming
out like that. I'm in Norwich, now. Around. Here and there. Of
course I'm safe – would I be calling you if I wasn't? My phone
was on silent, and, yeah, I was kind of angry. Would you? What
about work? Naughty girl, pulling a sickie when you've got your
big op coming up. Love you too. See you in about an hour then.
My phone's nearly out of battery, so I'll just wait in the coffee
shop for you. It's not like I'm inconspicuous, is it?"

 Tam rang off as my phone bleeped angrily, letting me know it
didn't appreciate being kept away from a charging point for so
long. I switched it off, shoved it in my pocket, and hobbled off in
search of a cash point, with a view to breakfast. It was going to be
okay – Tam was going to meet me, we were going to spend the
day together, become friends again. Everything would be alright.

 I needed to talk to Tam about the crew she was going to be
running, though. She needed to know how things worked on the
scene. I could help. Obviously I wouldn't be able to be part of her
operation, but I could be out and about, keep an eye on her and
her team. Look out for them, the way she'd looked out for me.

DI Mark Roscoe

"Where're we at with the Brewer case, Landon? I've just had Tam Freud ring in sick – first time in about two years, I think, so it must be bad – and Michelle and Danny are in court all day. I know you've been tied up with your fraud case, but did you get a chance to have a gander at it, at all?"

"Yes boss. I've got to interview the owner of Asbail's again, on the fraud job, but that shouldn't take more than an hour, all out. Then I'll go through the Brewer case again, see if there were any witnesses for the attack on the Area Car. You never know, we might get lucky – it might be the same knife, used by the same person, who's arrogant enough, or stupid enough, to leave evidence all over the place. Could be an easy win."

I gave a wry grin. "Could be, but don't hold your breath."

"I know. Worth hoping though, eh?"

"It's always worth hoping, Landon – it's what keeps us going in this dull world of ours."

I looked around at the remnants of my team, those who weren't in court or out on inquiries. They needed a break, all of them. Whenever I watched TV cop dramas, I always laughed at the simplicity of their working lives. One nice, juicy murder case, plenty of suspects, everyone with an intriguing, wholly plausible motive – what I wouldn't give for some of that, rather than every detective on my squad having a slew of different cases, most of them going nowhere, extremely reluctant witnesses, absolutely no motive for anyone who could conceivably have committed the crime to have done so. Everyone running on caffeine, and not much else.

No one had been that enthusiastic about the Brewer case. Innocent Mr. Nobody, person or persons unknown, no conceivable motive, no witnesses that we could find – it was the kind of nothing case that could linger for years, being pulled out and tinkered with every so often, with no one ever getting to court for it.

But then the Area Car had been attacked. Tony Raglan had been stabbed, and forensics said the blade used on him was a match for the blade that Brewer's post mortem had revealed did for him. Suddenly, everyone was on fire – because it was likely, though not definite, that the same man who'd stabbed Valiant Brewer had also stabbed one of our own.

Most criminals are caught because they make a mistake. Going for a copper was the mistake that Valiant Brewer's killer had made, assuming they were the same person. And I honestly wouldn't rate the odds of there being two violent murderers, both using exactly the same kind of knife – however common it happened to be – on the same ground, working at the same time. It was like the old joke; woman picks up a hitch hiker. Hitch hiker is grateful, says to the woman "I'm glad you didn't assume I was a serial killer, or something!" Woman shakes her head, focusing on the road. "Don't be ridiculous", she says; "The chances of two serial killers being in the same car, at the same time, are astronomical."

A lot of police work is done on gambles, hunches, and the law of probability. It's why we fail so often – but we'd fail a lot more if we tried to do it any other way. I'd prefer that we'd kept to the attitude that the public didn't need to know every detail of what the police did, and how they did it, but I could see why it had come to that – a few flies fouling everyone's honey, robbing us of the sweetness of being able to get on with out jobs outside of the public gaze. I supposed there was some sort of value to being in the public eye all the while. Accountability. One of the big buzzwords right now, or so it seemed.

When you kill a civilian, you become a murderer. We'll look for you, we'll hope you screw up, and we'll take a lot of satisfaction if we get a chance to bring you before a judge and jury. But, if you lie low, keep your mouth shut, and either don't kill again, or kill differently, we probably won't find you. Especially not if you were careful – if you wore gloves, if you've not had contact with the police before. Kill a copper, however, and you become... prey.

We'll hunt you to the ends of the earth. We'll keep hunting you, while our feet bleed, our lungs burn, and we tune out everything except you. Your crime. The insult and offence you perpetrated against us. We will hunt you, we will find you you – and we will break you, before we drag you before justice. We'll watch your damnation, and bay for your blood. And we won't let you rest, not even when some misguided parole board claims that you've "served your time". The minute you kill one of ours, you forfeit your life. We take whatever we want from you, because you took one of the most valuable things we had, and destroyed it. You want to get away with murder? Don't kill a cop.

I paced around the office, occasionally stopping to talk to officers about their caseload, new leads they'd had, what their snouts were saying; the day to day business of running an understaffed CID office.

I glanced at the clock on the wall. The hours were ticking by. We were losing time, and time was the best lead we had.

"I'm going to the hospital, see if Tony and Ryan can tell us anything."

There were murmurs of acknowledgement, but they didn't drown out the sound of fingers tapping keys, the hushed conversations on desk phones. I glanced round as I headed out the door. About half the coppers here had never known anything other than a recorded conversation with a snout on a desk phone. The other half twitched, remembering the days they'd simply used personal mobile phones, and things got written down if they felt like it. Or not bother if they had a touch of the green-eyed squirrel, wanting to hug their nuts to themselves. And that was just the women. No one on the team would remember the days when all we had was desk phones and notepads. No recording equipment, just code names and semi-literate scribbles. I remembered the days of mobile phones, where I'd first cut my teeth running a team of informants, but I didn't miss it. The recorded desk phone conversations were much more reliable, and we could get convictions, using the evidence contained in them, without compromising our sources.

Most of the time.

St. Ralph's was always busy, but always, strangely, restful.
Perhaps the busy-ness was what made it restful.

"Mr. Roscoe! You've come to see your two men, I presume?" I
smiled. Part of what made this place so soothing was the people
who worked here – and Sonia was the leading force of all who
worked at St. Ralph's.

"Yep. How are they?"

"Ryan Hartley will probably be able to go home tomorrow,
perhaps the day after. Tony, we'll need to keep in a little longer –
he's picked up a low-grade infection; we obviously want to make
sure that's flushed out before packing him off. Do you want me to
take you to them? They're on the same ward – two beds away
from each other, which is just as well, considering the hell Tony
raised when we let him be in the same room as that boy of his.
We're busy enough without that sort of nonsense." Her tone was
brusque, but her eyes sparkled. Sonia was like all of us; she cared
deeply for Tony Raglan. Another victim of the man's charm.

When Lothing nick had first been rocked by the news that big,
tough Tony Raglan, all-round man's man, batted for the other
side, I'd wondered – aloud, on a couple of occasions – how it was
that he could be so attractive to women. Not in the sense that they
desired him, the way they might some gym-bunny pop star, or
slick-suited businessman, but in the sense that they wanted to be
around him, they championed him, they wanted to make it clear
they were on his side. Over time, I came to realise that it was
precisely *because* Tony Raglan didn't desire women sexually that
they were drawn to him; whatever energy he gave out made it
clear he didn't want anything that women weren't prepared to
give, yet, at the same time, he had all of the strength and calm
competence women found attractive.

I'd seen more than a few discussions online, some quite vitriolic,
about why women felt threatened by men "simply being around",
but "straight blokes cope just fine with gays existing." From the

tone of that comment, and from things I'd seen and heard around the nick, in the aftermath of Tony Raglan's shooting five years ago, though, they didn't. I had a theory that it was all about confidence; if you were certain of yourself, your identity, and your place in the world, then someone else being 'other' in some way wouldn't even cause a ripple on your pond. If you were insecure and uncertain, however, someone having the boldness to stand in the full light of themselves, while you couldn't even put a foot outside the shadows of your unknowing, would seriously rock your boat.

It was the same with people like Colt Devereux – I'd been surprised at how ordinary he looked, but the fact that he hadn't always been the bloke who'd showed up in my CI|D offices didn't even scan. I knew who and what I was – who and what Colt Devereux, or anyone else, was didn't matter. I wasn't outraged at the number of LGBTQ people in the world (I had a feeling there were more letters, but I couldn't remember what they were); I was, however, shocked and bewildered at how there could be so many people whose identity was so fragile that another human being's mere existence sent them into a panicked rage.

"Tony – you have a visitor."

He looked pale, but determined. I smiled. "How you doing, big man?"

He made the effort to smile back. "You won't get rid of me that easily, guv."

I hadn't been surprised to learn that Tony Raglan had served time in the Met; it wasn't all that common for officers in divisional forces to call their DCIs "guv" - Tam Freud did, but she preferred formality in most things. Most people went with 'boss', out here.

"Damn. We'll have to make it a bullet, next time."

"Cannon ball, maybe – I dodged the last bullet, remember?"

"So you did. I hear Ryan's going to be okay?"

Tony pulled a mock-rueful face. "Him? Yeah – he only took a kicking, didn't he? I mean, that's no fun, but it's no big deal." Suddenly serious, he glanced along the ward. "You'll check in on him, yeah?"

"Of course."

"I feel like I let him down, y'know? It's daft, but I feel guilty that he got done over, that the car got trashed. Like I should've been better, done better."

He started coughing, then. I laid a hand on his shoulder, poured him a glass of water, helped him drink. "Take it easy. I'll let you rest, go and check in on the other reprobate." I stood up, paused. "It wasn't your fault, Tony. It was the fault of the gang who attacked you. The fault of the yobs who gave Ryan Hartley his kicking. The fault of the bastard who stabbed you. They're to blame, and we will find them."

PC Ryan Hartley
LB 680

"Boss – what're you doing here?"

The DI grinned. "Come to finish you off, obviously." He pulled up a chair, sat down, one leg flicked casually over the the other, ankle resting on knee.

"How're you doing?"

"Good – they reckon I'll be out of here tomorrow." I glanced up the ward; Tony Raglan looked as though he were sleeping. I caught snatches of coughing, saw the shifting of his head on the pillow, a glimpse of grey over the porcelain skull of the old man who was patiently waiting out the results of tests after he'd collapsed suddenly in the street. Derek; we'd chatted a fair bit, once the drugs had started to kick in, and I wasn't shot through with agony every time I lifted my head. Eighty two, and not all that bothered about dying, or so he claimed.

"That's good news. Look, Ryan, if you don't feel up to it, I get it, but we could really use a statement. Some descriptions?"

"I don't really remember much, boss; a lot of noise, mainly. Everyone seemed to kind of blur together, you know?" A thought struck me. "Surely the dashcam would've caught something? At least some of them, the ones right in front of the car?"

Roscoe pulled a face. "Dashcam's wrecked. I'll need to speak to Tony on my way out – I decided to let him rest for a bit, just now; he still seems quite poorly; if there's anything you can remember, anything at all? Because if he can't give us anything, we're reliant on residents of the street you were attacked on, and you know what people in Lothing are like."

"Yeah. The three wise monkeys on steroids, especially when it comes to helping the police."

"Exactly."

"I'll do my best, boss, but, like I say, it was a bit of a blur... I remember one guy in a red baseball cap, though. Blue hoody. Bright blue. I remember thinking they clashed, the hoody and the cap."

Roscoe gave me an encouraging smile. "Go on."

"I...he had a thin face. Clear skin. Really clear; I remember noticing that, particularly; hoodies and hygiene aren't your usual combination"

"No. That's good. Can you give me any idea of how many of them there were? Rough ages, male, female, black, white?"

"I don't remember there being any non-whites – I'd've noticed, I think. They still stand out a bit, round here. Am I allowed to say that?"

"You don't mean any harm by it, and it's the truth. Say what you want to me, lad."

"Thanks. Can you do me a favour, grab me a glass of water?"

"Sure." Roscoe poured, handed me the glass. "It's funny how we don't think twice about drinking water when we're in hospital, but the rest of the time, we baulk at the idea of simply taking what comes out of the tap."

I took a long gulp. "I know. I think, in hospital, everything's just naturally simpler, so water's the obvious option." I handed the glass back to Roscoe; my ribs were still too painful for reaching over to the locker beside my bed to be comfortable. "Cheers. I hate feeling helpless, needing everyone to do everything for me."

"We all do, but, unless you're incredibly lucky, or exceptionally lazy, it's part of the Job. Just ask Tony Raglan."

I pulled a face, shaking my head slowly. Stars danced, though not as brightly as they once had. "Yeah...he's been through it and then some., Poor guy." I frowned, trying hard to remember anything from the attack, anything that would help them catch the bastard who'd knifed one of our best lads. "I think...this is going to sound weird, but I think someone walked past, while it was happening, and took a photo. I'm almost certain that they weren't part of the group." My mind struggled for details. "Dark hair. Maybe mixed race, or just very tan. A white shirt – not a uniform shirt, just a standard white shirt. Sleeves rolled up. Some sort of bracelet – it glinted in the sunlight." I sank back against the pillows, exhausted. "Sorry, boss. That's no help, is it?"

"It is – you've done well. Was this a man or a woman?"

"A bloke. I'm sure of that. About five ten, five eleven. Slim. Maybe about your build – more muscle than me, but nowhere near as big as Tony."

Roscoe nodded. "That's great. If we can find him, we might just find the gang. And the one with the knife." He stood up. "Rest now, okay? Take it easy. Get well.."

Max

It felt strange, being back in Lothing. When I'd been released
from prison – six months, following an unfortunate occasion
which saw me caught up in some rich nob's fraud – I'd felt that
Lothing, with its narrow streets and narrower minds, would just
be another kind of prison. I'd spent too many years being spat at,
having abuse shouted at me, being threatened, being physically
assaulted, to want to go back after half a year locked up, with no
ability to avoid the aggression of others, no choice in what I did.
Lothing was more of the same, just with the illusion of freedom.
I shouldn't have even been on Lakeside, that day. It was a spur of
the moment thing; I'd seen some baby rabbits advertised on
Gumtree, and thought they looked cute; they'd be able to have the
run of the *Kahlo Dali*, I could set up little boxes of grass for
them, hang hay at random points. They'd be a kind of company.
I'd gone there to have a look at them. I'd fallen totally in love,
handed over the full price, and was walking back down the road,
making a note on my phone of everything I'd need to buy for
them. I was going to call them Ghillie and Tavistock; grand
names for grand creatures.
I'd looked up at the sound of sirens, a habit I'd got into when I'd
been dating Tony Raglan, and one I'd never been able to break
since. Then I saw the first brick. I ducked instinctively; it
wouldn't have been the first time someone had thrown a brick at
me for no reason other than they didn't happen to care for the
colour of my skin, so it wasn't unreasonable to assume it might be
happening again.
I'd looked up when I heard the shouting. I'd seen the crowd
around the Area Car. Seen Tony Raglan driving it. Looking back,
I couldn't see a point where I *thought* about taking photos; it had
been an automatic reaction, bringing up the phone, switching
from the notepad section to the camera with a couple of swipes.
Point. Click. Click. Click. A record. An indictment. Once I'd got
enough photos, I'd fled – walking fast without running. A man

with a purpose, but not someone to notice. A trick I'd mastered a long time ago, and one that had got me out of a lot of trouble.

I'd got back to the *Kahlo Dali,* and tried to calm myself down with work. When I'd first got out of the nick, I'd started making small collage pictures; a vase of white lilies, with a strip of crime scene tape across it. Different backgrounds, different shapes and styles and colours of vases. Sometimes the tape read CRIME SCENE, other times simply POLICE. The white lilies were always the same. The tape was always there. Tony Raglan's ghost, gone from my love life, but still haunting my work.

I smiled, the memory of the attack replaced by the more pleasant memory of the first painting I'd ever done of, and for, Tony.

A pig in a tutu rendered in crime scene tape and police batons – I'd had to paint the tape, in those days; no Ebay sellers enabling it to be dropped through my letter box for just two pounds forty-nine. A cityscape backdrop in ruins, buildings melting down to a sunless sea.

In Xanadu did Kubla Khan/A stately pleasure dome decree/Where Alph, the sacred river, ran/Through caverns measureless to man/Down to a sunless sea. I'd always remembered those few lines, and often thought of them. Recently, on Twitter, under the hashtag #MakePoetryBoring, I'd come across a spin on those lines from Coleridge's drug-induced ramblings that had made me smile, from a user calling themselves ScribeFM;

In Birmingham did Kenny Khan/A drug habit fast acquire/In chip paper streets that ran/Slick with the residue of man/Down to a tower block.

I'd liked that – it showed an imagination that was grounded in familiar reality, and a dash of talent. Most of us would never have more than a dash of talent. The hardest lesson I'd had to learn, the hardest lesson any of us had to learn, was how to refine that dash into a sustainable quantity of something usable and vital. The refining process could take years, with multiple mistakes and attempts along the way. I wasn't entirely certain I'd reached the end of the process myself.

Tony had laughed at the picture, and hung it on the living room wall. I wondered if it was still hanging there, wondered if Feroc knew the story behind it. Or had it been consigned to a cupboard somewhere – I couldn't imagine Tony throwing it away, even if Feroc had kicked up about it. I couldn't imagine it not being part of his life. But, then, I'd never been able to imagine him not being part of mine. It had still happened.

I'd pressed fingertips down on crime scene tape, watching the glue spread across the other side of the near-translucent tape. Smoothed the side of my hand across the front of the tape. Picked up the cardboard, laid it gently inside the frame, design against the glass. Cheap MDF behind it. Swung the clips home. I picked up the finished product. It worked. I could sell these at craft fairs, a fiver a time, all day long.

I'd bought twenty A4 frames from Poundland, the day before. The frames were filled before the end of the afternoon.

I glanced across at the built in unit, under the starboard deck. Twenty simplistic yet striking collages stared back. They looked good. Now, I just needed a fair to sell them at.

I glanced at my watch. Pets At Home would be open in about half an hour; it would take me at least that long to walk there. I checked the note on my phone, reminding myself of everything I needed to buy – hay, pellets, bowls – two food bowls, two water bowls – some toys, and an indoor cage, for when I wasn't on the boat. Some kind of bedding; sawdust, I supposed. I could always ask when I got to the shop. They should know.

I was excited about getting the rabbits. If I focused on that, I wouldn't have to think about what I'd seen, what had happened to Tony. I wondered if he was still in hospital, if he was in St. Ralph's. Wondered if I should go and see him. That was probably a bad idea; I hadn't intended to come back to Lothing, and I still wasn't sure I was going to stay. Seeing Tony, engaging with him again, would tie me here, whether I decided it was the right place to be or not.

I picked up my phone, tapping it against the palm of my hand. I should get the photographs to the police. I started scrolling, finding the clearest one, the last one I'd taken. Tony, staggering forward, as a jeering blond lad, with short spiked hair, stepped back, a blood-tipped knife gleaming just behind his shoulder. His jacket was distinctive; burgundy leather. Not many people round here would wear something like that. A couple of clicks, and it was done. Time to get washed, dressed, and gone. I imagined the rabbits, bouncing along the deck, and smiled at the thought. I was going to enjoy my shopping trip, and my future.

A future I didn't need to compromise by tying up my mooring ropes on Lothing's quay before I'd thought about other options.

DC Tam Freud

"Beck – hold up. Scroll back on that, would you?"
I leant over Beck's shoulder, staring at the screen. Beck glanced up. "Is that your boy, the one who got stabbed?"
"Yes."
"Looks like you've got a vigilante on your hands, then."
"Who shared that picture to the group?"
"A Peter Great, apparently." Beck hovered over the name. "Lives in Brighton, apparently."
"So...why's he sharing a photo taken in Lothing, to a Lothing Facebook group?"
Beck shrugged. "He was here on holiday? Might've decided to see justice done from the safety of home comforts, rather than having his life turned upside down by interacting with your lot?"
"One of my lot could have died out there, Beck. One of my lot could die every bloody time we go out into these streets. And you're so casual, like it's all some big joke, the idea that a copper could end up dead. Because, at the end of the day, you're just like everyone else. We're the big, bad wolves, hunting down poor, innocent lambs that just stumbled astray; if we all just disappeared, tomorrow, everyone would be so much happier. People could get as high as they liked, the poor would finally rise to supremacy, and all manner of things would be well. We're just capitalist poodles, barking the tune of oppression."
"Tam, that's not -"
"It is, though, Beck. I see it in the face of everyone I walk past. I hear it in the conversations that stop the moment people realise who sent me. It's all over social media – I can't get away from it. Everyone out there, they'd kill us if they thought they could get away with it. And even the good people would quietly applaud them. So don't tell me it's not like that. Don't tell me I'm being melodramatic, or overreacting. This trend of claiming we'll cause untold grief, we'll fuck your life up, we're all bent? It's getting people killed. It's stopping us from getting scum off the streets.

But sure – your anger transference is so much more important."
"Look, Tam, I can't help the fact that a lot of people have had a lot of grief off the police, okay? I can't help the fact that you have some very bad apples in your barrel. That's what people are reacting to, Tam – not you."

I looked at Beck, memories chasing shadows. "So – what are they reacting to when they turn on people like you, then, Beck?" I was expecting a shouting match. I thought Beck might storm out. I wasn't expecting what happened.

"Alright. You're right. I don't like judgements being made about me, which means I shouldn't be making them about other people. I get it. But how am I supposed to stop, Tam, when a lot of the people who hate you are kin to me? I don't want to be disloyal to you – god knows you've done more than enough to earn my loyalty – but I can't live my life without friends, Tam. Without people who know what it's like. I wouldn't ask that of you, wouldn't ask you to have nothing to do with the police, because of the way people like me feel about them, would I?"

"It's not the same thing, Beck."

"Yes, it is. It's exactly the same thing, Tam. How many normal people do you reckon would want to spend more than five minutes with me? People like me, Tam, we take our friends where we find them, and we don't tend to find the kind of friends we need in the most savoury of places. That's not our fault, Tam. It's society's fault. It's the fault of all the coppers who've laughed at people like me, who've ridiculed us, dismissed the crimes committed against us. Cops who, in plenty of cases, have actually assaulted us. You can't think that we should just get over that? That we should simply understand how it's only ever a few bad apples. It doesn't work like that for us, Tam – why should it for you?"

I stared at Beck. We'd been through so much together, but, now, it felt as though we were drifting apart. Drifting, or being pulled. It was an unsettling feeling. It struck me that this might well have been how Tony Raglan felt, before events overtook his caution and reserve, and everyone knew which way his desires fell. Did he feel the same disconnect that Beck did, as though he didn't belong with either world? Had he felt the same drift I was feeling now, a sense of falling through the cracks between worlds?

That was one of the hardest things about the world we lived in; whether it meant to or not, it created a barrier between us and all other possible worlds. It isolated us, forcing us to turn to each other for comfort. We tied ourselves up with other coppers, other people 'like us' – and then, as soon as something happened that could stain the great and glorious image of The Police Service, we turned on each other, tearing flesh as we severed bonds that might carry toxin through the whole. We were left alone, without the trust we needed to form other relationships. It was a rare thing to meet an ex-cop who was sane, stable, and functional. I sighed.

"Penny for your thoughts?"

I met Beck's gaze, shook my head slowly. "It's so messed up, isn't it?"

"What is?"

I sank back down on the sofa. "Everything. Everything's just got so..." I shook my head. "I don't know how to go on, Beck. I love my job, but I love you, too. I can't make a choice, Beck. Don't ask me to do that."

Beck got up, stumbling slightly. "You know I wouldn't. Even if I sometimes wish you'd choose, in spite of the pain."

"Like you made your choice?"

Beck turned. I was expecting fire in their eyes. Instead, there was melting ice, a softness it hurt to look at.

I turned away, pulling my mobile out of my pocket. "Guv? There's something I think you need to see. It's on Facebook." I walked hurriedly through to my bedroom, leaning over my desk as I passed it. I kept my laptop booted up. I tapped through. "I'm sending it across to you now." I paused. The clock ticked off the minutes. I kept the phone to my ear.

"No – that's the only photo that's been uploaded. I'm assuming this Peter Great was standing behind the group. To be honest, we're lucky he hung around long enough to take that photo. I don't know, guv. Great's profile claims he's from Brighton; maybe he wasn't in the area for long. Maybe he's got a record. Maybe he simply doesn't want to be caught up in the kind of circus we tend to bring to town." I winced; admitting Beck's assessment felt like a betrayal. "Definitely. I'll drop by the office, see what I can get on a quick spin through the computer. No, it's fine, honest, guv. I don't mind. I want to nail whoever did this to Tony and Ryan, and if that means coming in for a couple of hours on a Sunday, so be it. It'll be worth it for the collar."

God, I was starting to sound like Tony Raglan. Like Mark Roscoe. Like all the old timers. It had already started, the slow creep of an attitude that would eventually render me unfit for any company other than coppers. I didn't want that. I'd never wanted that; I'd always believed I could build a bridge between the worlds.

"Beck? I'm just going to the office for a bit, okay? Following up on that photo."

"Hope you find something."

"Yeah. Me too. Are you going to be alright?"

I stepped into the living room. Beck was sprawled on the sofa.

"I'm always alright, Tam. It's more convenient that way."

DC Colt Devereux

"So, how do you think you're going to like Lothing?"

"It'll be a change, boss, that's for sure." I licked my lips, wondering whether now was the right time to tell Warren what had been on my mind for a while.

"Colt? What's on your mind?"

No time like the present, it seemed. If the universe was arranging things, it had better be ready to deliver.

"Sir, I've been thinking for a while about putting in for a transfer. That's sort of what Killjoy was about, at least from my perspective, sir – earning back enough credibility to make it somewhere fresh."

Warren was nodding slowly. "I know, Colt. I understand it wasn't easy for you to come back here, and I appreciate that it's not been the best place for you to be since..."

Ah. So Maxwell had become a Nameless One. The Job was full of them – bad apples, rotten to the core, that we couldn't quite bring ourselves to publicly throw out. We dropped them quietly, a sensible distance from the barrel; far enough away to isolate the taint, close enough to pick them back up if the rot doesn't look like it will spread beyond a couple of blemishes, spots no one need ever see if we just kept them from seeing every side, kept them at arm's length. I wondered how close I'd come to being a Nameless One. I watched Warren without making eye contact, trying to stop my heart thudding quite so loudly.

"If Mark Roscoe wants you, after Nightshade, then I won't stand in your way. You didn't have to come back, and you did well on Killjoy. Personally, I'd like to see you spend a little more time on normal duties here, but if that's not what you want, then I understand."

Relief ran cold. I closed my eyes, then opened them, smiling. "That's alright, sir – I'm happy to serve my time here; I owe you that."

Warren shook his head. "You don't owe anyone anything, Colt.

You were a good copper before. You've proved you still are a good copper. You don't owe us anything."

He sounded as though he meant it. I met his gaze. "I want to stay, sir. For a while, at least. I'm not in any rush, but I would like to go somewhere where my past is less... present."

Warren nodded. "I understand, Colt. Believe me. You're brave, living the life you've chosen. Coming back here. Facing everyone. Staring down the whispers and the rumours. Bravery deserves a reward. See Nightshade through, and I'll talk to Roscoe; if he's got a place for you, and has no objection to you being on board, then serve out your four weeks, and go to Lothing, with my blessing, and an open door here, if things don't work out."

He held out his hand. I took it, feeling the gentle flame of energy exchanged between two human beings. And I felt a flicker of unease. This was madness. I needed to stay away from Tony Raglan, not get closer to him.

"Thank you, sir."

"And if you change your mind, it won't change the way I see you. I don't judge people harshly for thinking things through fully. Sometimes, what seems like the next right thing turns out to be a step down a blind alley. There's no shame in turning around and going back until you get your bearings again. Always remember that, whatever happens."

I'd had a lot of people, in different scenarios, tell me that over the years. For people like me, the words "You can always change your mind", were the soundtrack to our lives, whether we wanted them to be or not. Mostly, they were actually trying to plead with you, to *make* you change your mind. Sometimes, though, at times like this, it was reassuring. An offer of friendship. A welcome – a log fire kept burning, waiting for you to come home.

I was making a mistake. I knew that. But I was being drawn down this route by forces I couldn't control. I didn't have the strength or cunning to fight it, and, in all honesty, I wasn't sure I wanted to. Tony Raglan was almost like a drug – and keeping away was even less of an option than a junkie forgoing their next fix. And, just like a junkie, I was prepared to risk anything for a higher high. I was being foolish. Putting everything that mattered at risk, for something that might not work out in the end. Something that might drive everyone concerned insane. I was already mad to even be thinking about this, but the madness felt so right. I knew it was wrong, but it didn't *feel* wrong.

"I wish circumstances had been different for you, Colt. I really do." Warren sighed, a light smile flickering at his lips."But, times have changed. Perhaps they've changed just enough for men like you." The smile broadened. "One day, Colt, in one form or another, you'll be a long way ahead of those who wanted to hold you back."

"Thank you, sir." I wondered who they were; some of them I could guess, others had made themselves more than known.

"Good luck with Nightshade – let me know how it goes from a trenches point of view; if it works, if it's viable, we might run our own variant on a permanent basis." He gave a rueful grin. "Or, at least, apply for the budget to run our own version."

"Sir."

"Off you go, then – your caseload won't complete itself."

"Sir."

As I left Warren's office – colloquially known as 'the bunny hutch', for obvious reasons – my mind started to roam around possibilities. Including the possibility of leaving the Job – something I'd never even imagined before. Leaving the Job would take me right out of Tony Raglan's orbit. It would take me away from people who thought I had no business being out of my house, let alone working as a copper. Leaving my Job would allow me to reconnect with the trans community – a community that, understandably, couldn't trust me. That was the crux of all of this – the Job trusted me, but didn't accept me; the trans community would accept me, but couldn't trust me.

Tony Raglan was the only person I'd met since I'd started transition who'd offered acceptance and trust in equal measure.

That was a hard thing to let go of – and a compelling reason for continued folly.

Chris

I stared at the screen, taking in the photo that had been posted a couple of hours ago on one of the local groups. I'd recognised the guy as soon as I'd seen the snap, even though you couldn't see his face. Judging by the tags, so had several other people.

That's the thing about the graffiti scene – spend long enough on it, and you see a lot of things you shouldn't see, start to build up an understanding of networks and connections, debts and obligations.

I'd only ever heard this guy's street name, when others were greeting him, pleading with him, or begging him for mercy; Blood, after his oxblood coloured jacket. He wore matching boots, too. Several tags marked a James Marriott – presumably the name Blood's mother knew him by. Bit posh, for the kind of street scum he was.

I'd seen him, the night we passed the bloke who turned up dead on the beach. That'd been a shock – I'd had some ink done by Brewer, but hadn't recognised him at the time. I felt bad about that. Thing was, I'd seen Blood, standing outside the Pavilion. He'd looked like he was watching Brewer. I hadn't thought anything of it, that night – Blood was often around, and he never noticed the people who noticed him; high on his own supply, more than likely – but now? If this guy could stab a copper, he was capable of anything.

I got up, pacing the room, my laptop whirring away on the bed. My mum's voice; "You'll burn us all in our beds, one of these days - we'll come home, and there'll be a shell of a house, done to a crisp, everything gone." I never asked her how we could simultaneously be burned in our beds, and come home to a burnt-out house; my mother wasn't famous for her sense of humour. Wasn't famous for much, all told. A twittering ditz, ugly as sin, without an original or creative bone in her body. Not that anyone could tell her that, of course. She thought she was brilliant at everything, and people encouraged her, because she could be relied on to be daft enough to give something for nothing. Unless you were her son, of course; then you could whistle in the wind. Looking after your teenage lad didn't get you brownie points, not unless he was still at school, and having a terrible time with his exams.

That had been the last time my mother'd spoken to me. When I was doing my A-Levels, eighteen months ago. The last time she'd paid any attention to me. Apart from the hospital visit, where she got thrown out because of her yelling and sobbing. Served her right, but still didn't help me. Her mask had slipped, people had seen her for what she really was – but they just made excuses, papered over the cracks in their reality of "Isn't Elizabeth lovely?"

I was stuck with the bitch.

Not for long, though. I sat back down on the bed, picked up my laptop, and stared at Blood's mugshot. A plan was starting to form.

Nicole

"I saw that guy, the night... the night before we found out about Brewer getting killed."

"What guy?"

I handed over my phone. Charlie studied it for a moment, shrugged, and dropped it beside me. "How would you know? You can't see his face."

"Pretty unusual jacket, though."

"It was dark when we saw Brewer that night, Nic. It could've been anyone."

"It was this guy – James Marriott, according to a lot of the comments."

"So? Someone you know?"

"No, but -"

"Me neither. So; nothing to do with us. Right?"

I got up, pulling my hair into a sloppy pony tail. "I'm going out."

Charlie glanced up. "You've got work in a bit, haven't you?"

"Yeah. I need to go for a walk first, clear my head."

"Want me to come?"

I shook my head. "It's your day off. Enjoy it."

Charlie sprawled on the bed, grinning. "I intend to."

"Love you. Catch you later."

"Bye. Love you, too."

I raised a hand in farewell; Charlie pouted her lips, and waggled her boobs. I pulled a face, and swung out the door, and down the stairs. Despite the face-pulling, I was smiling. When you loved someone, even the sight of them trying to be a glamour model, when that particular ambition was about a million miles out of their league, couldn't make you wish they were anything other than themselves. I'd never understood the craze, particularly common among straights, for bitching about your partner every chance you got; if they annoyed you that much, why stay with them? We weren't living in the Victorian era, where people had to be concerned about appearances and gossip, after all. Charlie made me incredibly happy; I couldn't imagine living, laughing, and struggling alongside anyone else. Yes, I'd met other women I thought were attractive, but never anyone who made me feel the way Charlie did. I had ambitions, dreams, and goals, and I also had realistic plans for achieving at least the goals, and making a shot at the ambitions. But if nothing worked out? I had Charlie, and that was enough.

Charlie

I wasn't surprised that Nicole hadn't recognised Blood; she'd
somehow managed to avoid the worst of life on the streets,
despite having been homeless for a while. Drugs weren't her
scene at all, while they absolutely were Blood's. I'd done a bit of
blow in the past – and had learnt very quickly to stay away from
Blood. Drug dealers tended not to be the best people, but there
were drug dealers and drug dealers; some were mostly harmless
arseholes with a twisted sense of humour. Others were sadistic
bastards for whom dealing drugs was simply a wider part of a
focused, criminal lifestyle, a lifestyle that centred on causing
maximum harm. The first kind of dealer, you dealt with, and
moved on from as quickly as possible. The second? You did
everything you could to avoid them.

I'd avoided Blood, but everyone who had anything to do with the
street drug scene knew who he was. He was top of the tree when
it came to vicious bastards, and looked terrifyingly at home with
a knife in his hand.

I sat up, wrapping one of the throw blankets around myself,
shivering as I thought about Nicole. She wasn't naïve, but she
had the bizarre kind of confidence that I'd seen more than once in
people from middle class homes who'd ended up on the streets –
something that happened more often than you might think. In
middle class families, it often didn't take much for your family to
decide you were an embarrassment, and they'd be best off without
you. Kids were accessories, things you started to resent as soon as
the tax credits ran out, and which were there to make you look
good. A walking, talking version of the latest Gucci handbag, or
whatever it was that was top of the fashion must-have list right
now.

Nic would make a great mum. I hugged the throw tighter, and
started thinking about our future – which was a lot better for my
nerves than thinking about the past. I closed my eyes, feeling
suddenly tired and tearful. I scrubbed furiously at my eyes with

the back of my hand. I *hated* crying. Nic was one of those people who could cry elegantly. I wasn't; there was snot everywhere, sobbing, my throat hurt... I was a mess when I started crying. I couldn't remember the last time I'd cried, and I didn't know why I'd suddenly started now. It was completely out of the blue; there was no sense crying over someone like Blood, over what life was like on the streets. Crying wouldn't change it. It wouldn't change any of it.

I got up, the throw still draped around my shoulders. I walked across the room, and stood, staring out of the window, loosing any sense of time. It felt as though I'd ended up in a different world, somehow. Nothing seemed concrete; the clouds outside the window look like a kind of carpet, something I could open the window, reach out, and touch.

I glanced at my rucksack, crouched like a loyal dog at the end of the bed. Nic didn't like me going out tagging without her, and it wasn't the easiest thing to pull off during the day. I grabbed a fistful of of permanent markers off the desk, shrugged the throw to the floor, and headed out, shoving my feet into trainers, and grabbing a coat. It wouldn't be the kind of thing I normally did, it wasn't the kind of thing the Crew did, but I needed to get everything that was crowding up my mind out, in one form or another, and this seemed like the most constructive way.

As I locked the front door behind me, I felt the weight of my phone in my pocket; I wondered if I should text Nicole; I almost went for my phone, then thought better of it. I didn't tend to text her while she was at work; it would seem odd if I did now, and it would just end up worrying her.

It was colder than it had looked, those cotton-wool clouds not even offering half the warmth they'd promised when I'd been thinking about opening the window and reaching out to wrap myself in them.

The air stung, and the scent of the sea was sharper than I was used to, almost carrying blood.

Blood. I needed to find him. But I needed to get all the

screaming in my head into words that were graffitied onto something public.

I turned towards the bus station, and the toilets alongside it. It was a good starting point, the back of a closed door. The space to build up confidence,get that rush, the tingling fear of discovery crowding everything else out, heightening your senses, flowing through your veins, chased by the strange, sweet smell of marker fluid.

There were three sets of public toilets in Lothing. The last, you had to pay twenty pence for, but they were right on the seafront. Finish off the confidence building there, then straight down and over the sea wall, over the rocks to the cove known as Kiddies' Korner, and create something completely safe for work, that the kids of Lothing would enjoy. Then home, to wait for Nic, like a good little wife.

DI Mark Roscoe

"Tam – thanks for coming in."

Tam Freud shook her head lightly. "I couldn't've just stayed at home, knowing that we were losing time." She looked up, "I want this guy, guv. And I'll do whatever it takes to nail him."

I nodded. "It's appreciated. One development – there seems to be a consistent opinion that we're looking for a guy called James Marriott, although most people seem to know him by his street name – Blood. He's a regular guest downstairs, and one of the people we're very keen to meet."

"Drugs?"

"And all the rest. If it's illegal and profitable, our Mr. Marriott will be involved in it. In most cases, he'll be running it. And if it's not profitable when he comes across it? He'll spin it until it is – this guy was a marketing manager before he discovered the thug life, and realised he could be paid a hell of a lot more, for far less work."

Tam rolled her eyes. "Oh, the joys of capitalism."

"You said it. Anyone can do anything they want, and are encouraged to make as much money as possible. Unfortunately, the illegal ways to make a lot of money far outweigh the lawful, for most people. Especially in Lothing. I've done a brief skim for the guy who posted the photo, but we've got nothing. I'm waiting on Brighton to get back to me, see if they know anything about him."

I wasn't holding out much hope, but there was no need to tell Tam that. I tended to keep bad news from my team for as long as possible – no one likes to face the harsh reality that everything they're doing, all their efforts, are most likely going to prove futile. Tam glanced up, frowning.

"Guv... something's just struck me -"

The phone on my desk rang. "One sec – hold that thought." I darted into my office, snatching up the receiver. "Mark Roscoe. Yeah – you get anything? No? Yeah, that's what we had. The original blank slate, probably the last one left in Lothing. Rough? You don't know the half of it. Yeah. Thanks anyway." I put the phone down. Rubbing my forehead, I stepped back into the main office, the place I always felt most at home. "Right, Tam – you were saying?"

She looked up from a notepad, pen poised just above the paper. A hand brushed the paper, palm flat. The pen went behind her ear. "I was wondering, guv, why someone who'd seen a police officer being violently attacked would post a photo of the attacker to a public site under their real name? I mean, I wouldn't – it's asking for trouble."

I nodded. "I think you could be on to something. That was Brighton on the phone; they've got no record of a Paul Great either. So, I'm going to back your hunch – we're dealing with someone using an alias. Which means we need to find out what their real name is. Whoever they are, they saw the attack on the Area Car. If they got that photograph, they'll have seen it all. They may well be our only witness. Any thoughts on who they might actually be?"

Tam pushed the pad towards the centre of the desk. I pulled a chair across, and sat down, studying it. Tam tilted her head, a habit she had when she was fully engaged with something. She pointed at the centre of the page. I took in her neat, almost cramped handwriting, the script of a person who'd grown up afraid of being too untidy, of taking up too much space. Or perhaps simply someone concerned with others being able to easily read her notes if something unexpected happened to her.

"Well, I've only just got started – I hadn't thought about this until now. So... Paul tends to be linked with either Peter or John, it can also be feminised to Paula – if our poster is a woman, she may be using the male version of her name. Petra is a possibility, too, but that's less common. Great doesn't sound right as a surname... possibilities I've come up with so far are Grant, because it sounds similar, and Great's opposites – Small, Little, names like that. I'll come up with as many related names as I can." She nodded towards the A4 pad. "I thought, if I came up with enough names to list on one side of a page, then ran them through the computer, I'd get a fair few names scanned, but wouldn't waste too much time."

I nodded. "Good idea. If they don't have records, don't worry about them – it's likely we're looking for a regular visitor; anyone else would have had the decency to get in touch. And I'd suggest looking for someone local – I have a feeling the Brighton tag might be another red herring."

"Guv."

I stood up. "We'll get him, Tam."

PC Feroc Hanson
LB 599

The sound of the front door opening had me on my feet, heart pounding. The parrot started screaming.

"Tony!"

"A front door that opens straight into the living room, and you're still startled?"

I held up my book. "I was reading."

"Ah. That explains everything." Tony sat down, a grimace crossing his face.

"Are you supposed to be out of hospital? No one told me -"

Tony shook his head. "I'm fine. I needed to be at home. Nothing they can do there that I can't accomplish just as well here. Rest. Antibiotics. More rest. And yes, I do have a course of antibiotics. It may be against medical advice, but I did wait around long enough to get some halfway decent drugs." He laughed, or tried to; it came out as a sputtered cough, broken with a couple of short, sharp yelps.

I was at his side in seconds, one hand on his shoulder, the other on his chest, easing him back in the armchair. In the cage behind me, Idaho started to whistle anxiously. "Hey....hey..." My fingers found the wound in his chest, pressing gently down through his shirt. He winced, snarling in pain. No blood, though, and the area around the wound didn't feel any warmer than I'd have expected.

"How did you get back?"

"Taxi. Fer... this op, Nightshade...don't go. Get out of it, somehow." Tony's eyes were bright and wide. "I'm serious, Feroc. I've got a bad feeling about it. Something's brewing out there, and I don't want you getting caught in the crossfire."

"What's brewing? What do you think is going on?"

"The one who knifed me... I recognised him."

"Who?"

"James Marriott. Calls himself Blood."

"The drug dealer?"

"And anything else he can get his mitts on. The thing is, Blood's never played well with others. If he's running with a pack, firstly, he's leading it, and secondly, it means things are shifting... things are ramping up. I don't want you out there when it all kicks off."

"I might be out there anyway, Tony – it's my job, after all."

"But you'd be out with me. You'd have the back up of coppers who know what they're doing."

"Tam Freud does."

"Not like this she doesn't. She's never run an op before. There's too many of you never been under before. Too much potential for something to go wrong." Tony looked up. "I need you here, Feroc. I need you to be okay."

"I will be, Tony. Look, what's brought this on, eh?"

He looked exhausted. "I don't know." He sighed. I was stunned to see the glimmers of tears at the corners of his eyes. "I just... I can't lose you, Fer. I can't be on my own again."

"Tony... this isn't you. What's going on here?"

"I'm tired." The edge was back in his voice. He struggled to his feet, his breath catching in his chest. "I need to go and lie down."

I let him go, pulling my hand away as though I'd been burnt. Took his place in the armchair. Watched Tony stagger across the room, one leg dragging, shoulders bowed. Already, I could see that his hair was damp with sweat.

I knew better than to go after Tony when he was in this kind of mood. I sat still, listening, until I heard the bedroom door open, which told me Tony had made it upstairs without incident, then crossed back to the sofa, picked up my book, and started reading again, or trying to. I couldn't focus.

Damn Tony Raglan to hell; I shouldn't have to be this messed up because of him. He shouldn't have the power to affect me like this.

I put my book down, got to my feet. Tony Raglan owned the streets of Lothing. If he thought something was wrong, then it probably was.

I didn't know James Marriott – Blood – as well as Tony and

some of the others at Lothing, but I'd had enough dealings with him to know he wasn't good news. Men like Tony Raglan were the David Attenboroughs of the urban jungle – if he said Blood always worked alone, then there was something to worry about when the man started working with a gang. Something else started to nag at me; the few dealings I'd had with Blood, he'd never even swung for one of us. He'd been cocky, he'd been sure of himself, he'd been a pain in the backside, but he'd never even violently resisted arrest.

Why would he suddenly get involved with an aggressive, violent mob? Why would he suddenly take it into his head to stab a copper?" My blood ran cold as I realised something; a single knife strike, in the heat of the moment, shouldn't have done the damage it had.

James Marriott had been able to control his aim, and keep his focus, well enough to bring a small knife up and under the arm hole of Tony's stab vest, missing the ribs, and going straight for maximum impact. There weren't many people who could pull something like that off, not in those circumstances.

And those that could... had usually been trained to.

If Blood, historically a lone wolf, had found a pack...might that be because he'd been told to? By the same person who taught him how to wield a knife so well?

Suddenly, I felt cold – catching Tony's fear. I picked up my book, and headed upstairs.

PC Tony Raglan
LB 265

I heard Feroc coming up the stairs. It broke my heart, every time, the way he simply refused to leave me be. I'd learned a long time ago that it wasn't safe to ask for affection, or support; fortunately, since then, I'd found myself in a world, and among a tribe, where |I didn't have to.

"Tony?" Soft, gentle. A spoken caress, concerned that I might actually be sleeping. I doubted I'd sleep for several weeks, at least not properly, and certainly not if Feroc wasn't here. That was beside the point, though; it was the thought that counted. I sat up, wincing as the stitches tugged at my chest.

"Hey."

Feroc swung into bed beside me, long, lean legs stretched out. Runners' legs. "I'm sorry about just now – I'm a bit out of it. I don't know what I was thinking."

"You were thinking the exact same thing I was, when you were with Killjoy." Feroc brushed my ankle with the side of his foot, and turned to look at me. "That's the blessing and the curse of love – you have someone you never stop worrying about. I bet Max still worries about you, all these years on." He paused. "How's he doing? He must be out by now, after that business with Clifford-Alistair?"

I nodded. "He called me, a couple of weeks ago. He's in Brighton, now, renting a mooring there."

"He's not coming back to Lothing, then?"

"Why would he? What is there for him here, now?"

Feroc nodded, a sense of distance coming over him. "Do you ever feel like that, Tony? That there's nothing for you here?"

I felt as though I'd been stabbed again, the knife hitting my heart, this time. "No. I'll always have the streets. As long as I have those, I have everything." I turned to look fully at Feroc. "Why? Do you feel like that?"

He was quiet for a moment. "Sometimes. I think it's having

grown up where I did, with the family I did – I'd visited places on every continent before I was fifteen, Tony. I'd been to the most remote parts of the UK, and the busiest parts of Africa. London was somewhere we went a couple of times a month. It's hard to settle for Lothing."

"London's not all it's cracked up to be."

"I'd forgotten – you were with the Met for a while, weren't you?"

"Briefly. Couple of years. It didn't suit me. I mean, the action did – there was so much going on, it felt like you were going to war, rather than going to work... but it was a war you couldn't win. A war the government didn't want you to win. Doesn't matter who's in power, they want crime. They want a dysfunctional society, that's falling apart at the seams. They want a population that feels angry, frightened, resentful, and helpless. They want a force of guardians who are barely coping, who are constantly on the verge of giving up. They want people poor and desperate, greedy and hateful. Because that's a society they can divide. A society who'll believe that the ruling elite knows best. A society who'll consent to almost anything, if you spin it as making their individual, personal lives better."

Feroc shook his head. "I don't think the world's as black as you paint it, Tony. I can understand how it feels that way -"

"And when you've been part of the world for as long as I have, you'll understand how it *is* that way, and how nothing you or anyone else does will ever change it. It's why I don't vote – doesn't matter what they say; they're all lying, and they'll all ensure the status quo of fear and distrust and resentment never changes. They're only ever in it for themselves, however good a game they talk."

A smile played on Feroc's lips. "You know they say a pessimist is just a disappointed idealist?"

"Yeah, well – being a pessimist is an improvement. When I was with the Met, I was a nihilist. So were most of us – we just hadn't succumbed to anarchism, yet. Well; most of us hadn't."

"I can't see you as an anarchist, somehow – all grubby black t-

shirts and wild hair, tattoos, piercings, and a crappy little beard."
We both started laughing at the image. For me, that was the most
beautiful thing about being part of a couple – shared laughter. I
wondered if I'd laugh as much with Colt Devereux? Raglan-
Devereux; it had a ring to it I could never pull off with Raglan-
Hanson. Max and I had talked about the possibility – which was
all it had been, when we were together, and a dim, distant one at
that, of becoming a formal couple; it had been more of a joke of
wishful thinking than a discussion, back then, but we'd both
agreed that Rockford-Raglan sounded like a power-couple name.
Feroc and I had agreed to keep separate names, and, suddenly, I
felt as though that was a sign, proof that we weren't meant for
each other, that we wouldn't be together for ever. It was a daft
thought, a teenage-girl kind of thought, but it was still there. I
couldn't change it, and \I couldn't shake it.
They never talked about this when they talked about love.

Feroc was reading, the only sound the soft whisper of his fingers
on the pages, a kind of quiet dance.
"Fer?"
"Hm?" He glanced up.
"Can you read to me?"
He looked surprised, as well he might. I wasn't a toddler, in need
of a bedtime story, after all. Then he smiled.
"Sure. I'll go back to the start of this chapter – it won't make
sense, otherwise."
Feroc had a beautiful voice, smooth and restful, completely
accentless. Plenty of people thought they didn't have an accent;
Feroc genuinely didn't. It sounded green, his voice, a soft green,
like a watercolour painting of summer fields, edged with the
green of pine trees, and the scent of a forest breeze.
I closed my eyes, letting the colours of his voice dance, without
really hearing the words. I wished we could stay like this forever,
side by side, barely touching, bound by energy rather than
physicality, Feroc's voice weaving a spell around me, wrapping

me in a blanket of comfort that would always be warmer than anything I could buy. The stress and anxiety of the real world fell away; we were the only people left. There was no responsibility, no threat, just us, like this, forever.

It couldn't last, of course. I was startled out of my reverie, minutes or hours later, by the shrill, insistent ringing of my mobile. I moaned softly, swearing a little less softly as I reached over the the bedside table for the damn thing, stitches tugging. I glanced at the clock on the wall. It had only been about five minutes. There was clearly magic in Feroc's voice.

"Tony." I never answered with my full name, and I'd never advise anyone else to.

The line crackled, someone breathing hard. Panicked, not threatening. Finally; "Tony... it's Max. I think I've just done something really stupid. I need your help. Now. Please?"

PC Feroc Hanson
LB 599

"Where are you?"

I shot Tony a questioning look. He raised an eyebrow, and mouthed 'Max', bringing the phone down, and switching it to speaker. It was a gesture of trust I hadn't been expecting, but that I definitely appreciated. It had been clear, when we'd been dealing with the art fraud case, and before that, when Tony had been shot, and Max had arrived at St. Ralph's with his inappropriate flowers, that there was still something between the two men. Being let in on their conversation, now, allowed me to relax; whatever happened, Tony and I were a couple. We were strong together.

"I'm at the old Marquis. Tony, please, just get here. Don't bring anyone else with you."

"Look, Max, I need to know what's happened. Are you hurt? Do you need an ambulance?"

"No. Yes. No – no ambulance. Tony, please – we'll sort everything out when you get here, okay? Please, just come. The old Marquis. Quickly."

"Alright, Max, but I'm bringing Feroc with me – I *need* to, Max; I'm not fit to drive at the moment, alright? Neither of us is on duty, okay? But I have to bring Feroc with me. Alright? No, Max – I can't walk up there. Look, you didn't even have the decency to call me and let me know you were back in Lothing; the last I knew, you were living in Brighton. You don't get to call the shots now, right? I'll be there in about fifteen, twenty minutes – but I'm bringing Feroc with me. No, I *can't* get there sooner – not unless you let me call the nick, and get it blue-lighted. Right. I'll be there as soon as I can."

Tony ended the call with a sigh. "What's going on, Tony?"

He got up, wincing. "I don't know. I have a feeling I don't *want* to know. I'm sorry about this."

I was already on my feet. "Don't be. It's not down to you. Let's just get out there, see what's going on."

"I'll kill him."

"Not helpful."

"I don't care. He can't do this, Feroc. He can't just expect me to pick up the pieces of his life every time he screws up."

"Let's just find out what's going on, before we rush to judgement, okay?"

"You're too good for this world, Feroc."

I grinned. "I know. Now – let's go."

DC Tam Freud

Computers were supposed to make things easier. Try believing
that when you look up, only to realise that four hours of your life
have been wasted.

Two sides of a sheet of A4 of possible names for "Peter Great",
and I had two people with criminal records – a Paul Maxim, and
Petra Small. She was regularly run in for soliciting; it didn't seem
likely that she'd be bothered enough about having contact with us
to avoid reporting an attack like that. And Paul Maxim was
currently serving the final stretch of an eighteen-month sentence
for fraud, theft employee, and embezzlement. He couldn't have
seen anything, and, like Petra, would have come and told us about
it, if only to dance the I Told You So over how much worse than
him other people were, and why weren't we spending out time
preventing violent crime, rather than bothering hard working,
entreprenurial types like him.

I sat back, hands covering my face, trying not to scream.

And then something struck me.

Almost frantic, fingers trembling, I tapped a furious request. The
computer ground its gears. I ground my teeth. The screen flashed,
seemed to rotate, then filled with the info I'd asked for.

I scanned through, nodding, murmuring to myself, my heart rate
picking up. I hit Print, standing up in the same moment, hurrying
over to the printer as though I might lose the map that showed me
where all the world's treasure was buried.

After pacing for what felt like half an hour, but was probably
only a couple of minutes, the printer sighed, exhaling a sheaf of
paper, a printed replica of the webpage that was currently open.

I snatched the sheets up, reading as I walked.

"Guv – I think I've cracked it. It was clever; Peter Great is Max
Rockford."

"As in the Max Rockford who apparently used to date Tony
Raglan?" Roscoe ran a broad hand over the stubble on his jaw,
bitten nails caught in the steady glow of the strip light like a

guilty thing surprised. "You'd better be sure on this, before you make a move; what makes you think it's him?"

I handed over the papers. "When he was released, a little over three years ago, he gave the Prison Service that address." I pointed it out. "Near as dammit to Brighton. I actually recognise it, as it happens – it's a kind of housing co-operative; started by some old biddy who sold her house when she retired, and brought a boat and a whole bunch of moorings, all on the same stretch of the Ouse, where it skirts Haywards Heath. She rents the moorings for peppercorn rent to boat people – artists, many of them, some just people who like that way of life. She's even got an old cruise liner out there, that she puts up homeless in, for free. The council keep trying to fins a way to force her to move. Haven't managed it yet. There's a charitable trust ready to take over once she passes on." I took a deep breath, forcing myself to focus. "And the name – Peter means 'rock', Great translates to 'Max'..."

"It's tenuous, Tam. Really, really tenuous. If this is Max Rockford, why didn't he just come forward? Or try and stop the attack? He would have seen that it was Tony, would have seen what happened to him. How could he have just walked away from that?"

"I asked myself that, when I realised it could be him. I don't think he wants anyone to know he's back in Lothing. I wonder if he's started to make a name for himself in Brighton, and doesn't want to upset that particular applecart."

Roscoe shook his head. "I'm not buying it, not just yet. Tell me how he could have left Tony Raglan to die, for all he knew, and I might give you your head on this."

"We've got nothing else, guv."

"We've got Blood. I'll send a couple of uniform round to bring him in, see what he has to say for himself."

I felt my temper rising. "People like Blood don't crack, guv, and if we can't get a witness to place him there, any lawyer worth their salt is going to run rings round us with that photo, those tags. We need to talk to Max Rockford, at least to rule him out."

Roscoe sighed. "Alright. You've got 24hours. I'm going to get the uniforms to bring Blood in anyway, but I'll let you try and find Max. One day, Tam – if you haven't found him by then, you drop it, and we try it my way. Okay?"

"Guv." I could feel myself starting to grin, and had enough awareness to know that really wasn't a good idea; Mark Roscoe was pretty relaxed, but you could only push him so far, and I didn't want to risk losing the ground I'd gained. I knew I was right; Peter Great and Max Rockford were one and the same person. All I had to work out was the answer to DI Roscoe's question; why had Max gone to such lengths to avoid the police? Somehow, I had a feeling there was more to it than simply wanting to avoid Tony Raglan. Getting a statement that proved that James Marriott was the man with the knife, and that he was the same person known on the streets as Blood, was my first priority. Answering unanswered questions, however, definitely ran a close second.

PC Feroc Hanson
LB 599

"Wait here."

I pulled the handbrake on, a little more sharply than I'd intended. I glared at Tony.

"No. Whatever's going on, you're not dealing with it on your own." I was out of the car before I'd finished my sentence. Tony slammed the passenger door as he hurried to catch up.

"Feroc!"

"Tony! Tony! Thank the gods. Thank you. Please – over here." Max Rockford had done well on prison life, and whatever had come after it for him. He'd bulked up a little – more definition, a chiselled edge to his jaw – but the dusky tan of his skin, and the depth of his eyes, stopped him from looking hard. Behind him, I could see two cars, smashed against the metal fencing at the far side of the car park. The Marquis of Lorne had been closed and abandoned for as long as I could remember, although Tony and some of the others told some pretty hairy tales about what had gone down when it had been open. It made Lothing sound like the wild west, and, all things considered, the pub's closure was probably a good thing. Of course, coppers exaggerated – the human tendency to want our lives to sound more exciting than they were magnified by the need to justify, over and over again,the public need for the expense of a police force. Police *service* – we were just another branch of retail, now; Uniforms R Us.

"What the hell happened, Max?"

Max turned, looking back at the cars. "I found out who he was. The man who stabbed you. He was a bastard, Tony, in every possible way. I found his house, followed him when he came out this morning. I didn't mean to kill him..."

"So, how did that mess over there happen?"

"I don't know. I just lost it. I ran him off the road – the fencing was down, just on the corner – kids, probably, or junkies – and...

Tony, you've got to help me. I can't go back to prison. I'm just getting everything sorted."

I looked at Tony and saw the flicker of indecision on his face.

"Tony...." My voice was low. A warning. "Tony - "

"Shut up a minute, Fer. I need to think."

"No, you don't. We can't cover this up. You know we can't."

"Just let me see what's actually happened, first."

"Tony -"

He was already off, loping across the car park. I turned to Max, ice and fire chasing one another through my veins. "You – stay there. Right there. Don't move. Don't even cough, okay? You're an idiot, Max, and I won't let you drag Tony down for this. I won't let you destroy his life, too. It's not going to happen."

"I didn't mean -"

"No, Max – you didn't *think*."

Tony was walking back. There was something wrong about the way he moved, the way he looked.

"What? What is it?"

"I didn't really take in much, during the attack – I just went blank, operating on instinct. I was more concerned with where Ryan Hartley was, with what was happening to the car... but the guy with the knife... he was blond. I remember that. Bright blond hair, more white than blond, like he'd dyed it. The driver of that car? He's wearing a baseball cap, you wouldn't have been able to see his hair, from a distance. But he's got brown hair. Light brown." Tony turned to Max. "The man in that car isn't the man who stabbed me." He looked up at me. "Call it in."

"Tony!"

"No, Max. I can't cover this up. Someone's dead. Believe me, I know how much it messes you up, the knowledge that someone died because of you. I'm not letting you put yourself through that. *I'm* not living with it."

Tony took out his mobile, I slipped mine back into my pocket, and moved closer to him, resting a hand on his shoulder. He was doing the right thing, but that wouldn't stop it being incredibly hard for him.

"It's Tony Raglan, LB 265. I'm in the car park of the Marquis Of Lorne, on Lorne Road. I need to report a FATAC. It looks like the victim was run off the road. I have the other driver with me. He's got some superficial injuries, and he might have broken a couple of ribs – he's conscious and walking, but clearly in pain. Max. Max Rockford. I don't know the name of the other driver – I just took a quick look in the car, through the window, I didn't want to touch anything until scenes of crime have been out here. I didn't recognise him – but he's definitely dead. We'll need CID out here. And...can you give Inspector Wyckham a buzz? I'd like him to be here. Try Sergeant Gardner, if you can't get hold of him. Yeah, yeah, I can stay on scene, that's not a problem. Feroc Hanson's with me. Yeah, thanks – an ambulance, and a uniform unit. They'll need to stay with the injured driver at St. Ralph's. I'm off duty, and...there's a personal element. I know the injured driver. Very well, as it goes."

Tony ended the call, put his phone away, and looked blankly at Max. "There's nothing I could do, Max."

Max Rockford nodded, a single movement of his head. "It's okay. I shouldn't have even thought about asking you to do otherwise. You're not that man. I should never have tried to make you other than you are." He sighed, yelping a little. Some of the colour drained from his face, and he wrapped an arm across his chest. "I think you're right about the broken ribs." He started to sweat. Sirens howled, drawing closer. "I never told you, Tony, but..." he was struggling, pain catching up with him, as adrenaline ebbed. "...your integrity. That's why I fell for you; you were so....different. The people I knew, the people I still know... they see laws as recommendations, or challenges. They'll do whatever it takes to get by. Most of them are...well, 'chaotic good' is probably the best description. D&D is handy for words we need, but our regular language doesn't provide, isn't it? But you... you were always true good, Tony. And I hadn't come across that before."

The Area Car – or, rather, the expensive replacement for the smashed, twisted wreck of the Area Car – swung in, blue lights yelping and circling, an ambulance close behind. As the paramedics hit the ground, the CID car pulled in, a single blue light flashing on the roof.

DI Roscoe got out, Tam Freud following. Another car pulled in. The driver's door opened.

"Tony. Feroc. And this must be Max Rockford." Inspector Wyckham took in the scene. "It's all a bit of a mess, isn't it, lads?"

Cautions echoed. Blood pressure cuffs appeared. Crime scene tape unravelled. Radio chatter bounced across the pitted, windswept expanse.

I turned to Tony. He looked shattered.

"Tony?"

He glanced up. "Shona."

"We'll need a statement."

"Of course."

"Let's go back to your car, yeah? Get out of everyone's way for a bit."

Tony moved as though he were in a day dream. I followed close behind, watchful, but wary.

It was over. It was just beginning. The circus was back in town.

And the man who'd stabbed my lover was still at large. Armed, dangerous, and probably more than prepared to give it another go, if he got the chance.

I wasn't about to let him get that chance. Not if I could help it.

DI Mark Roscoe

"So, Max... why don't you just talk us through what happened today?"

Max Rockford looked shattered. That wasn't a common expression in the interview room. Arrogant, aggressive, hostile, strung out, blank; those looks, I was familiar with. Looking at Max Rockford, you could almost believe you were looking at a child. Someone who'd somehow got himself lost, and, cold and hungry, badly wanted to go home.

"I don't know... I mean, I *do* know... I just... I didn't mean to kill him."

"Do you mean you didn't mean to kill the man in the car, or you didn't mean to kill anyone?"

"I...I wanted to kill James Marriott. He goes by Blood on the streets. I thought he was driving the car. It was his car. Outside his house. I'd been waiting for him -"

"Max, I do need to remind you, you're still under caution. You can ask for a solicitor at any time. Do you understand?"

"Yes. But I don't want one. A solicitor. I screwed up, and someone's dead who probably shouldn't be. I want to get that sorted. Get it off my chest."

"Someone who 'probably' shouldn't be dead, Max? What do you mean?"

He swallowed hard,. Licked his lips. "I mean, if he's associated with James Marriott, he's hardly going to be an angel, is he?"

"The man in the car, the man you killed, was James Marriott's younger brother, Alex. No record, good job. Twenty years old. He hadn't spoken to his brother for two years, according to their mother. Lovely woman, at the end of her tether with James, Husband died of cancer eighteen months ago. Alex had gone to see James because his mum thought a reconciliation would be a good idea. She's not in the best of health, and she wanted to see her boys getting on again. Being brothers again. We don't know why Alex was driving his brother's car, but we do know that there are three cars registered to James Marriott, and none in Alex's name; it's likely the brothers had at least reached a partial truce, enough that James would feel inlined to help his kid brother out by giving him a car. He'd make the cost of another one, brand new, in a week, on his profits. It wasn't going to cost him anything to help his brother out, and, once he'd done him a favour, he might be able to call a couple back in return. I can imagine a man like James Marriott might find it very useful to have an acquaintance who wasn't known to police, can't you, Max?"

Truth be told, that thought had only just struck me, that Alex Marriott, identified ten minutes before this interview by his distraught mother, who'd collapsed, screaming, at the scene, might have been given a "gift" by a career criminal who'd seen the potential benefits of having someone with a clean sheet beholden to him. It would have started with small things, innocent requests, and would have built up to what Marriott actually needed and wanted. When kid brother protested, as all good men would, he would be reminded of the car, of all the other ways in which James would have "helped" him, investments that cost James "Blood" Marriott nothing, but which had the potential to bring him huge rewards.

Perhaps Alex Marriott was better off out of it. Perhaps, like Donnie Darko, his life would have only got worse if he'd lived, descending into a spiral of insanity and hopelessness.

"Do you have a Facebook account in the name of Peter Great, Max?"

He nodded. In previous years, he would have been prompted to speak aloud, 'for the tape'; we had DVD recording, now. There'd been all the usual objections, from both sides of the fence – coppers who didn't appreciate that, when you worked exactly to the book, courts didn't throw out your cases, or overturn convictions, and criminals and the criminal-adjacent who yelped and whined about how "their likeness or image" would be used. Never mind how come everyone was a critic all of a sudden; I wanted to know when everyone started taking courses in media and marketing. We'd even had the bloody human rights lobby get in on it – invasion of privacy, as though people's privacy wasn't invaded a hundred times a day, in subtle, unnoticed ways, every time they switched on their computer, or popped into town for a paper, pint of milk, and a fiver on the gee-gees. If you were where you were supposed to be, behaving yourself, what was your issue with someone knowing about it?

I brought my attention back to the interview. "Why is that? I mean, it's not your name, is it?"

"I've got a business page under my own name, I use it to sell my art. I don't want people to immediately find my personal account if they don't like my work. It's not all nice, middle-class abstracts, if you see what I mean?"

"Okay, I can understand that, but why post that photo of James Marriott to social media? Why not bring it to us?"

"You'd've taken days to work out who he was. I didn't want to wait that long."

"You like to serve your revenge white-hot, then?"

"I wanted him to pay for what he'd done – and the debt was already overdue."

I sat back in my chair, arms folded across my chest. "Thing is, Max, James Marriott has probably worked out that whoever killed his kid brother was actually after him. So, not only is he pissed off about his baby brother's abrupt demise, and looking for the scum who took him our, he's on his guard. Probably already left Lothing."

Max Rockford looked down at the table, fingers flexing and twisting, arm muscles jumping. Beneath the table, one feet beat a nervous tattoo.

"You're in a whole lot of trouble, Max, any way you look at it." I stood up, preparing to conclude the interview. "And you've probably made things worse for Tony Raglan. For all my officers."

I led him out, Tam Freud waiting until the door was closed, and the camera could clearly see an empty room, before switching off the equipment.

The custody officer looked up, a weary ex-cop who'd had to retire early on medical grounds, pleased to come back when we started loading up on civilians. Tom Grainger had seen it all, and disapproved of most of it. Aimee Gardner, on her way out, a bustle of uniform and chatter, paused. She'd been born at the wrong time, had Sergeant Gardner; should've been in the Force when a sergeant was essentially an office manager, ensuring the teams on the streets could get an arrest turned around quickly, looking after her relief, running interference between the blokes and the brass. Mind you, she'd probably disagree. She was a copper's copper, with a love of being out on the streets, making a difference.

"Max Rockford. I'm charging him with murder."

Tom Grainger's face didn't change. He wrote down the charge – an upgrade from the manslaughter of Max's arrest, and turned to him. "You still have the right to contact a solicitor, or to have one appointed for you, free of charge. You have the right to have someone notified that you are in custody." Max shook his head.

"It's okay. There's no one. I don't need a solicitor."

"That's what they all say. Now – anything changed from your arrest sheet? Allergies or illnesses you forgot to mention?" Another shake of the head.

"Right, then. Back to your room."

A couple, well-dressed, mid-thirties, came in through the front door. We kept the business end out of sight, which was just as well; prisoners were led to and from their cells without benefit of shoes – too easy to use as weapons, if someone got a strop on – and Joe Public tended to be somewhat appalled when they became aware of things like that, as though people didn't walk around their own houses without shoes on. If you were being bailed, released, or sent to court, you'd have your shoes taken out of the hutch beside your cell door, on the corridor side, and thrown at you, two coppers watching you put them on. If you were going to court, you didn't get your laces back.

"In you go. Anything you need?"

"Some toilet paper'd be nice. An actual roll, not just two sheets. An illusion that I'm a human being, rather than a caged monkey." Max Rockford looked up, deep brown eyes flashing with challenge as they met mine. "Unless that's what you think of me, of people who aren't quite white enough?"

I sighed. "I'll see about it, okay? You don't seem the type to try and block up the bog with it."

"What good would that do me? Just get me moved to another cell, wouldn't it? I just want to feel human. To wipe my arse if I need to take a dump. Okay?"

"Sure."

We regarded one another in silence. I sighed, and closed the door. I'd always hated the way we denied prisoners the basics. I mean, some of them weren't any better than animals, but not giving them toilet roll, for crying out loud? It wasn't just that stuff like that annoyed people – it was the kind of thing the keyboard warriors lapped up. The kind of thing the liberal newspapers loved to wring their hands over.

It was unnecessary humiliation, done out of a sadistic sense of spite. And it was more trouble than it was worth, every time.

PC Tony Raglan
LB 265

"Tony...stop it."

I paused, clenching my teeth as the jitters came over me again, almost immediately. I needed to keep moving. There was nothing I could do for Max, nothing I could do about any of it, but I could move. I could pace, while I was waiting to be interviewed by Yarmouth CID. Because of my previous relationship with Max, it had to be another nick, the impression of impartiality,. Well, less of an impression, with those knuckle draggers, and more of an actuality. Yarmouth hated us, and we returned the favour; somehow, I didn't hold out much hope of sympathy and cover ups from them.

"Look, you did the right thing, okay?"

"I nearly didn't. I wanted to help him. I was going to go along with a cover up."

"No, you weren't. You're not like that."

"So, why are the Yarmouth louts coming over, then?"

"It's just a formality, Tony. Ticking boxes, keeping the Press happy."

"Bastards. Sometimes, I think a free Press is more trouble than it's worth."

"You don't mean that."

"Stop telling me what I do and don't mean, Feroc – it's irritating at the best of times. And right now is far from one of the best times. Okay?"

Feroc sighed, and sat down at one of the tables in the canteen, doodling on a napkin. It made me think about straws, for some reason. I wondered why we'd fixated on plastic straws as a symbol of everything that was wrong with the world. I wondered why we weren't asking questions about why stuff we'd assumed we'd sent off be recycled was ending up in the ocean.

But of course, focusing on straws – commonly used by the elderly and the disabled – as the reason for cute little turtles and dolphins dying was born from the same premise as the one that had people claiming that trans people were the reason the NHS was broke, and people living their own personal expression of identity was the reason women wouldn't get their pensions when they'd been expecting them. Neither would I, now, but you didn't hear me complaining about it. What did people imagine they'd be doing with themselves that couldn't wait a couple of years? Another five years of work meant five years more cash to put towards whatever you'd apparently spent your entire working life waiting for.

It was pathetic, people hating their jobs so much that they spent forty years or more longing for the day they never had to go back. I had bad days – bad weeks, sometimes – everyone in this job did, but I couldn't imagine not doing it. I could imagine struggling to do it well, at sixty, but I couldn't imagine a life without it. In my book, if you didn't like something, you made the effort to change it. You didn't sit around whining about it and expecting someone else to sort everything for you. People were lazy and selfish, these days; they wanted everything handed to them on a plate, wanted the world to fall exactly in line with their whims. You saw it when people moaned about the place where they lived having "no decent shops, nothing to do" - what they meant was, they had to do more than step out of the front door to find shops and entertainment. There were plenty of shops in Lothing, plenty of places to while away a few hours, if you got off your arse and walked around a bit. But no one walked in Lothing; it's why they were all so keen for the council to spend whatever it took – a million, at the moment – to get a new crossing put in, bridging the tidal lake that gave the town its name. That, to me, was the clearest sign that most of the people in Lothing didn't pay their own council tax – what did they think would happen, in the years after that money was spent? In a decade, they'd be yowling for yet another crossing. Using public transport, walking, cycling – it never entered their heads that these were far cheaper ways of reducing the ballache of congestion on the existing bridge than simply building a new one. Lothing was one of the easiest places to walk around – if I didn't have to be anywhere in particular, or didn't have to bring anything too heavy or bulky back, I tended to walk; it was a pleasant way to engage with the town, and a lot less frustrating than the inevitable tailbacks whenever the bridge went up, or a train came through the level crossing out the back end of the town, where it yielded to the suburbs and the Suffolk side of the Broads.

I looked up as the canteen doors swung open. Inspector Wyckham gave a brief nod. "They're here, Tony. You okay?"

"Tired, sir. And I could use some painkillers. Other than that, I'll be fine."

"Good lad. You're sure you don't want to speak to your Fed Rep?"

"No. I haven't done anything wrong, sir."

Wyckham nodded, sadly. Just as we immediately read guilt in anyone who exercised their right to have a solicitor present, coppers who went to the Fed at the drop of a hat weren't trusted. It shouldn't be like that, but it was. I coped better than some of the younger officers; I'd been brought up to take care of myself and my problems, not run to other people sobbing about unfairness. It had got me this far, and, even with the insanity that was going on left, right, and centre on the socio-political scene, I had no doubt it would take me to the end of the line. Like all good Heathens, I hoped my next life would be in Valhalla. Like most good Heathens, my spirit would probably simply fade to the collective unconscious, fuelling fires for those who would come long after me.

I followed Wyckham out of the canteen, forcing myself not to look back at Feroc. I could feel him watching me, but I didn't want to see the pain in his eyes – hurt I'd caused.

That's what I did. I hurt people I cared about. I knew that was my failing, but, somehow, I couldn't stop doing it. I couldn't change my nature, couldn't start acting in ways that were best for everyone.

Feroc, Max, Colt; they'd all be better off without me. The Job would be glad enough to see the back of me, one of the last of the dinosaurs, keeping them from the slick, tech-savvy corporate entity they wanted to be.

James Marriott: Blood

Alex was dead.

I sat down, feeling the rage rising, setting my blood on fire. One of my runners had told me; he'd seen the smash, had come straight to my gaff, panicking that the lynchpin of Lothing's criminal fraternity, the one person he could rely on to get him out of this hellhole, was dead.

It had happened to the lad before. He'd been a runner for Matt Youngman, the cock who'd run this town before me. I'd scurried in Youngman's shadow for a couple of years, kept to the edges of his affairs – Youngman didn't trust anyone who wasn't black, a fucking joke, since the received wisdom is you can't be a victim of racial discrimination if you're white, so he never let me near anything vital. He kept his crew close, and kept it dark.

And then he fucked up. He shot that copper, lost everything, all because of some stupid girl. Some stupid *white* girl. He wouldn't let me in on his scene, but he'd let her into his legs. He'd lost his head over her, thrown everything he'd built up away over a fucking accident. I mean, yeah, the copper needed to be given a hiding – you lose your girl, you're going to give the bloke who took her from you a hiding. But, when that bloke's a copper, you don't kill him. Ideally, you don't kill him whoever he is, because women are ten a penny – if you've got money, you can get a girl, no bother. If you've got money, you're not looking for a happy ever after; you just want a quick leg over. A bit of fun. There's women all over who're well up for that. I mean, the copper didn't die, but that was more by luck than judgement. Youngman was inside, mandatory life. His record, he wasn't likely to be considered for parole anytime soon. Nature abhors a vacuum; so did I. And, unlike most dealers, I thought further ahead than my next wad, my next high. Being on the periphery of Matt Youngman's life had its advantages – like the fact that it had allowed me to build my own.

Networks in Norwich, Cambridge, Ipswich, Thetford, King's

Lynn, Peterborough, London. If a train or bus could get there from Lothing, so could I. I knew my cars were most likely flagged, so I travelled incognito by public transport whenever I needed to leave the area on business. I had plenty of time to go visiting, and all the dedication I needed to put in the work of proving myself, earning trust, and becoming a Name for the scene's Faces. And, unlike Matthew Youngman, I didn't blow it on show; I'd squirrelled and stashed until I had enough to buy a decent house. A modest but pleasant semi, in a decent part of Lothing. I had a fence, a garden, all the rooms I could want. No grotty tower block rabbit hutch for me. I was all about security, about things people couldn't take away from me.

And about diversification. Being involved in the dealing side of the drugs world brought you into contact with a lot of other business opportunities. I took advantage of the best of those that crossed my path, and, just as I'd done with Matt Youngman's leftover empire, I made them more than they were – and made a bit for myself at the same time. Entrepreneurial – that was me. Entrepreneurial, but careful. Matthew Youngman had lost everything because he made a stupid mistake. I hadn't made a mistake since I was fifteen years old. Twenty years of keeping one step ahead, and then I threw it all away. I still couldn't tell you why I'd got involved that day, but I had – and now Alex was dead.

One mistake. And now, I'd have to make a few more.

I tapped the piece of paper in front of me. I made a point of insisting that messages and information were written down, pen on paper, and handed directly to the person who needed them. No text messages, no WhatsApp. No phone calls. Nothing traceable. Nothing that could be used against you.

I booted up my laptop, and typed out a brief but formal letter. Hit print.

Pulled on a pair of latex gloves. Picked up a self-sealing envelope, a book of self-adhesive stamps. Letter folded.

Envelope. Picked up a pen. Clicked through to another website.

Carefully copied an address. Stamp on.
I paused to set the alarm, made sure the door was double locked, and started jogging, a snarl becoming a smile.

DC Tam Freud

I was shaking as I got up, reluctantly ready to face what had
proved to be a subdued gathering of the Nightshade task force.
Understandably so.

Colt Devereux and Feroc Hanson were the quietest, sitting side
by side at the back of the room, just outside the circle. Feroc had
his legs stretched out in front of him. I took in their length, their
muscled leanness. Colt had his arms folded across his chest, legs
crossed at the ankles, a strangely delicate pose for a man who'd
been through so much hardship.

I took a deep breath. This would be the first night we were out as
a 'crew', and, while this would be more about getting a feel for
how those who belonged to the night behaved, the ways in which
they were different to us, the ones who sought to control the
night.

"Right. So. Tonight's going to be mostly about observation. Walk
around – stick together, but not like glue. If you see people
working on graffiti, watch them; close enough to show you're
interested, not close enough to spook them. You're not Job, not
tonight, not any night you're out for Nightshade. You belong to
the night, you don't police it."

"What if we see criminal activity? Drug dealing, someone
breaking into somewhere?"

I glanced at Seamus Hanratty. "Report it if you can, without
drawing attention to yourself, or identifying yourself to the
switchboard. Take photos if it's safe to, but don't show out."

Seamus nodded, licking his lips. Colt glanced up, "I assume the
uniforms here know about us? About Nightshade, I mean?"

"They've been warned off interfering with any anti-social
behaviour. That's the safest way all round."

Colt looked away. I sensed the restlessness in the room. A cold,
focused rage that didn't want to be part of Nightshade. Everyone
here wanted to be hunting down the scum who put Ryan Hartley
and Tony Raglan in hospital. But the law of the pack was that,

whatever had gone before, there was work to be done in the here and now. James Marriott and his ilk would fall to us in time.

"Aimee and Feroc, as you two are the most artistic ones among us, any conversations that come up, you try and get the lead, but make sure it seems natural."

Aimee nodded, glancing back at Feroc. A subtle, certain movement, lines of power clearly visible. Aimee had the air and the power of someone who was going all the way. Recognising it in her, I noted its absence in myself.

I ran briskly through the remainder of the operational housekeeping, then opened the door, standing back. "Let's get out there, and do some good."

I followed them out, taking them all in, one by one, seeing not only the officer in front of me, but whatever history I knew of them, and, sometimes – as with Aimee Gardner – the future that lay ahead of them.

These glimpses of the future were the things that troubled me most. Sometimes, they were frightening. Always, they were... unsettling.

I wasn't a natural leader. I knew that now. But I'd get this team through Nightshade, and bring them back, send Colt Devereux home, in one piece. And then I was going to have to work out how to tell Roscoe that I didn't want to go for promotion. That I wasn't going to live up to his ambitions for me. I wasn't looking forward to that conversation, and, since I'd never been able to see my own future, I couldn't tell what the likely outcome would be. Best case scenario? He was completely understanding, and things carried on as they were, as they always had done. Worst case? I was looking for a new posting, unable to stay with a boss who wouldn't be able to keep his disappointment out of every interaction. Who would lace it through every word, a sharp edge he was just waiting for me to trip up and cut myself on.

I wondered if Colt Devereux ever felt like that – that people were just waiting for you to screw up? It couldn't be easy, living with his past.

I wondered how Colt and Beck would get on, whether I should introduce them. Once Nightshade was done, though. Only then.

Beck

I spent too much time on the internet. But why wouldn't I? It wasn't as though society gave people like me any other way of finding one another, was it? Other people got to wander up to people they could see face to face. They got to spend days, weeks, months, years, sharing confidences and watching how a new face behaved around old friends.

People like me? We had to trust in a screen name and an avatar. Had to leave ourselves open to abuse and manipulation. Had to risk being doxxed, having our addresses published, our employers contacted. And that was one of the better outcomes. The worst? We could end up dead. Raped, murdered, another tabloid prude fest. Another handwringing article in the *Guardian*, with a load of pseudo-academic bull. Another hashtag. Another 'crying with laughter' emoticon. Another 'angry' emoticon. Another statistic.

We weren't allowed to have real friends, because it might develop into something more, and what if people hadn't been told? And people like me? We weren't even allowed the friendship of so-called community, because our existence tainted their precious brand.

Even the online friendships were beginning to pale, though, everyone talking all the while about their drugs and their surgeries, seeking approval with photos that couldn't possibly have been their best, or most recent. Arguments over what made an identity, and what should get someone kicked out of the community, bared forever, and potentially doxxed. It seemed that being someone like me ticked all those boxes.

It was nearly eleven o'clock. I sighed, grabbed my cane, and, with my free hand, pushed myself back and up, staggering a little as I caught my balance. It didn't hurt – that was the upside of having your pelvis smashed; once you'd recovered enough to walk again, you didn't feel the pain that mobility caused you.

They'd told me I was lucky. I was regularly reminded that my recovery was nothing short of miraculous. It got to me, made me feel like I should be feeling all gooey-eyed and grateful. Well, no such luck. Sorry, not sorry.

I'd come to enjoy the sound of my cane as my weight rested on it. A kind of clinking squeak. It was soothing, almost relaxing. It took me fifteen squeak clinks to cross the living room, seven and a half to get from the living room to my bedroom. Three squeak clinks to the chest of drawers. Two squeak clinks and a half turn to the wardrobe.

I rarely went to the wardrobe, but I did this evening. I could open the drawers from the bed, sitting on the end of it, leaning forward. The wardrobe was a different proposition. I had to lean my weight against one side, and snatch open the other door.

I stared at the clothes, the soft pastels and striking, deep jewel tones. Different textures and cuts. Layers and lengths complementing and contrasting.

I felt the tears pricking my eyes. This would be my night, now. Staring at these. Trying them on. Trying to make them make me look normal.

But I couldn't be normal. I'd never be normal. Even with the most beautiful clothes in the world.

I reached into the wardrobe, balancing on my cane as I pushed my weight forward. I snatched at the crimson and silver I'd felt guilty about from the moment I first saw it. I'd had to have it.

I could still see the sales assistant's face, hear the brightness behind her smile.

"Someone's lucky night, eh?"

I could still remember how I'd blushed, stuttered some kind of response, handed over the cash, and bolted from the shop, without even waiting for a receipt.

I'd put the dress on as soon as I was safely behind a closed, locked door. It had looked beautiful. I'd spent at least fifteen minutes just stroking it, feeling the softness of the velvet, tracing the silk embroidery.

I'd taken it off in a hurry when I'd heard Tam's key in the lock. By the time she cracked open the door to ask if I wanted a coffee,

I was huddled under blankets, in track trousers and t-shirt, pleading exhaustion and nausea.

I'd slipped up, eventually, of course. Perhaps because I wanted to be caught.

She hadn't been surprised, angry, upset, or confused. She'd just asked calm, straightforward questions, listened to my answers, and, finally, quietly, go up, patted my hand, and made us both a cup of coffee.

She'd been that way the first time, too, all those years ago. While my mother screamed and threw things, and my dad tried to make it clear that he was on my side whilst appeasing his wife, Tam was nothing short of a rock, just holding me through the rows, patching up cuts and bruises, asking intelligent questions. She'd been so much more than I'd deserved. She still was.

Nicole

I'd opted out of going out with the Crew, and had headed to the skatepark, where graffiti was fully authorised, and I wouldn't be disturbed. I wanted to work on a large-scale piece, and the skatepark was the only place I knew I'd have the time, the only place it wouldn't get washed away by the council's high pressure hoses. The one place where people might actually be allowed to see it, and enjoy it.

I could handle my work being sprayed over; that was part of the fluid dynamics of the scene. Nothing was ever static. You got to be king for a day, and then other claims were placed prominently. It was a true democracy, with the edge of anarchy that true democracy will always carry with it. That slight edge, the whiff of mutiny, only ever lightly leashed, is why we'll never really be given genuine, honest democracy; the politicians are too afraid of all we might become if we weren't shut down, and shut up. If we weren't controlled by a carefully chosen set of options. If we were allowed to think fully and freely for ourselves, rather than being guided towards the decision some distant Other had already made, with a carefully woven impression that we had made that same decision freely, and with full knowledge of the facts; that it was what we wanted. I loved genuine democracy, and always would; what I couldn't stand was the sham where, if your face fit, or your pockets had plenty of well-filled depth, you could pretty much do whatever you pleased, while those who didn't look the part, who couldn't afford to, were made your whipping boys, your scapegoats, punished, always, for your transgressions, while you were celebrated as "daring", "edgy", "defiantly brave."

The bravest people I know are also the poorest, the ugliest, the least hopeful. They are brave because they live their best lives despite the disapproval of others. If you have money, connections, or looks, you are not 'brave'; no decision you make, no chance you take, will ever go that badly for you. Remember that, at your next book launch, your next solo exhibition, your next glamorous, fulfilling internship. You are not brave. We are. I'd just started my intended piece, brushing on the first, tentative strokes, when I noticed the group. They were just coming into the park stepping into the very edge of my peripheral vision. Charlie noticed them a second later, a brief nod telling me that she had it covered, that I should just keep working. I doubted that the newcomers were trouble, but when you're a woman, out in public after dusk, with your attention occupied, it paid to be sensibly cautious.

I liked working at night, starting when the evening light was just starting to be smudged away, and adapting my technique to compensate for the dimming light as night drew in. I could lose myself at night in a way I never really could when the sun set the ground rules; my work tended to take on an ethereal quality when I couldn't choose the light I would have preferred. I couldn't say it was "better" than my daysider work; it was different. You couldn't compare apples to oranges, and you couldn't compare different styles of work, either. They each spoke for themselves, and they would each speak to different people. Different times. Different places. Different feelings.

"You want something?" Charlie's voice jolted me out of my reverie. I glanced up. The crowd I'd noticed earlier, or three of them, anyway, were standing about three feet back, as close as Charlie would let them get. A black woman, and two lads, one tall, leanly muscled, with blond hair that threatened to fall off the edge and into scruffiness, well-dressed, in a casual way; a naughty little rich boy, playing at how he imagined the other half lived, the other shorter, stockier, a little softer, somehow. Blue jeans faded from wear, rather than a fashion designer's whim. Loose t-shirt that looked as though it had seen better days. A scuffed, battered leather jacket that, rather than giving him a rakish charm, just made him look like a down and out.

"Just taking a look. Not a crime, is it?" The stocky guy was bolshy, I'd give him that. I pushed myself up from the working crouch I favoured.

"Cool, Charlie. It's cool." I stepped forward, pushing hair out of my eyes. "I've not seen you before. I'm Nic."

"Colt. This is Aimee and Rocky. Rocky's my cousin. He's just moved to town. I didn't have anyone to run with before, so I didn't bother going out. Aimee lives down my street."

The young woman stepped forward, a cool, lithe grace about her. "I've not done this sort of thing before. I was just chillin', making the most of the weather. I seen Colt around, so I axed to hang with him, y'know?"

I frowned. It wasn't just that I wasn't all that keen on vernacular – although I wasn't, not really – it was also that the words didn't sound natural on this woman's lips. I wondered why she was playing at a patois that wasn't hers.

I turned to the other guy, the lean blond. "You don't look like a Rocky."

"Well..." he shrugged. "It's a sort of nickname. Because I'm nothing like the boxer from the films, right? It's ironic."

I nodded. "Right. Ironic. You got gear with you? Paints, cans?"

Rocky surprised me by pulling out a pack of permanent markers, a lazy grin on his face. "Where're you okay for me to start?"

I gestured to the inside back wall of the ramp. "Anywhere that isn't the centre of that."

"Right then." He moved forward with unhurried purpose, his cousin and the girl closing behind him. Charlie glanced at me. I pulled a face, an expression of puzzled uncertainty. I'd been sure they were police, or journalists, but they moved like us. Rocky had jumped up onto the lip of the ramp's curve, and was laid flat on his stomach, arm at full stretch above his head. He didn't need to look at the lines he was creating. That was the mark of someone with a bit of experience, at least.

I turned back to the other two, addressing the woman. "So – Aimee, right? What do you do?"

Aimee shrugged, exaggerated and elegant. "I draw. Like I said, I've not done anything on the scene. Just pen and ink stuff. Thought I'd simplify it for out here."

Her persona was slipping. That 'I've not' – it didn't fit with the attitude she'd been copping earlier. I was almost certain she wasn't a copper; she might be a journo, though. And we could do without them hanging around. In a way, journos were worse than cops. At least with a copper, once they'd either got the result they wanted, or accepted that it was never going to be a possibility, they tended to leave you alone. Journos were a lot more tenacious, and they had a thousand different angles. If they couldn't get you on one thing, they'd simply roll for damage on something else. Or write a bunch of crap, and see if any of it stuck.

There was a scuffle of gravel behind me. I turned. Rocky was leaning against the ramp, the pack of pens jutting out of his hip pocket.

I sauntered over, pulled myself up onto the lip of the ramp. I liked what I saw. Whoever and whatever he was, Rocky could do the work. He'd honed those skills somewhere. I doubted it was on the scene, but I couldn't believe there was anything too dubious about him.

Perhaps he'd been inside, had picked up the art habit in prison. No; that didn't seem likely, either, not looking at him.

I dropped down, smiling. "You're good."

"Thanks. I never doubted it, but new place, new crews... have to earn my cred all over again."

"Where were you, before?" I couldn't place his accent; it was bland, a little better cut than what you typically heard around here. "All over. My family moved a lot. But for the past couple of years, I've been fairly settled in London."

"Why would you leave London for Lothing?"

He looked sad, distant. "I wanted to be known again. To be familiar to someone. Does that make sense?"

I nodded. "You felt lonely in London, and you don't here?"

"Pretty much. Besides, my cousin lives here – family's family, y'know? I'd been a prat, hadn't had a lot to do with my family for years – my mother... she's not right in the head. She can be violent. My aunt, my grandparents, my dad, everyone – they protected her. They covered up for her. So I stopped talking to any of them. But then, when London didn't work out..."

He shrugged, glancing away. I understood. Families were complicated. I got it. And I knew better than to press any further. Whoever Rocky was, wherever he and Colt and Aimee came from, whatever brought them here, for the moment, it didn't matter. He'd fit in on the scene, his work was good – and I was beginning to think Charlie and I needed to break away from the Cancer Crew, especially if I wanted to be taken seriously by the wider art world, the one that paid. Perhaps training and protecting these newcomers while they found their feet on Lothing's scene was one way to do that.

PC Feroc Hanson
LB 599

I'd borrowed Tony's story. I hadn't intended to, hadn't even
realised I was going to, until I'd heard myself saying it. Perhaps
losing my name – Feroc was too recognisable – had made me
want to hold on to something that would always be mine. The
good thing about it was, thinking about Tony being so completely
alone in the world brought genuine tears to my eyes, a roughness
to my voice, that lent credence to this being my story, a damaged
past, and a present that was all about trying to make amends.
 It felt good, being out in the night, when Lothing as it really was
showed itself. It felt good to be stripped back – no uniforms, no
armour, just ordinary people in an ordinary place – and,
unexpectedly, it felt good, as far as I was concerned, to be
working, finally, as myself alone, rather than as Tony Raglan's
right hand man. I wasn't sure how I felt about that, about working
with other people, showing that I, as a copper in my own right,
was wholly and completely capable. That I didn't need Tony
Raglan watching over me to do my job, and do it well.
 That, far more than the risk of daft decisions made when your
judgement was clouded by romantic entanglements, was the
problem with getting involved with someone at the same nick;
your colleagues tended to assume that one of you was being
"looked after" by the other, that you couldn't function unless you
were a unit, working together. I needed to prove that I was as
good as Tony Raglan, on my own account, just as surely as it
seemed Colt Devereux was being asked to prove himself all over
again.
 As soon as I started bringing the lines of my drawing through, I
was lost in the beauty of how it felt to move my body in the way
art demanded. The feel of cool concrete pressing against the
muscle and bone of my torso, the slight friction and pressure of
my jeans as I shifted slightly through the work. The almost feline
feeling of leaping between the ground and the ramp. The scent of

markers in night air, sharp sweetness mingling with a cloying dampness, the scent of possibilities, the quietness of life at rest, and life just rousing itself for the night ahead. I felt almost as though I could close my eyes, and still draw something worthy of the name, simply from the energy and feel of the night. There was magic in moonlight, whatever anyone else thought, however hard they laughed. And tonight, the moon was full, wrapped in wispy clouds. It was a beautiful, powerful night. Tony would be charging his runes. Others would be Working rituals. Crystals, stones, sigils – all would be soaking up the bright brilliance, storing the moon's power as their own.

I remembered how I'd felt as I'd inked in the final lines, the feeling of freedom and flight as I'd jumped back down to earth. I felt like I belonged here. As though this was the life I should be living.

I'd felt like that about the Job, once. The memory was a shock, cold water hurled at the heat of a new passion. Was I, after all, so typical of my generation? Would I spend my life dancing between jobs, never able to settle anywhere?

"You're good. I like your style." Nicole's voice brought me back to the present, to the realities and responsibilities. I had to fit in here, with those who belonged to shadows and suspicion. Although the two girls seemed perfectly ordinary, I got the feeling there were certain kinds of people they distrusted instinctively. And I got the feeling, too, that coppers might come pretty high on their list of people to be cautious around. Caution could be a good thing – it made people lock their doors at night, think about how they were going to get home from events and parties that went on until the early hours, made people consider their options before making a choice. But it wasn't what you wanted from the normals around you when you were undercover. You needed them to behave naturally, to act without suspicion. That was the whole point – you were one of them, and you got to see them as they were, not as they wanted you to believe they could be. I needed to get Nicole and her friend to relax, and I wasn't at all sure how to go about it.

In the distance, across the park, I caught sight of Tam and Seamus, mucking about by the swings.

Nicole's friend, Charlie, was talking to Aimee; they both seemed alert, but relaxed, the way it should be.

"So, you didn't feel like coming out on your own, then?"

"Not really. Something like this, you want your mates around you, don't you? It's not really the kind of thing you do on your own."

Charlie nodded. "You're right there. That's what people miss, the kind of people who complain about it. It's a social activity, a way for those of us who can't easily get up to Norwich, who can't afford to go to this club and that club and the other club to form friendships. And it gets people outside, which is what everyone's always saying they want."

I was half-listening, half scanning the park. Suddenly, I tensed, my gaze focused on a small gathering in the bushes by the entrance. I could see the glow of cigarettes, the reflective stripes on tracksuits and trainers... and the shock of ice-white hair.

Nicole followed my gaze, and made a face. "C'mon. Let's get out of here." She herded us in the opposite direction, on a diagonal that took us away from the blond man and his group, and up to the entrance on the far side of the park. I couldn't be certain, but I was pretty sure I'd seen the blond guy's face. Pretty sure I'd been watching a drug deal.

"Who was that?"

Nicole shook her head. "No one you need to worry about."

"You were worried about him, though."

"It's nothing. He's no one. It's okay."

"Look – I've not been out on this scene, not around here. I need to know how to keep myself safe, who to watch out for."

"Blood – that guy – he's nothing to worry about. Stay out of his way, he'll stay out of yours."

"You can be sure on that, can you?"

"Look, he's harmless, okay? You don't need to worry about him."

"Blood – what kind of name is that?"

"Street name. Lot of people have them round here. It doesn't mean anything"

"You keep saying that, and it keeps making me think that it *does* mean something. Tell me the truth, Nicole – because it's not just me here; it's my cousin and our pal, too, you get me? I've got to protect them, y'know?"

Nicole paused, and turned to face me. There was a strange, ancient softness in her eyes. "I understand. They're family." She glanced at her friend, who'd walked with us in such as way that she'd never had to turn her back on the man Nicole called Blood. "It's the same with me and Charlie. We're family. We take care of each other."

She looked at me as though there was something I needed to understand. I nodded, understanding; Charlie and Nicole were the next generation to me and Tony. The bold, bright ones, who would fight the fires Tony's generation had run from, and that I was still wary of.

 "C'mon – let's go." Charlie yanked the gate open, and we stepped out, and onwards, into the night.

James Marriott: Blood

I got a kick out of seeing people's fear. I could almost smell it,
sometimes. As I watched the group head off, I noticed two other
people crossing from the other side of the park, clearly heading to
meet up with the group that were leaving. That made me curious,
and I started paying closer attention. Graffiti crews and addicts
stayed together. Whores travelled in pairs, not groups. Thieves
and vagabonds worked alone.

 Coppers, though... they travelled in packs, and were inclined to
split off and reform, covering as much ground as they could. I
waved away the waifs and strays that put a few quid extra in my
savings account, and set off at a light lope. I wondered if they
were on the track of the bastard who'd run my brother off the
road.

 Or that twat in a suit who'd put me in the position where
someone would want to run *me* off the road, and got Alex by
mistake.

 Either would be good enough for me. Both would be better.

I didn't intend to get to get too close – drawing the attention of
law enforcement was not a desirable activity for someone in my
line of business, but getting close enough to know what they
knew, without attracting notice, was an entirely reasonable way to
acquire information. The police made every effort to ensure they
had the right information – something you couldn't always rely
in with members of the public.

 The night was cool and dim, shadows creating their own artwork
on the canvas of the world. I liked it like this; it made people
notice my hair, dyed to a striking glacial. I liked to know people
had noticed me; it made it much more satisfying when I
successfully disappeared into the shadows I loved.

 I knew everyone who came to this park after dark. As I got closer
to the group, still keeping my distance, I recognised Charlie and
Nicole, the two dykes. They usually came here with another
woman, and three guys. They worked together, chilled together,

drank together.

The other five, two women and three men, I didn't know. They looked too old for the safety of a licensed graffiti area, and they were certainly too healthy to be customers of mine. I was guessing they were coppers – and I was determined to find out what they wanted. Why they were on this scene, and out of uniform. My business had always been to know whatever those with power knew, and I ran my business very, very well.

Michael Lamley

Puccini always went well with a glass of white wine, and a box of expensive chocolates. Rose pollen mingled with the old leather of my favourite armchair.

I had the casement window open, the silver velvet of the curtains rippling in the evening breeze. As I sipped my wine, I thought about the tattooed thug who would doubtless take the blame for the police officer getting stabbed. Alexander Clifford-Alistair had been a good friend of mine, and prison had broken him utterly. I'd been abroad when the whole business with the art fraud had happened. I'd given the dust time to settle, and returned a year ago, re-establishing Eastern Rise Investments as First Dawn Portfolios, contacting Alexander's old clients, and some new blood I had connections with. No matter how little I made in a month, ten percent of it went into Alexander's account. He'd been blacklisted from the financial services industry, and was struggling to find another job. I was hardly going to conscience him stacking shelves or flipping burgers for the minimum wage; he was better than that, and didn't live the kind of life whose expenses could be met by drudge work like that. I'd wangled him a couple of NEDs, two private sector, one public; I'd look for a charity Board next, create an impression of well-rounded competence. And, in time, I'd bring him onboard as a silent partner in First Dawn, keeping to the shadows, but with an equal share of the profits.

He was still a mess, not really fit for anything; I'd got the feeling he wouldn't recover until the officer who'd destroyed his life had his destroyed in turn. Alexander had described the man, and he'd proved easy enough to spot. The local youths were truly effortless to stir up – it was almost as if they wanted a criminal record. As though being arrested were the start of some deeply rewarding career option for them. It was quite sweet, really, how easily led they were, when they considered themselves so very independent.

The electric fire flickered, casting streaks of darker light against the navy walls. The music soared, stopped, and fell to fade. I finished my wine, got up, and closed the window. There would be rest for the wicked, after all.

Before I drew the curtains for the night, I glanced towards the glimmer of the sea, shining under the moonlight. With the window open, you could hear the soft whisper of the waves as the fell onto the shore. It sounded like secrets being shared.

Secrets were a compelling power. A source of energy that could keep a person going when all else failed. I traded in secrets. They were the pillars and the commandments of my world, and I would always be entranced by them. Secrets were the fountain of youth, the revenant of childhood that we carried into the adult world.

I smiled, imagining a thank you to the secrets that the waves brought to the shore. What is cast on the water will come back to your own shores. The eternal return of the same.

I pulled swathes of velvet across slowly, and went upstairs, pausing to lock the front and back doors, and set the alarm. On the landing, I stepped into the shaft of light that fell from the window of the spare room, highlighting the edge of the door, where it had been left ajar.

Alexander was asleep on his back, a blanket covering him to the waist, leaving his chest bare. I smiled softly. "It's sorted, Alexander. I sorted it all out for you." He turned his head, moaning softly in his sleep. I smiled, and stepped back onto the landing.

"It was a pleasure," I whispered, as I carried on along the corridor to my own room. Police Constable Tony Raglan was the kind of homosexual man that the rest of us could do without. Him and his little friend. I had no patience with slobs, or those who could do better, but chose not to. Such people needed to be taught a lesson. If a good hiding, and the stabbing of his boyfriend, convinced that young man to pursue a more appropriate career, with a more suitable partner, then that wasn't my fault. Some lessons simply had to be learned the hard way. Examples must be made, after all; we couldn't live in a world where everyone just did as they pleased, could we?

He would die from that stab wound... he just didn't know it, yet. I hoped he played safely; it would be a shame to lose the boy.

PC Tony Raglan
LB 265

I gulped water, wincing as I swallowed. I felt like I was burning up, and my throat felt as though it was closing in. I closed my eyes, struggling to catch my breath.

"You alright, Tony?" Bill Wyckham had come round to tell me that it had been decided that, all things considered, it would look better if I stayed away while the investigation into Max Rockford played out. As it was public knowledge I'd been stabbed, it would be easy to smooth over. I needed a little extra time to get fully fit, but intended to be back charged up and ready to go.

"Yeah. Probably just a reaction, my head catching up with everything that's happened. I'll be fine."

Wyckham frowned. "You're sure it was just the knife you were attacked with?"

"Yes, sir."

"And you didn't see it used on anyone else? It didn't have blood on it when you first saw it?"

"I didn't see it, sir -" I suddenly realised what Wyckham was driving at.

"You don't think..." I couldn't even get the words out.

Wyckham was already on his feet, taking his mobile phone out of his pocket. "I hope not. But I'm not taking chances." Someone had clearly answered the phone. "Inspector Bill Wyckham. Lima-Bravo eighty-one. Can you phone St. Ralph's, tell them I'm bringing a male, IC1, in for HIV testing. Suspected immediate, high viral load infection. He may have been stabbed with a knife that had already encountered dirty blood; he's showing flu-like symptoms... six days ago. Yeah. Yeah. Thanks, Callum. Yeah... it's Tony. Yeah, I know. I will."

While Wyckham had been on the phone, I'd got up, and gone over to Idaho's cage. We were whistling to each other, Idaho looking at me like he knew something was wrong.

"You ready, Tony?"

I was stroking Idaho, feeling like I was in a trance.

"Tony? Come on, eh?"

I stepped back, taking a deep breath.

"Yeah. Let's get this over with."

As I followed my boss out of my home, the darkness of the night felt weirdly appropriate. I'd been surprised to see Wyckham, surprised that he'd come to see me after a night shift, rather than going straight home. Now, I was pleased he hadn't left it until the morning; I don't think I could have coped with stepping out into bright sunlight for the start of something like this. It was better that it was night, even if it did mean I'd be waiting around for hours at the hospital.

As I got into the passenger side of Wyckham's car, he turned to me, one hand on the ignition. "Do you want to try and get hold of Feroc?"

I shook my head. "No, boss. I don't want to compromise Nightshade. I don't want him worried. It might be for nothing, anyway. This might just be a cold."

Wyckham nodded. "I think you've made the right choice. See what the test says."

I closed my eyes. "At least they can get it sorted quickly these days. Drop on a strip, something like this."

"Yes. Best thing for all concerned."

"Okay... you'll just feel a sharp scratch. Okay?"

I nodded, glancing away.

"Don't get faint at the sight of blood, do you?"

I shook my head. "No. I see enough of it."

"Of course." The nurse smiled. He looked shattered.

"Long shift?"

"I'll be alright. Home in a couple hours."

"Well, that's one thing." I clocked the ring, a slim gold band, on the third finger of his left hand. "Someone waiting for you?"

He laughed. "Is there a full moon, did you notice?"

"I don't think so."

"Well, in that case, there might be; my wife's a consultant psychiatrist. She's on call tonight. With luck, she won't have been called out."

"Arggh!" I hissed, feeling my lips draw back over my teeth. The nurse raised an eyebrow.

"Oh, do calm down. Always the big boys who make the most fuss." I winced again, as a spray, cold and sharp, was misted over the wound. A cotton bud was pushed down where the blood welled. "Hold that in place for me." The sound of tape tearing. The feel of adhesive against skin.

"Right. I'll be back as soon as this shows it's true colours."

I felt sick. "Okay."

Wyckham's hand closed over my shoulder. The pressure through his fingers was comforting. "Deep breaths, okay? Breathe for me. Come on, big fella. Take it steady."

I turned to Wyckham, feeling the fear fully for the first time. "It's going to be okay, isn't it, sir?"

"I'm not going to tell you that, Tony. You know that. Never make promises you can't keep."

I hung my head. "Sir."

"I'll stay here with you. Once we've got the results, I'll take you home, wait with you there until Feroc gets back."

"Thanks."

This wasn't the first time I'd had a HIV test, and it probably wouldn't be the last. The worst thing was having to wait in a private room. Nothing to see except the clock on the wall. No one else around. It felt like being in a twilight zone. Footsteps and conversation flowed by, seeming to come from a million miles away.

It was the waiting that got to me, every time.

"Mr. Tony Raglan?"

I jerked awake, my mouth feeling dry. I blinked, and started to get up.

"Easy there, Tiger." The nurse came over, and sat down beside me. "Now – do you want the good news, or the bad news?"

PC Feroc Hanson
LB 599

As dawn started to consider breaking, I was sat on the seawall, looking out over a lightening ripple of waves. Nicole and Charlie had introduced us to the friends they regularly went out graffiting with – the Cancer Crew.

"We R Cancer – that your tag?"

The apparent leader of the group, a guy called Chris, nodded, swigging from a can of energy drink. "Yeah."

"What's it mean?"

"Everything and nothing, really. Whatever people want it to mean. Taken together, the first name initial of everyone in the crew spells 'CANCER', so, once we were all running together, we became the Cancer Crew. It has a certain ring to it, and people talk about it." He grinned. "It's gone viral online."

"Nice one, mate."

"Yeah, we were pretty chuffed. Since Banksy, it's been really tough to get anything else from the scene talked about. Like we're all just copying him. Like graffiti didn't exist before he rocked up, and started flogging it to the middle classes."

I shook my head. "It's bollocks, that. I mean, you hear the way they talk about us, all the time, then the minute there's something of ours that one of their precious broadsheet columnists raves about, they're all over the person the papers are lauding like a cheap suit, creating an avalanche that basically buries everyone else. That's the crux of capitalism, fella – only a certain number of people are allowed to succeed. The rest of us have to be kept down, crushed, subdued. Good slaves to bad masters."

I noticed Aimee Gardner, stifling a giggle, and wondered how it must sound to her, hearing a white guy talking about being a slave. Mind you, she did tend to have a sense of humour about such things.

"Tell me about it." I took out my phone as the first full shards of what promised to be a bright, vibrant day broke over the surface of the water in front of us. We'd come out at around ten o'clock last night, and, from the quality of the light, it was about an hour before sunrise. I checked my phone; 3.32am. Over five hours, and yet it had passed so quickly, I would have sworn that it had only been a couple of hours, at most.

I liked these people, liked the way the night seemed when you lived it, rather than worked it. But I hadn't forgotten the point of Nightshade; other than the almost-encounter with Blood, back at the skateboard park, we'd seen a couple of sex workers, what had looked like a much lower-level drug deal – cannabis, probably – and some racers who may or may not have been joy riding in stolen cars. Charlie and Nicole had always herded us away from the sound of sirens; we were going to need to avoid them, the next few nights, if we had any chance of getting on with the job we were here for. That made me feel more despondent than it should have done; not getting the intel that the budget was being spent in the hopes of would be worse, though.

The other woman in the Cancer Crew, Evie, got up. "I'm going to head off, guys. See you around, yeah?"

Nicole glanced at her watch. Charlie nodded. They both stood up. "We should be going, too." Nicole smiled. "I won't be out tomorrow – I'm covering a mate's shift at a local bar. You probably won't see Charlie, either. I'm not sure what the guys are doing?"

She glanced at Chris, who shook his head. "It's my Mum's birthday – my big sister'll kill me if I'm not there." He tapped a short tattoo on the back of the bench. "But you've seen some of the sites, now – you on Facebook?"

I hadn't thought about that. Time for some fast footwork. "Nah. I never saw the point, y'know? Old fashioned, me."

"I'm on there – Lady Garden." I tried not to let my surprise show. Seamus Hanratty barked a laugh.

"Aye, and I'm Padraig Murphy." He winked. "Got a couple of ladies I'd rather couldn't track me down too easy, y'know?" Chris offered a high-five. "Too right, my man." He turned to Colt.

"What about you, bro?"

Colt shook his head. "Nah. I was on it, but got fed up with it. Bunch of whinging kids, getting butt hurt over everything. Who needs that hassle?"

"Boy's got sense." Adam vaulted the bench, his brother following him. "Catch you all around, maybe."

We watched them as they sauntered off, breaking apart at the crossing, Chris heading south, the other two crossing the road and turning north.

Tam stood up, stretching. "Well, I think we should give it another half hour or so; no one'll be misbehaving once the light comes through, so we may as well head home and get some sleep."

"Nice short night shift, boys." Aimee was going through what looked like yoga poses. I took in the way her limbs moved, long, lean, with a supple, subtle strength.

I got up, flexing my back, grinning. "Lady Garden?"

Aimee arched an eyebrow. "Why not? Let's me have a daily giggle at desperate men, and brings...well, a little something I want my way. Anyway, what about Seamus? Fake name on Facebook, Shay? Tut tut, slapped wrist."

"I was telling the truth – there's ladies who made the mistake of thinking I was a gentleman, once upon a time. Tried to tie me down. I don't need that grief, y'know?" He grinned. "We can't all have a cosy little marriage to the Wolf of Lothing, now, can we?" He stood up, sauntering a loose, looping circle, the way he always did. "What about you, Colt? You got someone?"

Colt blushed, looking out to sea as he got to his feet. "Not right now, no."

"Why not? Good looking lad like you? Is it boys or girls you like? I'm not judging, see? I can set you up with someone – I know loads of people, both sides of the duvet, know what I mean?"

Colt gave a tight smile, but wasn't quite quick enough to hide the trace of hopelessness in his eyes.

"I'm not looking for anyone right now."

"Sure?" Seamus turned. "What about you, Tam? Maybe you and Colt here could get together?"

Tam shook her head. "Nope – young, free, and single, me."

"Well, if you ever fancy a touch of the Irish, you know where to find me, right?"

"Wrong." Tam was heading along the seafront, towards the rougher, seedier south town. We all fell into a loose, ragged line behind her.

"Ah, sure, and with that hair, you'll want a laddie like me for your wee'ns, won't you?"

"I don't mix business and pleasure, Seamus. And you shouldn't, either."

"Plenty we shouldn't do – but life'd be boring if we didn't."

We wandered, in a close approximation of aimlessness, for another hour. Environment Agency might be interested in the couple of people we'd noticed barbecuing fish on the beach, but, then again, they might have landed species well within the size limit. They probably hadn't, but that wasn't our business. A couple more drug deals, a house that seemed to have a purpose other than sheltering happy families. The beginnings of a picture that would hopefully start to become a lot more complete after another couple of nights spent doing our own thing, heading to the places Nicole and Charlie had kept us away from; hospitality, and care of those under your protection, in any other circumstances. In these circumstances? A hindrance, more than a help.

****

As I drew closer to the house on Excelsior Street, I slowed, noticing Bill Wyckham's car. That surprised me; he would've been on late turn. I could imagine him wanting to check on Tony, but he should have been home and in bed by now.

I let myself in, starting to worry.

Tony was asleep on the sofa. Bill Wyckham was talking quietly to

Idaho. He turned, startled, as he heard the door; presumably someone who lived with the luxury of some kind of entrance hall, and wasn't used to someone stepping off the street into their living room.

Tony moaned in his sleep, tossing his head. I moved over to the sofa, picking up a throw from the armchair, and kneeling to lay it over him. I turned to face my inspector, the question clear in my eyes.

Bill Wyckham inclined his head, indicating the back room. I nodded, and followed him through, closing the door softly.

"Sir?"

"I dropped in to see how Tony was getting on...we ended up having to swing by St. Ralph's."

"What? Why? What's wrong with Tony?"

Bill Wyckham pulled one of the wicker chairs round, and gestured to me to sit down. I dropped like a stone, gazing up at him, needing an explanation, reassurance.

"Nothing's wrong, Feroc. He's just a little under the weather, they reckon. Stress reaction. He'll be fine."

"If he's just under the weather, why the hospital visit? And – not that I mean anything by it, sir – but why are you still here?"

"Like I said, Tony wasn't feeling too great when I got here... his symptoms, given that he was stabbed by someone who's known for involvement in drugs -"

"HIV? Tony's got HIV?"

"Calm down. He hasn't, that's the point. We went to St. Ralph's to get tested."

I was on my feet, pacing. "But we won't know for months yet! He could be dying!"

"Feroc...calm down. Yes, he's got to go back for tests in three months, but they're almost certain he hasn't been infected; because of the way any infection would have been introduced, they would have expected an unmistakable viral load to show up on the first test. It's ninety-nine percent that he's going to be fine."

"But there's still that one percent, isn't there?" My voice was soft with sadness. My boss and I stared at one another in silence.

"I meant to ask Tony – the picture with the pig in the tutu, over the fireplace?"

I smiled. "Tony's. A present from an ex."

"Ah."

We both spun round when the door opened.

"Fer?"

"Tony." My heart broke at the sound of his voice, soft and thick with sleep.

"I didn't hear you come in."

"You were asleep. I didn't want to wake you."

Tony grinned. "I'm awake now, though."

I stepped forward, matching his smile. "So you are."

Bill Wyckham gave a discreet cough. "I'd best be getting along – the wife'll be wondering what's become of me." He turned to go. "Take care, lads."

We were too wrapped up in one another to hear the door close behind him.

"Bed?" I raised an eyebrow. Tony shook his head.

"Not like that. I just... can you just hold me, keep me company?"

I stood up on tip toe, kissing him gently on the lips, feeling the flow of energy and warmth.

"Of course I can. Anything you want."

"Tell me about Nightshade. How much longer is it running?"

I shrugged, wrapping my arms tighter round him. "Until we've got some solid intel, I suppose."

"I missed you tonight."

"I know. But it's good for us to work apart from time to time. I missed you, when you were away on Killjoy, but you came back. And Nightshade's a lot less dangerous."

Tony stepped out of my embrace. "Nothing's ever less dangerous in this job, Feroc; it's just dangerous in a different way." He glanced back into the living room. "I'd better go and lock the door, if we're taking this upstairs."

Sergeant Aimee Gardner
LB 761

I was already looking forward to tomorrow night. Tam Freud
would have myself, Feroc, and Seamus for the next three nights.
That should be long enough to start building a picture of the
hotspots, an idea of what was going on, and where we should be
targeting.

I was intrigued by the Cancer Crew, especially Nicole; she
seemed the most intelligent of the group. Charlie, too. The others
came across as your typical, childish reactionaries, spouting anti-
authoritarian sentiments without understanding the intricacies of
circumstances beyond the petty lives of individuals. The world
seemed so straightforward and simple, when you thought you
could just extrapolate from your immediate experience, and
assume that what works for you and your 2.4 kids will work for a
diverse and difficult nation state, with arrangements and
agreements that are only ever half admitted.

Lothing at night felt different when you walked through it as
though you belonged to it, rather than as a controlling force. I'd
noticed it during the day, too, the times I was off duty, and
completely 'switched off', browsing shops, or enjoying half an
hour on the beach. That bothered me, a little; I didn't want to like
some kind of overseer, controlling an unruly pack of restless
natives. I didn't want to think of members of the public *as*
restless natives. I hadn't joined the Police to sit in judgement on
people who were often dealing with lives that were falling apart
around them. I wasn't sure why I had joined the Job, if I were
honest; perhaps that was why the idea of going for promotion
bothered me; I had been brought up to act with integrity, and I
didn't feel that being in a job that didn't really gel with me any
more was living in integrity.

I loved the Job, but it was changing, and I wasn't sure I liked
what it was becoming.

I wasn't ready to resign, but Tony Raglan's stabbing had made me realise I wasn't ready for the next step, either.

But Nightshade... I'd only been out for a few hours, not even a full shift, but I'd felt as though I was making a difference, as though the work I was doing mattered. I couldn't remember the last time I'd felt like that with a uniform on.

I wondered if Tony Raglan could.

PC Tony Raglan
LB 265

"So... what brings you here, sarge?"

Aimee Gardner bit into a croissant, shaking her head. "No rank, no pack drill, Tony. We're off duty." Pastry flakes clung to the corners of her mouth; it made her look cute, as though she had never, would never, be nothing more than a pretty little rich girl with nothing more to do with her day than lunch and shop. Anyone who brought into that illusion would have been in for a short, sharp shock, though – probably administered hot on the heels of their first racist or misogynistic comment.

Aimee Gardner didn't need the Equality Act; she could look after herself, mostly without even smudging her makeup.

I'd been pleased to see her when I'd answered the knock at the door, shortly after three o'clock. We'd been friends for a long while, Aimee and I, and, recently, I'd felt as though we were losing touch, growing apart. It happened when people made rank; inevitably, their circle shifted. You had less in common with one another, less to talk about, especially if you hadn't made time for general chit chat between working hours. Talking about something other than the Job was vital, but most of us lost the habit a few years in; or we never got the knack of it to begin with.

"So... I missed the fitness assessment, courtesy of a knife that was two inches off being fatal. Feroc assures me I'd've dropped dead of a heart attack inside of five minutes."

Aimee chuckled. "He's right. Although my money would have been on two minutes."

"Seriously, though – how was it?"

Aimee shook her head. "Usual thing. Bleep test to a light jog, slalom runs, bit of weights. More a brisk warm-up than a fitness test."

"Yeah, well... we're hardly out on the streets, these days." I gulped down coffee, slathered jam onto my own croissant.

"Except for you two, of course. Feroc seems to be enjoying the concept of Nightshade."

Aimee nodded.

"So am I. It feels...it feels *right*. Like something we could do all
the time, keep a lid on things without turning the heat up. Be
visible, without being oppressive. I'm hoping we'll see our
friendly neighbourhood drug dealers in the same spots over the
next couple of nights – that would be a result, all on its own,
really; we'd know where to spread our resources."

"So, for the moment, at least, a policeman's lot is a very happy
one?"

Feroc nodded. "I think we should make it a regular thing, maybe
with two or three rotating crews out. It's a lot safer – and a lot less
unfair on the women – than having coppers pretending to be sex
workers, and it actually brings us into contact with the younger
generation, which is what we want."

"You know they'd never approve that. Budgets, constraints... a
preference for redecorating top-floor offices, rather than putting
boots on the street."

"Yeah..." I'd never seen Feroc look so disheartened. It made me
worry for him, worry about what the Job was doing to him.

I'd fallen for Feroc's passion, his determination to make the
world a better place. I'd been entranced by his youthful energy,
his hope and optimism. I didn't want him to lose that. I didn't
want him to end up like me.

"Anyone want another coffee?" It was a redundant question –
coppers always wanted coffee. Caffeine and sugar;, that was
pretty much all that kept us going, ninety percent of the time.

"I'll get it." Feroc was already on his feet, rubbing my shoulder.

"I'm not an invalid, Fer."

He was already over by the breakfast bar. "You were stabbed a
week ago. You need to rest, let that wound heal."

"Rest, yes – not turn to mush as I sit here doing nothing."

Feroc glanced round. "As though you're normally doing twenty
mile runs?"

I snorted. "Twenty mile run? That's nothing. I wouldn't even make a dent in a full tank of petrol for that." Everyone laughed. The kettle whistled. Life, for the moment, was good.

DI Mark Roscoe

"Tam – how did the first night of the rest of your life go?"
She looked up, thoughtful. "Not bad, actually, guv. Obviously,
we'll need at least a couple more nights, to see if they stick to the
same place, but there were certainly at least three people dealing
drugs. Oh, and uniform might want to think about having patrols
on the beach."
Colt Devereux had come in again, and was making himself
useful sorting out filing, and answering desk phones, which rang
more often than they should, in these digital days. I called across
to him. "What about you? You get on alright with our little lot?"
"Yes, boss." He paused, studying our Prom Noms board. "This
guy – the guy with the dyed white hair? What's he wanted for?"
Everyone in the room looked up. Silence fell. I cleared my
throat, wanting to break it gently, before the harshness of speech.
"Tony Raglan's stabbing... we think this guy had the knife." I
paused, processing. "Why? Did you see him, last night?"
Colt nodded. "I think so. I'm pretty sure Feroc did, too – he was
in the skatepark. I'm pretty sure he was dealing, and it seemed
serious stuff, not just a bit of dope."
"Right. That's good. You're all going out again tonight, aren't
you?"
"Yes, boss."
"Swing by the skatepark again. You were there at ten, right?"
Tam nodded. "A little after."
"Make it a little earlier tonight, and a little later tomorrow. I want
to try and narrow down to a set time frame, so I can tell uniform
when to go and pick him up."
Colt had a strange look on his face. Focused and distant all at
once. "You're sure he's the one? The man who stabbed Tony?"
I nodded. "We had a photograph of him holding the knife. That
doesn't leave a lot of room for doubt." I turned to Tam. "Do we
have anything, yet, on the Val Brewer murder? The same kind of
knife was used, wasn't it?"

"Yes, guv. There doesn't appear to be any obvious link between James Marriott and Val Brewer – Marriott does have tattoos, but he's not listed as a client of Brewer's studio."

"We'll ask him about them when we bring him in. We need to know if he's had any dealings with Brewer – even if he simply looked at some art work one time, then went and got it done somewhere else. If he bought a bottle of antiseptic from him. If he left a review of the studio. Anything, no matter how small. It'll be the little things that trip us up – and the little things that trip our man Blood up."

I looked around the room. "That goes for everyone, okay? Rattle your snouts' cages, make a nuisance of yourselves, ask the awkward questions, and -"

The chorus went up; "Don't ignore the obvious!"

I grinned. "That's my team. This one's for Tony Raglan, remember – so, make it good, and make it stick."

Michael Lamley

"Morning, Michael. What are the horrors of the day?"
I folded the paper, setting it aside, a stark white blot on the grey leather landscape of the sofa. "Opportunities, Alexander. As horrors everywhere always are."
"What about that murder, a few days ago? The body on the beach? I never did keep an eye on developments, as far as that one went."
I got up, and went over to the sleek, white Mac in the corner of the room, booting up the internet, and clicking through until I found the page I wanted. "Here we are..." My throat went suddenly dry. I licked my lips. "Nothing much. Very quiet, actually. Makes me think our friends the police have a suspect they don't want to warn off."
Alexander had picked up my discarded newspaper, and was flicking through it. "Michael."
I turned. He was staring at an article, looking bewildered. "What is it?"
"This piece, about the stabbing of that cretin of a policeman – they're saying that they believe the same knife was used in the killing on the ..."
He trailed off, staring at me. Realisation dawning. "My god, Michael...Tell me I'm wrong. Tell me you didn't..."
I sighed, and sauntered back across the room, setting in a casual sprawl on the sofa.
"I wish I could. I'm sure you'll understand, though. You see, he lost money, through Eastern Rise... He saw us together, in Waterstones... He was... a little bit upset. And then I got a telephone call from our lovely local rag, asking me how I found being a homosexual businessman. They could only have got that information from friend Valiant. As you can imagine, I was just a little bit annoyed. So, I started following him, working out his routine." I shrugged. "Then, one night, I simply...took advantage of a fortuitous arrangement of events." I sighed. "I'd been putting

off doing what you'd asked of me – little bit of the jitters, I'm afraid. When I had Valiant Brewer's routine down, I thought, 'Why not kill him? It will be easier, the next time.' And do you know? Killing Valiant was effortless. He was drunk – not staggering, but certainly tipsy. I challenged him. We had a rather... unseemly row by the fountains. He *laughed* at me, Alexander. I punched him. It hurt rather more than I was expecting. I was going to come home. Give it all up as a bad job. But then I saw him, staggering, saw the blood drips on the ground. It..." Another shrug. "It sparked something primal and feral in me. I went after him. I stabbed him, And then I battered him. It felt as though I were possessed, as though something else had control of my body. My arms. My legs. I kicked him, several times. Then I threw his body onto the rocks, and walked away." I smiled, sipping coffee. "And the next time, it actually *was* easier. What? Alexander – oh, for heaven's sake, don't look at me like – Alex! Wait!"

The front door slammed shut as I took the corner from the lounge to the hallway. I shoved my feet into loafers, wrenched the door open, and threw myself into the street, running after Alexander, closing the gap between us.

I was close enough to reach out and grab his shoulder. I heard the rumble of a lorry approaching. I grabbed. Alexander fell, almost in slow motion. Brakes squealed. People shouted.

I kept walking.

Sergeant Gavin Medcalf
LB 23

"Right, girls and boys – we've just had word of a FATAC – HGV and an IC1 male. Interestingly, the victim has been identified as one Alexander Clifford-Alistair. He's been a guest here before; art fraud, facilitated by his company, Eastern Rise Investments. He served eighteen months of a three year sentence. Since his release, he's been living at Lamley Heights, off Church Lane, with a Mr. Michael Lamley – who conveniently took over Eastern Rise Investments, now trading as First Dawn Portfolios. Tony, take Caro, and go to the scene; London Road."
"Sarge."
I watched the two of them head out. It was Tony Raglan's first day back, and Wyckham had asked me to keep an eye on him. By rights, following the schedule that had been in place before he went sick, he should have been on nights; days tended to be safer, though. And better staffed.
Tony should be alright. He looked well enough, and no one had ever had cause to doubt his commitment to the Job. He'd be alright. And Caro would look after him. She had her head screwed on, that one; been in the Army before coming to us. Used to ordering men and horses about. Tony Raglan wouldn't be a problem for her.
I finished assigning duties to the rest of the team, following them out, There were rumours of a demo at the Britten Centre; I intended to look in on it, make sure it didn't get out of hand. I glanced at my notes, reminding myself of what, exactly, today's rabble had a problem with.
Oh, joy... some nonsense about the town centre not being sufficiently thrilling for the masses. Should be delightful fun; shepherding a bunch of entitled children who wanted more and more shops they couldn't afford, just so they could mooch and fantasise.
Give me honest coppers any day.

PC Tony Raglan
LB 265

"Tony – this woman saw something interesting."
I looked up. Caro stood beside a middle-aged woman, smartly dressed, hair neatly styled, good shoes.
"Okay Caro, thanks." I smiled at the woman. "If we could start with your name?"
"Harriet. Harriet Weller. I live just along the road there, Laurel House. I was just coming back from the carboot sale, up on the playing fields – I always love rootling about; I like old china, you see...Oh, sorry...that's not relevant, is it?"
"If you could just tell me what you saw earlier?"
"Of course. Well, the man who died – he was being chased."
"Chased?"
"Yes. By another man. Average height, slender build, light blond hair. Very smartly dressed. He... well, he pushed the other man. He reached out, took him by the shoulder, and... pushed him. Deliberately pushed him in front of the lorry." Harriet Weller's hand flew to her mouth. "I mean... maybe it was an accident..."
"Did you see where this man went?"
"He just kept walking... as though nothing had happened." She looked around. "I think... I think I've seen him before. I think he lives in the house up there, with the crimson door."
I followed her pointing finger, then glanced at Caro. "Stay with her – I'll go and check it out."
I'd just reached the house when a shout rang out. I turned, and jogged back down the road. A blur of motion caught my eye. Blond hair. Lavendar shirt. I broke into a run, trying to ignore the pain in my chest.
He swerved across the road. I crossed at a run, an intersecting angle. We fell to the ground together. He looked up, his face drained.
"You're supposed to be dead."
"You should read the local papers." I yanked him to his feet,

slamming cuffs home. "You're under arrest on suspicion of murder, attempted murder, and assault on police with an offensive weapon."

"You'll never prove it."

I gave a broad grin."Oh, I will – we have body cameras, these days. Come on – get in the car; mind your head."

DC Colt Devereux

"That's Nicole."

"Don't get your hopes up – she may not have seen anything."

"Maybe not. I have a feeling she did, though."

I jogged over, feeling the chill as evening turned to night. "Hey."

"Hey – you out again?"

"We're just hanging out for a bit. It's a nice spot here."

"Yeah. It can be."

I held up my phone, cover story ready. "Do you know this guy? He's offered to quote for some building work, but, well... he doesn't look much like a builder." I handed Nicole the phone. She handed it back.

"Yes." Her voice was quiet. "I saw him following a man who was killed here a couple of weeks ago. I didn't thing anything of it, at the time... He might be a builder, but I wouldn't hire him."

"No... Did you tell the cops?"

She shook her head. "No. Do you think I should?"

"This guy's dangerous. Sometimes, you can let things slide. Other times? No way. This is one of those other times, right?"

Nicole nodded. "I suppose...if I can stop him killing someone else..."

I smiled. "Exactly."

Inspector Bill Wyckham
LB 81

"...so, she came in, just a random off the street, said she needed to talk about the body on the beach. Turned out, same time as she was describing Lamley, he was already confessing." I shook my head, incredulous. Across the canteen table, Tony Raglan sipped his coffee, a thoughtful depth to his eyes that I hadn't seen before.   I supposed it was not unreasonable that processing the arrest – on a wholly unrelated charge – of the man who'd stabbed you would make you a little introspective.

"And he did it because I nicked Clifford-Alistair what, two, three years ago? That's why he stabbed me, and Brewer was his test run? This was all over some bloody scam merchant?"

"Yep. Apparently, they'd been a couple for over fifteen years. Your Mr. Hyphenated was very upset about his life being turned upside down."

Tony snorted. *He* was upset?!" He shook his head. "Thing is, I genuinely couldn't remember anything about the stabbing, but, as soon as I saw him, I got a flashback to the attack. I saw him there; I had noticed him – he'd looked out of place. I just...lost that memory, for a while."

"It happens."

"So...how did he get Blood to take the knife?"

"Blood Marriott was very quick to tell us that, after we lifted him and a couple of small time dealers. He wouldn't stop going on about how he hadn't stabbed that copper, he'd been stupid, got drunk; his defences were down. Our pal Lamley high-fives him, pressing the knife into his hand. He grasps it instinctively..."

"And Max?"

Wyckham sighed. "He did kill Alex Marriott, Tony. There's no getting around that."

"Sir."

"I'm sorry, Tony."

"It's okay. It's the Job.

"He asked if you'd keep an eye on his boat?"

"Of course."

Tony leaned back, finished his coffee. "Nightshade did well."

"Yes, it did. Three active dealing sites, two houses being used as brothels, and an unlicensed gambling club. Things we may never have been able to pinpoint accurately, easily, without going out and being part of the night."

"That's good, then."

We sat in silence, feeling, rather than seeing, the earth spinning. After several long moments, I got to my feet. "Come on. Let's get you home."

"You don't have to – I'm fine -"

"Home. Now. Rest. Come on.

To my surprise, Tony Raglan followed me meekly to the car. Now – I wasn't expecting that.

In the driving seat, I glanced at Tony. "You okay?"

"Tired, sir. Nothing more."

"Tell me when it becomes more, won't you?"

"Sir."

It was going to be okay. We'd had a good day.

Beck

"So... is that your undercover thing over, then?"

Tam looked up from the crossword she was in the middle of. "For now, yes. They're talking about running it as a stretch of three nights once a month, but I'll believe that when I see it." She put her pen down, turning to look fully at me. "What about you, Beck?"

"What about me?"

"Do you want to... would you be able to...?"

"Pick up where I left off with things? Probably. But I'm not sure I want to, any more"

"You're not?"

I shook my head. "I was reading about the guy you were working with, Colt? I don't think I want to go through that. What he's been through. I think I'm going to focus on learning how to live in both worlds, how I can use that energy to create something unique."

Tam smiled. "I think that's a great idea. If you ever change your mind, or your feelings change... I'll try and be more supportive than I was before."

I got up, sauntering to the sink with my bowl, pausing to look over her shoulder. "Can't say fairer than that." I leaned closer to her crossword. "Three across? 'Expressive Tolkeinian grunt; this is what you heard'? Awkward. Orc-word. Sixteen across? 'This politician,with his tidal enclosure, offering sanctuary?' Ambition."

Tam looked up. "Thanks – how did you get so good at cryptic crosswords?"

I took my plate to the sink, grinning over my shoulder. "You forget, kiddo; my whole life's a cryptic crossword. And I think I might just get to like it that way."

PC Feroc Hanson
LB 599

"So, how was undercover work, then?"

"Yeah... I think... I don't think I want to go deep cover, that seems like it would be more pressure than I could handle. But doing more short-term ops like Nightshade...I'd be up for that."

"You think you'd want to stay in the Job, if you could go off on a jaunt like Nightshade every few months?"

I nodded. "I've been thinking about putting in for an attachment to specialist unit. Get some different experience under my belt, make some new contacts."

Tony finished his coffee, looking up as he pushed his mug away. "If that's what you want."

"It might mean being away from home."

"I'm sure I'll cope. He smiled, a little sadly. "This is your life, Feroc. I think I realised that, while you were out with Tam Freud and the others. I can't ask you to always be by my side, and I can't limit your ambitions because that suits me better. I don't want you to end up resenting me, and in order to avoid that, I have to let you be yourself. Do the things you want to." He got up, pacing, the way he always did when there was something on his mind. "I've had my time; I'm just treading water, now. You've got decades ahead of you, and it's my responsibility to allow you to make them count. To allow you to enjoy them." He turned to face me, leaning against the wall. I smiled at the aura of casual threat the pose cast around him. "Got anywhere in mind, attachment-wise?"

I nodded. "Yes; I thought I'd see if I could spend a couple of weeks with the Arts and Antiques team – they've not long been reformed, after Grenfell...there's only three of them, I think. They could probably use some help."

"Big business, art crime. You could make a name for yourself."

"I don't want to make a name for myself, Tony," I got up, and went to stand beside him, both of us exuding casual reflection."I

want to make a life for myself. At work as well as at home."
"As long as I can still be part of it, of every aspect of it." There
was a sadness in Tony's voice that startled me. I turned, laid the
backs of three fingers on his shoulder.
"Of course you'll be part of it. Always."
He smiled, though it didn't quite reach his eyes. "That's alright,
then."